P9-DHJ-308

RUSSIA

Y

Prague

Vienna

AUSTRIA-
HUNGARY

BLACK
SEA

SERBIA

Constantinople

OTTOMAN
EMPIRE

·LEVIATHAN·

Also by Scott Westerfeld

Uglies

Pretties

Specials

Extras

And the book that explains it all:

Bogus to Bubbly:
An Insider's Guide to the World of Uglies

LEVIATHAN

Written by

MR. SCOTT WESTERFELD

Illustrated by Mr. Keith Thompson

SIMON PULSE

New York · London · Toronto · Sydney

This book is a work of fiction. Any references
to historical events, real people, or real locales are used fictitiously.
Other names, characters, places, and incidents are the product of the author's
imagination, and any resemblance to actual events or locales or persons,
living or dead, is entirely coincidental.

SIMON PULSE

An imprint of Simon & Schuster Children's Publishing Division
1230 Avenue of the Americas, New York, NY 10020
First Simon Pulse hardcover edition October 2009
Copyright © 2009 by Scott Westerfeld
All rights reserved, including the right of reproduction
in whole or in part in any form.
SIMON PULSE and colophon are registered trademarks
of Simon & Schuster, Inc.
For information about special discounts for bulk purchases, please contact
Simon & Schuster Special Sales at 1-866-506-1949 or
business@simonandschuster.com.
The Simon & Schuster Speakers Bureau can bring authors to your live event.
For more information or to book an event contact the Simon & Schuster
Speakers Bureau at 1-866-248-3049 or visit our website at www.simonspeakers.com.
Designed by Mike Rosamilia
The text of this book was set in Hoefler Text.
Manufactured in the United States of America
2 4 6 8 10 9 7 5 3 1
Library of Congress Cataloging-in-Publication Data
Westerfeld, Scott.
Leviathan / by Scott Westerfeld ; illustrated by Keith Thompson. —
1st Simon Pulse hardcover ed.
p. cm.
Summary: In an alternate 1914 Europe, fifteen-year-old Austrian Prince
Alek, on the run from the Clanker powers who are attempting to take over
the globe using mechanical machinery, forms an uneasy alliance with
Deryn, who, disguised as a boy to join the British Air Service, is
learning to fly genetically engineered beasts.
ISBN 978-1-4169-7173-3 (hardcover)
[1. Science fiction. 2. Imaginary creatures—Fiction. 3. Princes—Fiction.
4. War—Fiction. 5. Genetic engineering—Fiction.]
I. Thompson, Keith, 1982– ill. II. Title.
PZ7.W5197Lev 2009   [Fic]—dc22
2009000881
ISBN 978-1-4169-8706-2 (eBook)

To my NYC writing crew,
for knowing the importance of Craft

ONE

The Austrian horses glinted in the moonlight, their riders standing tall in the saddle, swords raised. Behind them two ranks of diesel-powered walking machines stood ready to fire, cannon aimed over the heads of the cavalry. A zeppelin scouted no-man's-land at the center of the battlefield, its metal skin sparkling.

The French and British infantry crouched behind their fortifications—a letter opener, an ink jar, and a line of fountain pens—knowing they stood no chance against the might of the Austro-Hungarian Empire. But a row of Darwinist monsters loomed behind them, ready to devour any who dared retreat.

The attack had almost begun when Prince Aleksandar thought he heard someone outside his door. . . .

He took a guilty step toward his bed—then froze in place, listening hard. Trees stirred in a soft breeze

outside, but otherwise the night was silent. Mother and Father were in Sarajevo, after all. The servants wouldn't dare disturb his sleep.

Alek turned back to his desk and began to move the cavalry forward, grinning as the battle neared its climax. The Austrian walkers had completed their bombardment, and it was time for the tin horses to finish off the woefully outnumbered French. It had taken all night to set up the attack, using an imperial tactics manual borrowed from Father's study.

It seemed only fair that Alek have some fun while his parents were off watching military maneuvers. He'd begged to be taken along, to see the mustered ranks of soldiers striding past in real life, to feel the rumble of massed fighting machines through the soles of his boots.

It was Mother, of course, who had forbidden it—his studies were more important than "parades," as she called them. She didn't understand that military exercises had more to teach him than musty old tutors and their books. One day soon Alek might be piloting one of those machines.

War was coming, after all. Everyone said so.

The last tin cavalry unit had just crashed into the French lines when the soft sound came from the hallway again: jingling, like a ring of keys.

Alek turned, peering at the gap beneath his bed chamber's double doors. Shadows shifted along the sliver of moonlight, and he heard the hiss of whispers.

Someone was right outside.

Silent in bare feet, he swiftly crossed the cold marble floor, sliding into bed just as the door creaked open. Alek narrowed his eyes to a slit, wondering which of the servants was checking on him.

Moonlight spilled into the room, making the tin soldiers on his desk glitter. Someone slipped inside, graceful and dead silent. The figure paused, staring at Alek for a moment, then crept toward his dresser. Alek heard the wooden rasp of a drawer sliding open.

His heart raced. None of the servants would dare steal from him!

But what if the intruder were something worse than

a thief? His father's warnings echoed in his ears. . . .

You have had enemies from the day you were born.

A bell cord hung next to his bed, but his parents' rooms were empty. With Father and his bodyguard in Sarajevo, the closest sentries were quartered at the other end of the trophy hall, fifty meters away.

Alek slid one hand under his pillow, until his fingers touched the cold steel of his hunting knife. He lay there holding his breath, grasping the handle tightly, repeating to himself his father's other watchword.

Surprise is more valuable than strength.

Another figure came through the door then, boots clomping, a piloting jacket's metal clips jingling like keys on a ring. The figure tromped straight toward his bed.

"Young master! Wake up!"

Alek let go of the knife, expelling a sigh of relief. It was just old Otto Klopp, his master of mechaniks.

The first figure began rifling through the dresser, pulling at clothes.

"The young prince has been awake all along," Wildcount Volger's low voice said. "A bit of advice, Your Highness? When pretending to be asleep, it is advisable not to hold one's breath."

Alek sat up and scowled. His fencing master had an annoying knack for seeing through deception.

"What's the meaning of this?"

"You're to come with us, young master," Otto mumbled, studying the marble floor. "The archduke's orders."

"My father? He's back already?"

"He left instructions," Count Volger said with the same infuriating tone he used during fencing lessons. He tossed a pair of Alek's trousers and a piloting jacket onto the bed.

Alek stared at them, half outraged and half confused.

"Like young Mozart," Otto said softly. "In the archduke's stories."

Alek frowned, remembering Father's favorite tales about the great composer's upbringing. Supposedly Mozart's tutors would wake him in the middle of the night, when his mind was raw and defenseless, and thrust musical lessons upon him. It all sounded rather disrespectful to Alek.

He reached for the trousers. "You're going to make me compose a *fugue*?"

"An amusing thought," Count Volger said. "But please make haste."

"We have a walker waiting behind the stables, young master." Otto's worried face made an attempt at a smile. "You're to take the helm."

"A walker?" Alek's eyes widened. Piloting was one part of his studies he'd gladly get out of bed for. He slipped quickly into the clothes.

"Yes, your first night lesson!" Otto said, handing Alek his boots.

Alek pulled them on and stood, then fetched his favorite pilot's gloves from the dresser, his footsteps echoing on the marble floor.

"Quietly now." Count Volger stood by the chamber doors. He cracked them and peered out into the hall.

"We're to sneak out, Your Highness!" Otto whispered. "Good fun, this lesson! Just like young Mozart!"

The three of them crept down the trophy hall, Master Klopp still clomping, Volger gliding along in silence. Paintings of Alek's ancestors, the family who had ruled Austria for six hundred years, lined the hallway, their subjects staring down with unreadable expressions. The antlers of his father's hunting trophies cast tangled shadows, like a moonlit forest. Every footstep was magnified by the stillness of the castle, and questions echoed in Alek's mind.

Wasn't it dangerous, piloting a walker at night? And why was his fencing master coming along? Count Volger preferred swords and horses over soulless mechaniks, and had little tolerance for commoners like old Otto. Master Klopp had been hired for his piloting skills, not his family name.

"Volger . . . ," Alek began.

"*Quiet*, boy!" the wildcount spat.

Anger flashed inside Alek, and a curse almost burst

from his mouth, even if it ruined their stupid game of sneaking out.

It was always like this. To the servants he might be "the young archduke," but nobles like Volger never let Alek forget his position. Thanks to his mother's common blood, he wasn't fit to inherit royal lands and titles. His father might be heir to an empire of fifty million souls, but Alek was heir to nothing.

Volger himself was only a wildcount—no farmlands to his name, just a bit of forest—but even he could feel superior to the son of a lady-in-waiting.

Alek managed to stay quiet, though, letting his anger cool as they stole through the vast and darkened banquet kitchens. Years of insults had taught him how to bite his tongue, and disrespect was easier to swallow with the prospect of piloting ahead.

One day he would have his revenge. Father had promised. The marriage contract would be changed somehow, and Alek's blood made royal.

Even if it meant defying the emperor himself.

∘ TWO ∘

By the time they reached the stables, Alek's only
concern was tripping in the darkness. The moon was less
than half full, and the estate's hunting forests stretched
like a black sea across the valley. At this hour even the
lights of Prague had died out to a mere inkling.

When Alek saw the walker, a soft cry escaped his lips.

It stood taller than the stable's roof, its two metal feet
sunk deep into the soil of the riding paddock. It looked
like one of the Darwinist monsters skulking in the darkness.

This wasn't some training machine—it was a real engine
of war, a Cyklop Stormwalker. A cannon was mounted in its
belly, and the stubby noses of two Spandau machine guns
sprouted from its head, which was as big as a smokehouse.

Before tonight Alek had piloted only unarmed runabouts and four-legged training corvettes. Even with his

"STEALING AWAY."

sixteenth birthday almost here, Mother always insisted that he was too young for war machines.

"I'm supposed to pilot *that?*" Alek heard his own voice break. "My old runabout wouldn't come up to its knee!"

Otto Klopp's gloved hand patted his shoulder heavily. "Don't worry, young Mozart. I'll be at your side."

Count Volger called up to the machine, and its engines rumbled to life, the ground trembling under Alek's feet. Moonlight shivered from the wet leaves in the camouflage nets draped over the Stormwalker, and the mutter of nervous horses came from the stable.

The belly hatch swung open and a chain ladder tumbled out, unrolling as it fell. Count Volger stilled it from swinging, then planted a boot on the lowermost metal rung to hold it steady.

"Young master, if you please."

Alek stared up at the machine. He tried to imagine guiding this monster through the darkness, crushing trees, buildings, and anything else unlucky enough to be in his path.

Otto Klopp leaned closer. "Your father the archduke has thrown us a challenge, me and you. He wants you ready to pilot any machine in the House Guard, even in the middle of the night."

Alek swallowed. Father always said that, with war on the horizon, everyone in the household had to be prepared. And it made sense to begin training while Mother was away.

If Alek crashed the walker, the worst bruises might fade before the princess Sophie returned.

But Alek still hesitated. The belly hatch of the rumbling machine looked like the jaws of some giant predator bending down to take a bite.

"Of course, we cannot force you, Your Serene Highness," Count Volger said, amusement in his voice. "We can always explain to your father that you were too scared."

"I'm *not* scared." Alek grabbed the ladder and hoisted himself up. The sawtooth rungs gripped his gloves as Alek climbed past the anti-boarding spikes arrayed along the walker's belly. He crawled into the machine's dark maw, the smell of kerosene and sweat filling his nose, the engines' rhythm trembling in his bones.

"Welcome aboard, Your Highness," a voice said. Two men waited in the gunners' cabin, steel helmets glittering. A Stormwalker carried a crew of five, Alek recalled. This wasn't some little three-man runabout. He almost forgot to return their salutes.

Count Volger was close behind him on the ladder, so Alek kept climbing up into the command cabin. He took the pilot's seat, strapping himself in as Klopp and Volger followed.

He placed his hands on the saunters, feeling the machine's awesome power trembling in his fingers. Strange to think that these two small levers could control the walker's huge metal legs.

"Vision at full," Klopp said, cranking the viewport open as wide as it would go. The cool night air spilled into the Stormwalker's cabin, and moonlight fell across dozens of switches and levers.

The four-legged corvette he'd piloted the month before had needed only control saunters, a fuel gauge, and a compass. But now uncountable needles were arrayed before him, shivering like nervous whiskers.

What were they all *for*?

He pulled his eyes from the controls and stared through the viewport. The distance to the ground gave him a queasy feeling, like peering down from a hayloft with thoughts of jumping.

The edge of the forest loomed only twenty meters away. Did they really expect him to pilot this machine through those dense trees and tangled roots . . . *at night*?

"At your pleasure, young master," Count Volger said, sounding bored already.

Alek set his jaw, resolving not to provide the man with any more amusement. He eased the saunters forward, and the huge Daimler engines changed pitch as steel gears bit, grinding into motion.

The Stormwalker rose from its crouch slowly, the ground slipping still farther away. Alek could see across the treetops now, all the way to shimmering Prague.

He pulled the left saunter back and pushed the right forward. The machine lumbered into motion with an inhumanly large step, pressing him back into the pilot's seat.

The right pedal rose a little as the walker's foot hit soft ground, nudging Alek's boot. He twisted at the saunters, transferring weight from one foot to the other. The cabin swayed like a tree house in a high wind, lurching back and forth with each giant step. A chorus of hissing came from the engines below, gauges dancing as the Stormwalker's pneumatic joints strained against the machine's weight.

"Good . . . excellent," Otto muttered from the commander's seat. "Watch your knee pressure, though."

Alek dared a glance down at the controls, but had no idea what Master Klopp was talking about. *Knee pressure? How could anyone keep track of all those needles without driving the whole contraption into a tree?*

"Better," the man said a few steps later. Alek nodded dumbly, overjoyed that he hadn't tipped them over yet.

Already the forest was looming up, filling the wide-open viewport with a dark tangle of shapes. The first glistening branches swept past, thwacking at the viewport, spattering Alek with cold showers of dew.

"Shouldn't we spark up the running lights?" he asked.

Klopp shook his head. "Remember, young master? We're pretending we don't want to be spotted."

"Revolting way to travel," Volger muttered, and Alek wondered again why the man was here. Was there to be a *fencing* lesson after this? What sort of warrior-Mozart was his father trying to make him into?

The shriek of grinding gears filled the cabin. The left pedal snapped up against Alek's foot, and the whole machine tipped ominously forward.

"You're caught, young master!" Otto said, hands ready to snatch the saunters away.

"I *know*!" Alek cried, twisting at the controls. He slammed the machine's right foot down midstride, its knee joint spitting air like a train whistle. The Stormwalker wavered drunkenly for a moment, threatening to fall. But long seconds later Alek felt the machine's weight settle into the moss and dirt. It was balanced with one foot stretching back, like a fencer posing after a lunge.

He pushed on both saunters, the left leg pulling at whatever had entangled it, the right straining forward. The Daimler engines groaned, and metal joints hissed. Finally a shudder passed through the cabin, along with the satisfying sound of roots tearing from the ground— the Stormwalker rising up. It stood high for a moment, like a chicken on one leg, then stepped forward again.

Alek's shaking hands guided the walker through its next few strides.

"Well done, young master!" Otto cried. He clapped his hands once.

"Thank you, Klopp," Alek said in a dry voice, feeling sweat trickle down his face. His hands clenched the saunters tight, but the machine was walking smoothly again.

Gradually he forgot that he was at the controls, feeling the steps as if they were his own. The sway of the cabin settled into his body, the rhythms of gears and pneumatics not so different from his runabout's, only louder. Alek had even begun to see patterns in the flickering needles of the control panel—a few leapt into the red with every footfall, easing back as the walker straightened. Knee pressure, indeed.

But the sheer power of the machine kept him anxious. Heat from the engines built in the cabin, the night air blowing in like cold fingers. Alek tried to imagine what piloting would be like in battle, with the viewport half shut against flying bullets and shrapnel.

Finally the pine branches cleared before them, and Klopp said, "Turn here and we'll have better footing, young master."

"Isn't this one of Mother's riding paths?" Alek said. "She'll have my hide if we track it up!" Whenever one of Princess Sophie's horses stumbled on a walker footprint, Master Klopp, Alek, and even Father felt her wrath for days.

But he eased back on the throttle, grateful for a moment of rest, bringing the Stormwalker to a halt on the trail. Inside his piloting jacket Alek was soaked with sweat.

"Disagreeable in every way, Your Highness," Volger said. "But necessary if we're to make good time tonight."

Alek turned to Otto Klopp and frowned. "Make good time? But this is just practice. We're not *going* anywhere, are we?"

Klopp didn't answer, his eyes glancing up at the count. Alek pulled his hands from the saunters and swiveled the pilot's chair around.

"Volger, what's going on?"

The wildcount stared down at him in silence, and Alek felt suddenly very alone out here in the darkness.

His mind began to replay his father's warnings: How some nobles believed that Alek's muddled lineage threatened the empire. That one day the insults might turn into something worse. . . .

But these men *couldn't* be traitors. Volger had held a sword to his throat a thousand times in fencing practice, and his master of mechaniks? Unthinkable.

"Where are we going, Otto? Explain this *at once*."

"You're to come with us, Your Highness," Otto Klopp said softly.

"We have to get as far away from Prague as possible," Volger said. "Your father's orders."

"But my father isn't even . . ." Alek gritted his teeth and swore. What a *fool* he'd been, tempted into the forest with tales of midnight piloting, like luring a child with candy. The whole household was asleep, his parents away in Sarajevo.

Alek's arms were still tired from fighting to keep the Stormwalker upright, and strapped into the pilot's chair he could hardly draw his knife. He closed his eyes—he'd left the weapon back in his room, under the pillow.

"The archduke left instructions," Count Volger said.

"You're *lying!*" Alek shouted.

"I wish we were, young master." Volger reached into his riding jacket.

A surge of panic swept into Alek, cutting through his despair. His hands shot to the unfamiliar controls, searching for the distress whistle's cord. They couldn't be far from home yet. Surely *someone* would hear the Stormwalker's shriek.

Otto jumped into motion, grabbing Alek's arms. Volger swept a flask from his jacket and forced its open mouth to Alek's face. A sweet smell filled the cabin, sending his mind spinning. He tried not to breathe, struggling against the larger men.

Then his fingers found the distress cord and pulled—

But Master Klopp's hands were already at the controls, spilling the Stormwalker's pneumatic pressure. The whistle let out only a miserable descending wail, like a teakettle pulled from the fire.

Alek still struggled, holding his breath for what felt like minutes, but finally his lungs rebelled. He scooped in a ragged breath, the sharp scent of chemicals filling his head . . .

A cascade of bright spots fell across the instruments, and a weight seemed to lift from Alek's shoulders. He felt as though he were floating free of the men's grasp, free of the seat straps—free of gravity, even.

"My father will have your heads," he managed to croak.

"Alas not, Your Highness," Count Volger said. "Your parents are both dead, murdered this night in Sarajevo."

Alek tried to laugh at this absurd statement, but the world twisted sideways under him, darkness and silence crashing down.

° THREE °

"Wake up, you ninny!"

Deryn Sharp opened one eye . . . and found herself staring at etched lines streaming past an airbeast's body, like a river's course around an island—an airflow diagram. Lifting her head from the aeronautics manual, she discovered that the open page was stuck to her face.

"You stayed up all night!" The voice of her brother, Jaspert, battered her ears again. "I told you to get some sleep!"

Deryn gently peeled the page from her cheek and frowned—a smudge of drool had disfigured the diagram. She wondered if sleeping with her head in the manual had stuffed still more aeronautics into her brain.

"Obviously I *did* get some sleep, Jaspert, seeing as you found me snoring."

"Aye, but not properly in bed." He was moving around

the small rented room in the darkness, piecing together a clean airman's uniform. "One more hour of studying, you said, and you've burnt our last candle down to a squick!"

Deryn rubbed at her eyes, looking around the small, depressing room. It was always damp and smelled of horse clart from the stables below. Hopefully last night would be the last time she slept here, in bed or not. "Doesn't matter. The Service has its own candles."

"Aye, if you pass the test."

Deryn snorted. She'd studied only because she hadn't

been able to sleep, half excited about finally taking the airman middy's test, half terrified that someone would see through her disguise. "No need to worry about that, Jaspert. I'll pass."

Her brother nodded slowly, a mischievous expression crossing his face. "Aye, maybe you're a crack hand with sextants and aerology. And maybe you can draw any airbeast in the fleet. But there's one test I haven't mentioned. It's not about book learning—more what they call 'air sense.'"

"*Air sense?*" Deryn said. "Are you winding me up?"

"It's a dark secret of the Service." Jaspert leaned forward, his voice dropping to a whisper. "I've risked expulsion for daring to mention it to a civilian."

"You are full of *clart*, Jaspert Sharp!"

"I can say no more." He pulled his still-buttoned shirt over his head, and when his face emerged, it had broken into a smile.

Deryn scowled, still not sure if he was kidding. As if she weren't nervous enough.

Jaspert tied his airman's neckerchief. "Get your slops on and we'll see what you look like. All that studying's going to waste if your tailoring don't persuade them."

Deryn stared sullenly down at the pile of borrowed clothes. After all her studying and everything she'd learned when her father was alive, the middy's test would be easy. But what was in her head wouldn't matter unless she could fool the Air Service boffins into believing her name was Dylan, not Deryn.

She'd resewn Jaspert's old clothes to alter their shape, and she was plenty tall—taller than most boys of midshipman's age. But height and shape weren't everything. A month of practicing on the streets of London and in front of the mirror had convinced her of that.

Boys had something else . . . a sort of *swagger* about them.

When she was dressed, Deryn gazed at her reflection in a darkened window. Her usual self stared back: female and fifteen. The careful tailoring only made her look queerly skinny, not so much a boy as some tattie bogle set out in old clothes to scare the crows.

"Well?" she said finally. "Do I pass as a Dylan?"

Jaspert's eyes drifted up and down, but he said nothing.

"I'm plenty tall for sixteen, right?" she pleaded.

Finally he nodded. "Aye, I suppose you'll pass. It's just lucky you've no diddies to speak of."

Deryn's jaw dropped open, her arms crossing over her chest. "And you're a bum-rag covered in clart!"

Jaspert laughed, slapping her hard on the back. "That's the spirit. I'll have you swearing like a navy lad yet."

The London omnibuses were much fancier than those back in Scotland—faster, too. The one that took them to the airship field at Wormwood Scrubs was drawn by a hippo-esque the breadth of two oxen across the shoulders. The huge, powerful beast had them nearing the Scrubs before dawn had broken.

Deryn stared out the window, watching the movements of treetops and windblown trash for hints about the day's weather. The horizon was red, and the *Manual of Aerology* claimed, *Red sky in morning, sailors take warning.* But Da had always said that was just an old wives' tale. It was when you saw a dog eating grass that you knew the heavens were about to split.

Not that a drop of rain mattered—the tests today would be indoors. It was book learning the Air Service demanded from their young midshipmen: navigation and aerodynamics. But staring at the sky was safer than reading the glances of the other passengers.

Since getting on the bus with Jaspert, Deryn's skin had itched with wondering what she looked like to strangers. Could they see through her boy's slops and shorn hair? Did they really think she was a young recruit on his way to the Air Proving Ground? Or did she look like some lassie with a few screws loose, playing dress-up in her brother's old clothes?

The omnibus's next to last stop was at the Scrubs' famous prison. Most of the passengers disembarked there, women carrying lunch pails and gifts for their men inside. The sight of barred windows made Deryn's stomach churn.

How much trouble would Jaspert be in if this ruse went wrong? Enough to lose his position in the Service? To send him to jail, even?

It just wasn't *fair*, her being born a girl! She knew more about aeronautics than Da had ever crammed into Jaspert's attic. On top of which, she had a better head for heights than her brother.

The worst thing was, if the boffins didn't let her into the Service, she'd be spending tonight in that horrible rented room again, and headed back to Scotland by tomorrow.

Her mother and the aunties were waiting there, certain that this mad scheme wouldn't work and ready to stuff Deryn back into skirts and corsets. No more dreams of flying, no more studying, no more *swearing*! And the last of her inheritance wasted on this trip to London.

She glared at the three boys riding in the front of the bus, jostling each other and giggling nervously as the proving ground drew closer, happy as a box of birds. The tallest hardly came up to Deryn's shoulder. They couldn't be so much stronger, and she didn't credit that they were as smart or as brave. So why should *they* be allowed into the king's service and not her?

Deryn Sharp gritted her teeth, resolving that no one would see through her disguise.

There couldn't be *that* much trick to it, being a stupid boy.

⊙　　⊙　　⊙

The line of recruits on the ascension field weren't impressive. Most looked barely sixteen, sent off by their families to find fortune and advancement. A few older boys were mixed in with the others, probably middies coming over from the navy.

Looking at their anxious faces, Deryn was glad to have had a father who'd taken her up in hot-air balloons. She'd seen the ground from on high plenty of times. But that didn't keep her nerves from playing up. She almost reached for Jaspert's hand before realizing how *that* would look.

"All right, *Dylan*," he said quietly as they neared the desk. "Just remember what I told you."

Deryn snorted. Last night Jaspert had demonstrated how a proper boy checked his fingernails—looking at his palm, fingers bent, whereas girls looked at the backs of their hands, fingers splayed.

"Aye, Jaspert," she said. "But if they ask me to do my nails, don't you think the jig's up already?"

He didn't laugh. "Just don't draw attention to yourself, right?"

Deryn said nothing more, following him to the long table set up outside a white hangar tent. Three officers sat behind it, accepting letters of introduction from the recruits.

"Ah, Coxswain Sharp!" one said. He wore the uniform

of a flight lieutenant, but also the curve-brimmed bowler hat of a boffin.

Jaspert saluted him smartly. "Lieutenant Cook, may I present my cousin Dylan."

When Cook held out his hand to Deryn, she felt the moment of British pride that boffins always gave her. Here was a man who'd reached into the very chains of life and worked them to suit his purposes.

She gave his hand the firmest shake she could. "Nice to meet you, sir."

"Always a pleasure to meet a Sharp fellow," the boffin said, then chuckled at his own joke. "Your cousin speaks highly of your comprehension of aeronautics and aerology."

Deryn cleared her throat, using the soft, low voice she'd been practicing for weeks. "My da—that is, my uncle—taught us all about ballooning."

"Ah, yes, a brave man." He shook his head. "A tragedy he isn't here to see the triumphs of living flight."

"Aye, he would've loved it, sir." Da had gone up in only hot-air balloons, not hydrogen breathers like the Service used.

Jaspert gave her a nudge, and Deryn remembered the letter of recommendation. She pulled it from her jacket and offered it to Flight Lieutenant Cook. He pretended to study it, which was silly because he'd written it himself as a favor to Jaspert, but even boffins had to follow Royal Navy form.

"This seems to be in order." His eyes drifted up from the letter and traveled across Deryn's borrowed outfit, looking troubled for a moment by what he saw.

She stood stiffly under his gaze, wondering what she'd done wrong. Was it her hair? Her voice? Had the hand-shake somehow gone amiss?

"Bit spindly, aren't you?" the boffin finally said.

"Aye, sir. I suppose so."

His face broke into a smile. "Well, we had to fatten up your cousin too. Mr. Sharp, please join the line!"

◦ FOUR ◦

The sun was just starting to creep above the tree line when the proper military men arrived. They rolled across the field in an all-terrain carriage drawn by two lupine tigeresques, pulling up smartly before the line of recruits. The beasts' muscles bulged under the leather straps of the carriage rig, and when one shook itself like a monstrous house cat, sweat flew in all directions.

In the corners of her vision Deryn saw the boys around her stiffen. Then the carriage driver set the tigers growling with a snap of his whip, and a nervous murmur traveled down the line.

A man in a flight captain's uniform stood in the open carriage, a riding crop under one arm. "Gentlemen, welcome to Wormwood Scrubs. I trust none of you is frightened by the fabrications of natural philosophy?"

No one answered. Fabricated beasts were everywhere

"ADDRESSING THE APPLICANTS."

in London, of course, but nothing so magnificent as these half-wolf tigers, all sinews and claws, a crafty intelligence lurking in their eyes.

Deryn kept her eyes forward, though she was dying to take a closer look at the tigeresques. Before today she'd seen military fabs only in the zoo.

"Barking spiders!" the young boy next to her whispered. He was nearly as tall as her, and his short blond hair stuck straight up into the air. "I'd hate to see those two get loose."

Deryn resisted the urge to explain that lupines were the tamest of the fabs. Wolves were really just a kind of dog, and could be trained almost as easily. Airbeasts came from trickier stock, of course.

When no one stepped forward to admit their fear, the flight captain said, "Excellent. Then you won't mind a closer look."

The driver's whip snapped again, and the carriage rumbled across the broken field, the nearest tiger passing within arm's reach of the volunteers. The snarling beasts were too much for three boys at the other end of the line. They broke ranks and ran shrieking back toward the open gates of the Scrubs.

Deryn kept her eyes focused directly ahead as the tigers passed, but a whiff of them—a mix of wet dog and raw meat—sent shivers down her spine.

"Not bad, not bad," the flight captain said. "I'm glad

to see so few of our young men succumbing to common superstition."

Deryn snorted. A few people—Monkey Luddites, they were called—were afraid of Darwinist beasties on principle. They thought that crossbreeding natural creatures was more blasphemy than science, even if fabs had been the backbone of the British Empire for the last fifty years.

She wondered for a moment if these tigers were the secret test Jaspert had warned her about, and smirked. If so, it had been a pure dawdle.

"But your nerves of steel may not last the day, gentlemen," the flight captain said. "Before moving on we'd like to discover if you have a head for heights. Coxswain?"

"About-*face!*" shouted an airman. With a muddled bit of shuffling, the line of boys turned itself about to face the hangar tent. Deryn saw that Jaspert was still here, hanging off to one side with the boffins. They were all wearing clart-snaffling grins.

Then the hangar's tent flaps split apart, and Deryn's jaw dropped open. . . .

An airbeast was inside: a Huxley ascender, its tentacles in the grips of a dozen ground men. The beast pulsed and trembled as they drew it gently out, setting its translucent gasbag shimmering with the red light of the rising sun.

"A medusa," gasped the boy next to her.

Deryn nodded. This was the first hydrogen breather

ever fabricated, nothing like the giant living airships of today, with their gondolas, engines, and observation decks.

The Huxley was made from the life chains of medusae—jellyfish and other venomous sea creatures—and was practically as dangerous. One wrong puff of wind could spook a Huxley, sending it diving for the ground like a bird headed for worms. The creatures' fishy guts could survive almost any fall, but their human passengers were rarely so lucky.

Then Deryn saw a pilot's rig hanging from the airbeast, and her eyes widened still farther.

Was this the test of "air sense" Jaspert had been hinting at? And he'd let her believe he'd only been kidding! *That bum-rag.*

"You lucky young gents will be taking a ride this morning," the flight captain said from behind them. "Not a long one: only up a thousand feet or so and then back down . . . after ten minutes lofting in the air. Believe me, you'll see London as you never have before!"

Deryn felt a smile creeping across her lips. Finally, a chance to see the world from on high again, just like in one of Da's balloons.

"To those of you who'd prefer not to," the flight captain finished, "we bid fond farewells."

"Any of you little blighters want out?" shouted the coxswain from the end of the line. "Then get out *now*! Otherwise, it's skyward with you!"

After a short pause another dozen boys departed. They didn't run screaming this time, just slunk toward the gates in a huddled pack, a few pale and frightened faces glancing back at the pulsing, hovering monster. Deryn realized with pride that almost half the volunteers were gone.

"Right, then." The flight captain stepped in front of the line. "Now that the Monkey Luddites have been cleared out, who'd like to go first?"

Without hesitation, without a thought of what Jaspert had said about not drawing attention, and with the last squick of nerves in her belly gone, Deryn Sharp took one step forward.

"Please, sir. I'd like to fly."

The pilot's rig held her snugly, the contraption swaying gently under the medusa's body. Leather straps passed under her arms and around her waist, then were clipped to the curved seat that she perched on like a horseman riding sidesaddle. Deryn had worried that the coxswain would discover her secret as he buckled her in, but Jaspert had been right about one thing: There wasn't much to give her away.

"Just ride it up, laddie," the man said quietly. "Enjoy the view and wait for us to pull you down. Most of all, don't do *anything* to upset the beastie."

"Aye, sir." She swallowed.

"If you start to panic, or if you think something's gone wrong, just throw this." He pressed a thick roll of yellow cloth into her hand, then tied one end around her wrist. "And we'll wind you down steady and fast."

Deryn clutched it tightly. "Don't worry. I won't panic."

"That's what they all say." He smiled, and pressed into her other hand a cord leading to a pair of water bags harnessed to the creature's tentacles. "But if by any chance you do anything *completely* stupid, the Huxley may go into a dive. If the ground's coming up too fast, just give this a tug."

"It spills the water out, making the beast lighter," Deryn said, nodding. Just like the sandbags on Da's balloons.

"Very clever, laddie," the coxswain said. "But cleverness is no substitute for air sense, which is Service talk for *keeping your barking head*. Understand?"

"Yes, *sir*," Deryn said. She couldn't wait to get off the ground, the flightless years since Da's accident suddenly heavy in her chest.

The coxswain stepped back and blew a short pattern on his whistle. As the final note shrieked, the ground men let go of the Huxley's tentacles all together.

The straps cut into her as the airbeast rose, like being scooped up in a giant net. A moment later the feeling of ascent vanished, as if the earth itself were dropping away. . . .

Down below, the line of boys stared up in undisguised

"ASCENDING."

awe. Jaspert was grinning like a loon, and even the boffins' faces showed squicks of fascination. Deryn felt brilliant, rising through the air at the center of everyone's attention, like an acrobat aloft on a swing. She wanted to make a speech:

"Hey, all you sods, I can fly and you can't! A natural airman, in case you haven't noticed. And in conclusion, I'd like to add that I'm a girl and you can all get stuffed!"

The four airmen at the winch were letting the cable out quickly, and soon the upturned faces blurred with distance. Larger geometries came into view: the worn curves of an old cricket oval on the ascension field, the network of roads and railways surrounding the Scrubs, the wings of the prison pointing southward like a huge pitchfork.

Deryn looked up and saw the medusa's body alight with the sunrise, pulsing veins and arteries running like iridescent ivy through its translucent flesh. The tentacles drifted in the soft breezes around her, capturing pollen and insects and sucking them into the stomach sack above.

Hydrogen breathers didn't really breathe hydrogen, of course. They *exhaled* it: burped it into their own gasbags. The bacteria in their stomachs broke down food into pure elements—oxygen, carbon, and, most important, lighter-than-air hydrogen.

It should have been nauseating, Deryn supposed, hanging suspended from all those gaseous dead insects. Or terrifying, with nothing but a few leather straps between her and a quarter mile of tumbling to a terrible death. But she felt as grand as an eagle on the wing.

The smoky outline of central London rose up toward the east, divided by the winding, shimmering snake of the River Thames. Soon she could make out the green expanse of Hyde Park and Kensington Gardens. It was like looking down on a living map: the omnibuses crawling along like bugs, sailboats fluttering as they tacked against the breeze.

Then, just as the spire of St. Paul's Cathedral rose into view, a shiver passed through the rig.

Deryn scowled. Were her ten minutes up *already*?

She looked down, but the line leading to the ground hung slack. They weren't reeling her in just yet.

The jolt came again, and Deryn saw a few of the tentacles around her clench, coiling like ribbons scraped between a pair of scissors. They were slowly gathering back into a single strand.

The Huxley was nervous.

Deryn swung herself from side to side, ignoring the majesty of London to search the horizon for whatever was spooking the airbeast.

Then she spotted it: a dark shapeless mass in the north, a rolling wave of clouds spreading across the sky. Its leading

edge crept forward steadily, blackening the northern sub-
urbs with rain.

Deryn felt the hairs on her arms tingling.

She dropped her gaze to the Scrubs, wondering if the
tiny airmen down there could see the storm front too,
and would start to reel her in. But the proving ground still
glowed with light from the rising sun. From down there
they would see only clear skies above, as cheery as a picnic.

Deryn waved a hand. Could they even see her well
enough? But of course they'd only think she was larking
about.

"Bum-rag!" she swore, and glared at the roll of yellow
cloth tied to her wrist. A real ascender scout would have
semaphore flags, or at least a message lizard that could
scamper down the line. But all they'd given her was a panic
signal.

And Deryn Sharp was *not* panicking!

At least, she didn't think she was. . . .

She stared at the blackness in the sky, wondering if it
were only a last bit of night the sunrise hadn't chased away.
What if she had no air sense at all, and the height had gone
to her head?

Deryn closed her eyes, took a deep breath, and counted
to ten.

When she opened them again, the clouds were still
there—closer.

The Huxley trembled again, and Deryn smelled lightning in the air. The approaching squall was definitely real. The aerology manual had been right after all: *Red sky in morning, sailors take warning.*

She stared again at the yellow cloth. If the officers below saw it unfurl, they'd think she was panicking. Then she'd have to explain that it hadn't been terror, just a coolheaded observation that rough weather was coming. Maybe they'd commend her for making the right decision.

But what if the squall changed course? Or faded to a drizzle before it arrived at the Scrubs?

Deryn clenched her teeth, wondering how long she'd been up here. Weren't ten minutes almost up? Or had her sense of time gone crook in the vast, cold sky?

Her eyes darted back and forth between the rolled-up yellow cloth and the approaching storm, wondering what a *boy* would do.

○ FIVE ○

When Prince Aleksandar awoke, his tongue was coated with sickly sweetness. The awful taste overpowered his other senses; he couldn't see or hear or even think, as if his brain were drenched in sugary brine.

Gradually his head cleared—he smelled kerosene and heard tree branches thrashing past outside. The world rocked dizzily around him, hard-edged and metallic.

Then Alek began to remember: the midnight piloting lesson, his teachers turning on him, and finally the sweet-smelling chemical that had knocked him out. He was still in the Stormwalker, still moving away from home. All of it had really happened. . . . He'd been kidnapped.

At least he was still alive. Maybe they planned to ransom him. Humiliating, he supposed, but better than dying.

His kidnappers evidently didn't think Alek was much of a threat. They hadn't tied him up. Someone had even thought to put a blanket between him and the rocking metal floor.

He opened his eyes and saw shifting patches of light, a grid of swaying shadows cast by a ventilation grill. Neat racks of explosive shells lined the walls, and the hiss of pneumatics was louder than ever. He was in the belly of the Stormwalker—the gunners' station.

"Your Highness?" came a nervous voice.

Alek pulled himself up from the blanket, squinting through the darkness. One of the crewmen sat bolt upright against a rack of shells, wide-eyed and at attention. Traitor or not, the man probably had never been alone with a prince before. He didn't look much older than twenty.

"Where are we?" Alek said, trying to use the steely tone of command his father had taught him.

"I . . . suppose I don't know exactly, Your Highness."

Alek frowned, but the man had a point. There wasn't much to see down here except through the gun sight of the 57-millimeter cannon. "Where are we headed, then?"

The crewman swallowed, then reached a hand up toward the communicating hatch. "I'll get Count Volger."

"No," Alek snapped, and the man froze.

Aleksandar smiled grimly. At least someone in this machine remembered his station.

"What's your name?"

The man saluted. "Corporal Bauer, sir."

"All right, Bauer," he said in a calm, even voice. "I'm ordering you to let me go. I can drop out the belly hatch while we're still moving. You can follow and help me get home. I'll make sure my father rewards you. You'll be a hero, instead of a traitor."

"Your father . . ." The man's face fell. "I'm so sorry."

Like a long echo rolling in from a distance, Alek's mind replayed what Count Volger had said as the chemical had taken hold—something about his parents being dead.

"No," he said again, but the tone of command was gone. Suddenly the metal confines of the Stormwalker's belly felt crushingly small. In his own ears Alek's voice sounded broken now, like a child's. "Please let me go."

But the man looked away, embarrassed, reaching up to rap on the hatchway with an oily wrench.

"Your father made preparations before he left for Sarajevo," Count Volger said. "In case the worst happened."

Alek didn't answer. He was staring out the Stormwalker's viewport from the commander's chair, watching the tops of young hornbeam trees roll past. Beside him Otto Klopp guided the machine with steady, perfect motions of the saunters.

Dawn was breaking, the horizon turning bloodred. They were still deep in the forest, heading west on a narrow carriage path.

"He was a wise man," Klopp said. "He knew that going so close to Serbia would be dangerous."

"But threats couldn't keep the archduke from his duty," Count Volger said.

"Duty?" Alek held his throbbing head; he could still taste the chemicals in his mouth. "But my mother . . . He would never take her into danger."

Count Volger sighed. "Whenever Princess Sophie could participate in affairs of state, your father was happy."

Alek shut his eyes. It always pained Father when Sophie wasn't allowed to stand beside him at official receptions. More punishment for loving a woman who wasn't royal.

The thought of his parents dead was absurd. "This is a trick to keep me quiet. You're all *lying!*"

No one answered. The cabin resonated with the growl of Daimler engines and the scrape of branches against camouflage netting. Volger stood silent, his face thoughtful. The leather hand straps hanging from the ceiling swung in time with the walker's gait. Strangely, part of Alek's mind could focus only on Klopp's hands on the controls, marveling at his mastery of the machine.

"The Serbs wouldn't dare kill my parents," Alek said softly.

"I have other suspects in mind," Volger said flatly. "Those who want war among the great powers. But we have no time to theorize now, Aleksandar. Our first task is to get you to safety."

Alek stared out the walker's viewport again. Volger had addressed him as simply Aleksandar, without any title, as if he were a commoner. But somehow the insult had lost its power.

"Assassins struck twice in the morning," Volger said. "Serb schoolboys hardly older than you, first with bombs and then with pistols. Both times they failed. Then last night a feast was given in your father's honor, and he was toasted for his bravery. But poison took your parents in the night."

Alek imagined them lying dead beside each other, and the hollowness inside him grew. But the story didn't make sense at all. The assassins would have come for Alek himself—the half royal, the lady-in-waiting's son. Not his father, whose blood was pure.

"If they're really dead, why does anyone still care about me? I'm *nothing* now."

"Some might think differently." Count Volger crouched next to the command chair. He stared out the window alongside Alek, his voice dropping to a whisper. "Emperor Franz Joseph is eighty-three years old. If he dies soon, some might turn to you in these anxious times."

"He hated my mother more than any of them." Alek closed his eyes again. The red-tinged forest outside was too bleak to stare at anymore. A patch of uneven ground set the cabin shuddering, as if the world were unsteady in its path around the sun. "I just want to go home."

"Not until we can be sure it's safe, young master," said Otto Klopp. "We promised your father."

"What do promises matter if he's—"

"Silence!" Volger cried.

Aleksandar looked up at him in shock. He opened his mouth to protest, but the wildcount's hand clenched his shoulder.

"Cut the engines!"

Master Klopp wrenched the Stormwalker to a halt, cycling the Daimlers down to a low rumble. The hiss of pneumatics settled around them.

Alek's ears rang in the sudden quiet, his body shuddering with echoes of the walker's motion. Through the viewport the leaves were motionless, the air without a breath of wind. No birds sang, as if the forest had been startled into silence by the walker's abrupt halt.

Volger's eyes closed.

Then Alek felt it. The slightest shudder passed through the metal frame of the Stormwalker—the tread of something larger, heavier. Something that shook the earth.

Count Volger stood, opening the hatchway overhead. Dawn light spilled in as he pulled himself halfway out.

The shudder came again. Through the viewport Alek

saw the tremor passing through the forest, leaves shivering in its wake. It unsettled the pit of his stomach, like an angry look from his father.

"Your Highness," Volger called, "if you would join me."

Alek stood and balanced on the commander's chair, hoisting himself up through the hatch.

Outside, his eyes squinted against the half-risen sun; dawn had turned the sky a deep orange around them. The Stormwalker stood a little taller than the young hornbeam trees, and the horizon seemed enormous after hours of peering through the viewport.

Volger pointed back the way they had come. "There are your enemies, Prince Aleksandar."

Alek squinted against the rising sun. The other machine was kilometers away, towering twice as tall as the trees. Her six huge legs moved unhurriedly, but men scurried like ants across the gun deck, raising signal flags and manning the turrets. Along her flank stretched the letters of her name: S.M.S. *Beowulf*.

Alek watched a massive foot plant itself upon the forest floor. Long seconds later another tremor arrived, rippling across the trees around them and up through the Stormwalker's metal frame. As the next step fell, a distant treetop flailed and then vanished, torn down by the giant walker's stride.

The red and black stripes of the Kaiser's Landforce

Jack flew from her spar deck, whipping in the breeze.

"A German land dreadnought," Alek said softly. "But aren't we still in Austria-Hungary?"

"Yes," Volger said, "but all those who want chaos and war are hunting us, Your Highness. Or do you still doubt me?"

But what if it's a rescue mission? Alek thought. Maybe his kidnappers had been lying after all, and Father and Mother were still alive. A vast search for Alek had been launched, with the German land navy helping! Why else would this monstrosity be allowed on Austrian soil?

Then Alek saw that the machine was changing direction, slowly turning sideways across the sunrise. . . .

He held up his hand and waved. "Here! Over *here!*"

"They already see us, Your Highness," Count Volger said quietly.

Alek was still waving when the first broadside erupted, bright flashes rippling along the dreadnought's flank, puffs of cannon smoke swelling into a hazy veil around her. The sound followed moments later—a rolling thunder that broke into sharp, tearing bursts from every direction. The treetops churned around them, concussions shaking the Stormwalker and throwing clouds of leaves into the sky.

Then Volger was dragging him back down into the cabin, the engines roaring back to life.

"Load the cannon!" Master Klopp cried to the men below.

"THE S.M.S. *BEOWULF*."

Alek found himself deposited into the commander's chair as the machine began to move. He struggled with the seat straps, but a terrible thought took hold of his mind, freezing his fingers.

If they're trying to kill me . . . it's all true.

Count Volger crouched beside him, yelling over the rumble of engines and gunfire. "Take heart at this impoliteness, Alek. It proves that you are still a threat to the throne."

◦ SIX ◦

The second broadside of cannon shells fell closer, a spray of gravel and wooden splinters rattling against the viewport's grill, the smaller pieces spilling through.

Alek spat dirt from his mouth.

"Vision to half!" Master Klopp cried, then cursed. The two crewmen were below, and Volger was halfway up through the hatch again, his legs dangling from the ceiling.

Klopp glanced apologetically at Alek. "If you please, Your Highness."

"Certainly, Master Klopp," Alek said. He unbuckled and pulled himself up from the commander's chair. The cabin rocked and swayed, and he grasped the straps overhead to keep his footing.

He tried to turn the viewport's crank, but it wouldn't budge. Taking it with both hands, Alek strained harder, until the massive armored visor grudgingly closed a few centimeters.

Another broadside shook the earth beneath them, and the walker staggered forward. Count Volger's riding boots flailed, kicking Alek in the back of the head.

"They can still see us!" Volger shouted from above. "We're too tall!"

Master Klopp twisted at the saunters, hunkering the Stormwalker lower. The hornbeam trees rose up in the viewport, the walker's clumsy gait sending Volger's boots swinging again. For an astonished moment Alek watched Klopp's hands on the controls—he'd never seen a walker shuffle along in a crouch like this.

Of course, he'd never imagined a Cyklop Stormwalker having to hide from anything. But against a dreadnought this walker was practically a toy.

Grunting and heaving, Alek managed to close the right viewport to half. He reached for the other crank.

"Young master, the antenna!" Klopp cried out.

"Yes, of course!" The Stormwalker's wireless antenna stretched up above the trees, the archducal flag snapping in the breeze. But Alek had no idea how to lower it. He looked around the cabin, wishing he'd paid more attention to the crewmen when learning how to pilot.

Finally he spotted a windlass beside the wireless set. As he darted for it, Volger's dangling boots delivered another blow to his shoulder. The windlass spun wildly the moment Alek unlocked it, the antenna telescoping closed a few centimeters from his ear.

He started back for the commander's seat, then saw that the left viewport was still open. He reached across the lurching cabin and began to crank it tighter.

Volger dropped back into the cabin, closing the hatch above him against a sudden rain of dirt and pebbles. "We're out of sight now."

Another broadside rumbled in the distance, followed by more explosions flickering among the trees ahead. Debris struck the Stormwalker, but the viewport's grills were squeezed as tight as a comb's teeth now; only the fine dust of pulverized forest floor filtered through.

Alek felt a moment of satisfaction—he'd done something useful. This was his first real battle, when only hours before, he'd been playing with tin soldiers. The rumble of explosions and the shriek of engines somehow filled the hollowness inside him.

The Stormwalker was thrashing through dense forest now. Of course—any cleared path would be clearly visible from the *Beowulf*'s lookout towers.

Alek's heart was beating fast as he slipped back into the commander's chair and watched Klopp's hands on the saunters. His long hours of piloting practice seemed suddenly trifling. All that time in runabouts had been pretend-play, and this was real.

Volger crouched between the chairs to peer forward, his face blackened with dirt and sweat. Blood flowed from a scratch above one eye, shining bright red in the gloom of the shuttered cabin.

"I believe I suggested a smaller landship, Master Klopp."

Klopp barked a laugh, still struggling to keep the Stormwalker low to the ground. "Don't appreciate the extra armor, Volger? A runabout would've been blown off her feet by that last broadside."

The forest rumbled again, but the explosions came from well behind and off to the right. The dreadnought had lost sight of them for now.

"The sun was rising behind the *Beowulf*. So we're headed west," Alek said. "We should turn left. The pines and firs down in the south are much taller than these hornbeams."

"Well remembered, Your Highness," Master Klopp said, adjusting his course.

Alek clapped him on the shoulder. "You were right to choose a Stormwalker, Klopp. We'd be dead now, otherwise."

"We'd be halfway to Switzerland, you mean," Volger said, managing to sound as if this were some fencing lesson that Alek was failing to comprehend. "In a runabout half this size, or on horses, they wouldn't have spotted us in the first place."

Alek glared up at the wildcount, but before he could open his mouth, the intercom popped.

"Loaded and ready, sir."

Alek dropped his gaze toward the cabin floor. "Those two would have been more use up here. There's not much they can do with that peashooter against a dreadnought."

"True, Your Highness," Klopp said. "But she'll have escorts—smaller, faster ships moving below tree height. We may get a whiff of them sooner than you think."

"Ah, quite right." Alek closed his mouth and swallowed. The rush of battle was beginning to fade, and his hands were shaking.

All he'd done was turn a few cranks; the others had handled everything important. The bruises left by Volger's swinging boots still throbbed, reminders of how Alek had mostly managed to get in the way.

He leaned back into the commander's chair. As the simple, overwhelming fear of being shot at faded, the emptiness was rushing back. . . .

Alek wished that it were him bleeding instead of Volger—anything to distract himself from the truth welling up in his mind.

"She's lost our range," Klopp said. "No big guns for a count of thirty."

"They've turned to give chase," Volger said. "But wait

till their scouts spot us. She'll swing around for another broadside soon enough."

Alek cast about for something to say, but found himself in the grip of a silent panic, his vision blurring with tears. The attack had swept away his last doubts.

His father was dead; his mother too. Both gone forever.

His Serene Highness, Prince Aleksandar of Hohenberg, was alone now. He might never see his home again. The armed forces of two empires were hunting him, set against one walker and four men.

Volger and Klopp fell silent, and when Alek turned, he saw his despair reflected in their faces. He clenched the hand rests of the commander's chair, fighting to breathe.

His father would've known what to say in this situation: a short and forceful speech, praising the men for their efforts, urging them to carry on. But Alek could only stare into the forest, blinking away tears.

If he didn't say something, the emptiness would swallow him.

A burst of gunfire broke out in the trees ahead, cutting through the grind of the engines. The walker twisted to a new heading, and Count Volger jumped to his feet again.

"Horse scouts, I reckon!" Master Klopp said. "They have stables on the *Beowulf.*"

A shower of bullets rattled against the Stormwalker's visor, louder than any spray of dirt and pebbles. Alek imagined metal projectiles ripping through the armor and cutting into him, and his heart began to race again.

The awful emptiness lifted a little. . . .

A huge *boom* shook the walker in its track, and a billow of smoke rose across the viewport, its choking stench spilling into the cabin. For a moment Alek thought they'd been hit, but then an explosion answered from the distance, followed by the crack of trees and the awful cries of horses.

"That was *us!*" he murmured. The men below had fired the Stormwalker's cannon.

As the echoes died, Volger called, "Do you know how to load a Spandau machine gun, Alek?"

Prince Aleksandar knew nothing of the sort, but already his hands were moving to unbuckle his seat straps.

○ SEVEN ○

They were just beginning to reel in Deryn when the storm struck.

The ground men had noticed the darkening sky. They were scrambling about the field, securing the hangar tent with extra spikes, getting the recruits under cover. Four men strained at the ascender's winch, pulling Deryn down steady and fast. A dozen ground crew waited to grab the beast's tentacles when it was low enough.

But she was still five hundred feet up when the first sheets of rain arrived. The cold drops fell diagonally, hitting her dangling feet even under the cover of the airbeast. Its tentacles coiled tighter, and she wondered how long the medusa would take this pounding before it spilled its hydrogen, hurling itself toward the ground.

"Stay calm, beastie," Deryn said softly. "They're bringing us in."

A wild gust caught the medusa's airbag, and it billowed like a full sail. Deryn swung out into the full force of the storm, her boy-slops instantly soaked with freezing rain.

Then the cable snapped taut, whipping the beast earthward like a kite without enough string. It dropped toward houses and backyard gardens, down to just above the high prison walls. Directly beneath Deryn people scurried along the wet streets, shoulders hunched, unaware of the monster overhead.

Another gust of wind struck, and the Huxley was forced low enough that Deryn could see the ribs of umbrellas below.

"Oh, beastie. This isn't good."

The medusa swelled again, trying to regain its lift, and leveled off a few dozen feet above the rooftops. The cable strained against the wind for a moment, then loosened. The ground men were giving them slack, Deryn reckoned, letting them climb a bit more, like a fisherman trying to keep a catch on the line.

But that extra cable was more weight to carry, and she and the Huxley were both heavy with rain. She could spill the water ballast, but once it was gone, there'd be nothing left to slow their fall if the beastie panicked.

The cable was scraping across the prison's rooftops now, snapping against shingles and drainpipes. Deryn saw it snag on one of the smoking chimneys, and her eyes widened. . . .

No *wonder* the ground men were letting out more cable—they were keeping her away from the prison. If a chimney spark drifted up and reached the Huxley's airbag, the hydrogen would ignite, the ascender exploding in a massive fireball, rain or no rain.

The cable snagged again, sending a jolt through the Huxley. The creature spooked, its tentacles coiling tight, and dropped again.

Deryn clutched the ballast cord, gritting her teeth. She might survive a wind-tossed landing herself, but the shingled rooftops and backyard fences below would shred the creature to pieces. And it would be all Deryn Sharp's fault for not warning the ground men when she'd had the chance.

Some air sense.

"Okay, beastie," she called up. "I may have got you into this mess, but I'm gonna get you out, too. And I'm telling you: Now's not the time to panic!"

The creature made no promises, but Deryn pulled the ballast cords anyway. The bags snapped open, spilling their water into the storm.

Slowly the airbeast began to climb.

The ground men gave a cheer and set upon the winch, furiously hauling the airbeast in against the wind. The captain was supervising, shouting orders from the back of the all-terrain carriage. The tigeresques looked miserable in the rain, like a pair of house cats standing under a faucet.

With a few more turns of the winch the medusa was over the proving grounds, safely away from the prison's smoking chimneys.

But then the wind switched direction. The airbeast billowed again, pulled in a half circle toward the other end of the Scrubs.

The Huxley let out a screech above the wind, like the horrible sound when one of Da's air bladders would spring a leak.

"No, beastie! We're almost safe!" Deryn shouted.

But the medusa had been tossed about once too often. Its gasbag was contracting, the tentacles coiled as tight as rattlesnakes.

Deryn Sharp smelled the hydrogen spilling into the air, the scent like bitter almonds. She was falling . . .

But the wind still carried them, changing direction without rhyme or reason. It tossed the airbeast about like a crumpled piece of paper, pulling Deryn behind it.

They had to be heavier than air by now, but in a gale like this, Deryn fancied you could fly a bowler hat on a bit of string.

At the other end of the cable the ground men were watching helplessly, the flight captain ducking as the gyrating cable sliced overhead. If they tried to crank her any closer, they'd pull the airbeast straight down into the ground.

Jaspert was running across the field toward her, cupping his hands to his mouth and shouting something. . . .

She caught the sound of his voice, but the wind whipped the words away.

Deryn's feet now dangled a few yards above the ground, which raced by as if she were on horseback. She peeled off her heavy, sodden jacket and tossed it overboard.

The prison loomed close again as the Huxley sped along. Smashing into its walls at this speed would turn her and the airbeast into bloody splotches.

Her fingers scrambled at the pilot's rig, searching for a way to escape the harness. Deryn reckoned her chances were better dropping onto muddy grass than crashing into a wall. And with her weight gone the Huxley would rise back into the air.

Of course, that clart-rag of a coxswain hadn't bothered showing her how to unbuckle the rig. The leather straps were swollen with rain, cinched as tight as a duck's bum. Evidently the Service didn't trust recruits not to wriggle out in a panic and fall to their deaths.

Then Deryn saw the knot over her head—the cable that bound the airbeast to the ground!

She looked at the cable stretched out between her and the winch . . . about three hundred feet of it now. That length of rain-soaked hemp *had* to weigh more than one skinny wee lassie and her wet clothes.

If she could set the Huxley free, it might still have enough hydrogen to carry her up to safety.

But the ground was rising again, shining wet grass and puddles blurring past just beneath her feet—the prison walls ahead. Reaching up with one hand, Deryn felt the half-familiar shape of the knot. . . .

It was nothing but a backhanded mooring hitch! She remembered Jaspert telling her how Air Service riggers used sailor's knots, the same ones she'd tied a thousand times on Da's balloons!

As Deryn struggled to free the wet cable from its knot, her boots struck the ground with a bone-jarring thud, skidding across the wet grass.

But the real danger wasn't below—it was the approaching prison walls. Deryn and the Huxley were seconds away from smashing into that shining expanse of wet stone.

Finally her fingers pushed the cable's working end free. The knot spilled, the rope twisting like a live thing, skinning her fingers as it slipped from the steel ring.

As the weight of three hundred feet of wet hemp dropped away, the airbeast soared, clearing the prison walls with yards to spare.

Deryn's breath caught as a belching chimney passed beneath her feet. She imagined raindrops tumbling down its mouth to the coal fires below, spitting steam, the sparks rising up to ignite the angry mass of hydrogen over her head.

But the wind whipped the sparks away—moments later the Huxley had cleared the southernmost prison buildings.

As she climbed, Deryn heard a hoarse cheer from below.

The ground men raised their arms in triumph. Jaspert was beaming, cupping both hands to his face and shouting something that sounded congratulatory, as if to say she'd done exactly what he'd told her!

"It was *my* barking idea, Jaspert Sharp," she muttered, sucking her rope-burned fingers.

Of course, she was still in the middle of a storm, strapped to an irritable Huxley, both of them soaring across a stretch of London with precious few spots to land.

And how *was* Deryn meant to land this beastie? She had no way to vent hydrogen, no more ballast in case the creature spooked, and no clue if anyone had ever free-ballooned with a Huxley before and lived to tell the tale.

Still . . . at least she was flying. If she ever came down alive, the boffins would have to admit as how she'd passed this test.

Boy or not, Deryn Sharp had shown a squick of air sense after all.

∘ EIGHT ∘

The storm felt strangely still.

She remembered the sensation from Da's hot-air balloons. Cut free from its tether, the medusa had exactly matched the speed of the wind. The air felt motionless, the earth turning below on a giant lathe.

Dark clouds still boiled around her, giving the Huxley an occasional spin. But worse were the flickers in the distance. One sure way to set a hydrogen breather aflame was to hit it with *lightning*. Deryn distracted herself by watching London pass beneath, all matchbox houses and winding streets, the factories with their sealed smokestacks.

She remembered how Da had said London looked in the days before old Darwin had worked his magic. A pall of coal smoke had covered the entire city, along with a fog so thick that streetlamps were lit during the day. During the worst of the steam age so much soot and ash had decorated the nearby countryside that butterflies had evolved black splotches on their wings for camouflage.

But before Deryn had been born, the great coal-fired engines had been overtaken by fabricated beasties, muscles and sinews replacing boilers and gears. These days the only chimney smoke came from ovens, not huge factories, and the storm had cleared even that murk from the air.

Deryn could see fabs wherever she looked. Over Buckingham Palace a flock of strafing hawks patrolled in spirals, carrying nets that would slice the wings off any aeroplane that ventured too close. Messenger terns criss-crossed the Square Mile, undeterred by the weather. The streets were full of draft animals: hippoesques and equine breeds, an elephantine dragging a sledge full of bricks through the rain. The storm that had almost snuffed out her Huxley had barely slowed the city down.

Deryn wished she had her sketch pad, to capture the tangle of streets and beasts and buildings below. She'd first started drawing up in one of Da's balloons, trying to capture the wonders of flight.

As the clouds gradually broke apart, the Huxley slid across a shaft of light. Deryn stretched in the warmth, and set to squelching water out of her cold, damp clothes.

The houses below were getting smaller, the teeming umbrella tops blurring into the wet streets. As it dried, the Huxley was climbing.

Deryn frowned. To descend in a balloon, you vented hot air from the top. But Huxleys were primitive ascenders, designed to be tethered at all times.

What was she supposed to do, *talk* the beastie down?

"Oi!" she shouted. "You there!"

The nearest tentacle curled a bit, but that was all.

"Beastie! I'm *talking to you!*"

No reaction.

Deryn scowled. An hour ago the Huxley had been so *easy* to spook! Perhaps one annoyed lassie's cries didn't amount to much after the terrific storm.

"You're a big, bloated bum-rag!" she shouted, swinging her feet to rock the pilot's rig. "And I'm getting bored of your company! Let! Me! Down!"

The tentacles uncurled, like a cat stretching in the sun.

"That's just brilliant," she grumbled. "I'll add rudeness to your defects."

Passing through another patch of sun, the medusa made a soft sighing noise, expanding its airbag to dry itself.

Deryn felt herself drifting higher.

She groaned, looking at the blue skies ahead. She could see all the way to the farmlands of Surrey now. And past that would be the English Channel.

For two long years Deryn had wanted nothing more than to go aloft again, like when Da had been alive—and here she was, marooned in the sky. Maybe this was punishment for acting like a boy, just like her mum had always warned.

The wind steadied, pushing the beast toward France.

It was going to be a long day.

The Huxley noticed it first.

The pilot's rig jolted under Deryn, like a carriage going over a pothole. Shaken from a catnap, she glared up at the Huxley.

"Getting bored?"

The airbeast seemed to be glowing, the sun shining straight down through iridescent skin. It was noon, so she'd been aloft more than six hours. The English Channel sparkled not far ahead, set against a perfect sky. They'd left London's gray clouds far behind.

Deryn scowled and stretched.

"Barking lovely weather," she croaked. Her lips were parched and her bum was very, very sore.

Then she saw the tentacles coiling around her.

"What now?" she moaned, though she'd have welcomed a flock of birds attacking them, as long as it brought the beastie down. A bumpy landing was better than hanging here till she died of thirst.

Deryn scanned the horizon and saw nothing. But she felt a trembling in the leather cords of her pilot's rig and heard the thrum of engines in the air.

Her eyes widened.

A huge airbeast was emerging from the gray clouds behind her, its reflective silver topside glistening in the sunlight.

The thing was gigantic—larger than St. Paul's Cathedral, longer than the oceangoing dreadnought *Orion* that she'd seen in the Thames the week before. The shining cylinder was shaped like a zeppelin, but the flanks pulsed with the motion of its cilia, and the air around it swarmed with symbiotic bats and birds.

The medusa made an unhappy whistling sound.

"No, beastie. Don't fret!" she called softly. "They're here to help!"

At least, Deryn assumed they were. But she hadn't been expecting anything quite so *big* to come hunting her down.

The airship drew closer, until Deryn could make out the gondola suspended from the beastie's belly. The foot-tall letters under the bridge windows came slowly into focus. . . . *Leviathan.*

She swallowed. "And barking famous, these friends are."

The *Leviathan* had been the first of the great hydrogen breathers fabricated to rival the kaiser's zeppelins. A few beasties had grown larger since, but no other had yet made the trip to India and back, breaking German airship records all the way.

The *Leviathan*'s body was made from the life threads

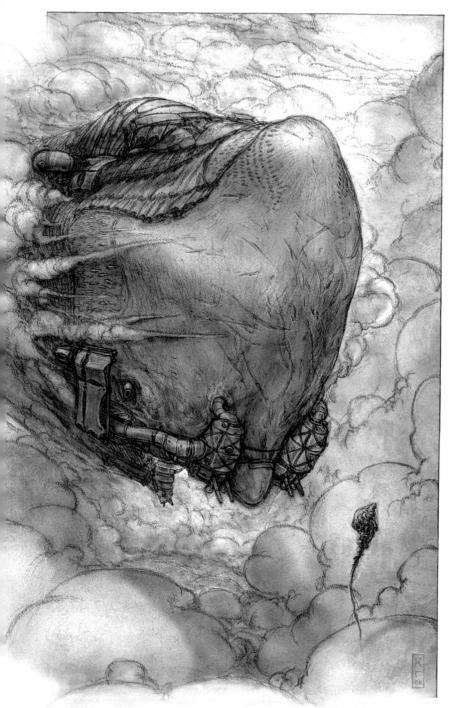

"THE *LEVIATHAN* APPROACHES."

of a whale, but a hundred other species were tangled into its design, countless creatures fitting together like the gears of a stopwatch. Flocks of fabricated birds swarmed around it—scouts, fighters, and predators to gather food. Deryn saw message lizards and other beasties scampering across its skin.

According to her aerology manual, the big hydrogen breathers were modeled on the tiny South American islands where Darwin had made his famous discoveries. The *Leviathan* wasn't one beastie, but a vast web of life in ever shifting balance.

The motivator engines changed pitch, nudging the creature's nose up. The airbeast obeyed, cilia along its flanks undulating like a sea of grass in the wind—a host of tiny oars rowing backward, slowing the *Leviathan* almost to a halt.

The huge shape drifted slowly overhead, blotting out the sky. Its belly was all mottled grays, camouflage for night raids.

In the sudden coolness of the huge shadow, Deryn stared up, spellbound. This vast, fantastic creature had actually come to rescue *her*.

The Huxley shuddered again, wondering where the sun had gone.

"Hush, beastie. It's nothing but your big cousin."

Deryn heard calls from above, and she saw movement.

A rope tumbled into view, unrolling past her. Another followed, then a dozen more, until Deryn was surrounded by an upside-down forest of swaying ropes.

She stretched out for one, but the width of the air-beast's gasbag kept the rope out of reach. Deryn swung the pilot's rig, trying to get closer.

Her motion made the Huxley's tentacles curl up tight, resulting in a sickening lurch downward.

"Aye, so *now* you want to head down?" she complained. "Just useless, you are."

The airship's engines changed pitch again, and the dangling lines reappeared, still out of reach. But then the engines overhead set up a grinding pattern, on-off, on-off . . . and the ropes began to sway in rhythm with the sound.

That was one clever pilot up there.

The ropes swung closer with every pulse of the engines. Deryn stretched out one arm as far as she could. . . .

Finally her reaching fingers caught hold. She pulled the rope in, knotting it to the ring over her rig—then frowned.

Were they going to hoist her up into the gondola? Wouldn't that flip the Huxley upside down?

But the line stayed slack, and a few moments later a message lizard made its way down. Its tiny webbed hands cupped the rope as though it were a thin tree branch. The lizard's bright green skin seemed to glow in the shadows below the airship.

It spoke with a posh accent, the deep voice uncanny from such a wee body.

"Mr. Sharp, I presume?" The lizard let out a throaty chuckle.

Gobsmacked as she was, Deryn almost answered. Of course, the message lizard was only repeating what one of the officers overhead had said to it.

"Greetings from the *Leviathan*," it continued. "Our apologies for the delay. Bad weather and all that." It made a noise like a man clearing his throat, and Deryn half expected the lizard to raise a tiny fist to its mouth. "But here we are at last. We'll be taking you in on the dorsal side, of course—standard procedure."

The lizard paused, and Deryn pondered what "dorsal" might mean.

"Ah, yes. I'm told you're just a sprog. Well done, getting lost on your first flight."

Deryn rolled her eyes. First a bag of gas and insect guts had carted her halfway across England, and now she was getting cheek from a barking *lizard*!

"I expect you don't know standard procedure. Well, it's quite simple, really. We'll drop below you, then come up under and bring you in with the dorsal winch. Any questions?"

The message lizard stared up at her expectantly, blinking its wee black eyes.

"No questions, sir. I'm ready," Deryn said, remembering to use her boy's voice. She wasn't about to admit she didn't know what "dorsal" meant.

The message lizard didn't move, just blinked again.

"So . . . standard procedure it is?" she added.

The lizard waited another moment, but when Deryn said nothing more, it scampered back up the rope to repeat her words to whoever was at the other end.

A minute later the other ropes were all hoisted away, but the line attached to her pilot's rig was given more slack. It looped down almost out of sight, a quarter mile of rope, it looked like. Then the airship's idling engines sprang to life again.

The huge shadow pulled back against the wind, so that the sun broke out from behind its nose, half blinding Deryn. The airship dropped then, venting hydrogen with a sound like rushing water, steadily descending till the officers in the bridge windows were dead even with her, only twenty yards away.

One smiled and gave a crisp salute, and Deryn returned it.

The *Leviathan* dropped still farther, and the Huxley whined a bit when one huge eye drew level with them.

"Don't you give me any more bother," Deryn murmured.

She was watching keenly, noting how the airship's huge harness wrapped around its body, holding the gondolas in place. The straps were connected by a network of ropes, like the rigging of a sailing ship. Strange six-legged beasties climbed alongside the crewmen in the ropes, snuffling the airbeast's skin.

Those had to be the hydrogen sniffers she'd read about, searching the membrane for leaks.

When the *Leviathan*'s vast silver expanse slipped beneath her, Deryn saw that the other end of her rope was now attached to a winch on the creature's spine.

So "dorsal" was just Service-speak for "backside."

The winch was small and aluminum, made as light as possible, like everything on an airship. Two men cranked it, drawing up the slack quickly enough. Soon Deryn and her nervous Huxley were descending toward the *Leviathan*'s silver back.

A few minutes later a half dozen crewmen grabbed the tentacles of the medusa and hauled it down. Deryn found herself released from the pilot's rig, stumbling with numbed legs onto the squishy surface of the *Leviathan*'s inflated skin.

"Welcome aboard, Mr. Sharp," said the young officer in charge.

Deryn tried to stand up straight, but pain shot down her spine. She wriggled her toes inside Jaspert's boots, trying to erase the pins and needles in her feet.

"Thank you, sir," she managed.

"You all right there?" the officer asked.

"Aye, sir. Just a bit numb in my, um, dorsal areas."

The officer laughed. "Long flight, eh?"

"Aye, sir. A bit." She sheepishly returned his salute.

He was smiling, at least. All the crewmen looked rather jolly as they checked over the medusa. Deryn supposed it wasn't often they were called upon to rescue recruits from the sky.

A man in a coxswain's uniform clapped her on the back. "Your Huxley's in good shape after a storm like that. You must have a way with the beasties, Mr. Sharp."

"Thank you, sir," she said. The men at the winch were running the Huxley back up, towing it in the *Leviathan*'s wake.

"Not many middies spend half their first day aloft," the officer said.

"I'm not a middy exactly, sir. Haven't taken the tests yet." Deryn glanced longingly around the topside, praying they would let her explore the ship while they took her back to the Scrubs. She'd be ready to walk again in just a few more minutes. . . .

The coxswain laughed. "Solving a few aeronautics problems shouldn't be too hard after free-ballooning in a Huxley. And with this trouble brewing, I expect the Service will be looking for a few more lads."

Deryn frowned. "Trouble, sir?"

The officer nodded. "Ah, yes. I suppose you haven't heard. Some Austrian duke and duchess got themselves killed last night. There may be a bit of a ruckus on the Continent."

She blinked. "I'm sorry, sir. I don't understand."

The officer shrugged. "Not sure what it's got to do with Britain myself, but we've been put on alert. Now that we've got you sorted, we're headed straight over to France, in case the Clankers try to start something." He smiled. "I expect you'll be with us a few days. Hope that isn't a bother."

Deryn's eyes widened. As sensation returned to her legs, she could feel the rumble of the engines in the airbeast's skin. From the spine of the *Leviathan*, its silver flanks sloping away into oblivion, the sky was huge in all directions.

A few days, the man had said—a hundred more hours in this perfect sky. Deryn saluted again, trying to hide her grin.

"No, sir. No bother at all."

• NINE •

Alek awoke to the chatter of Morse code.

Wood creaked as he stirred, and a damp smell filled his
nose. Dust swirled in shafts of sunlight streaming through
the half-rotten walls. He sat up and blinked, staring at the
hay covering his clothes.

Prince Aleksandar had never slept in a barn before.
Of course, he'd done a lot of new things in the last two
weeks.

Klopp, Bauer, and Master Engineer Hoffman were
snoring nearby. The Stormwalker crouched in the half-
lit barn, its head almost level with the hayloft. Alek had
maneuvered the machine inside late last night, shuffling
at half height in the darkness to squeeze it in. A tricky bit
of piloting.

Morse code crackled again through the walker's open
viewport.

Count Volger, of course. The man was allergic to sleep.

The gap between the hayloft and the walker's head was barely the length of a sword, an easy jump.

Alek landed softly, his bare feet silent on the metal armor. He eased himself over the edge to peek in through the viewport. Volger sat facing away in the commander's chair, a wireless earphone pressed against his head.

Slowly, silently, Alek lowered one foot to the edge of the viewport. . . .

"Careful not to fall, Your Highness."

Alek sighed, wondering if he would ever manage to sneak up on his fencing master. He slid through the viewport and dropped into the pilot's chair.

"Don't you ever sleep, Count?"

"Not with that racket." Volger glared out at the hayloft.

"You mean the snoring?" Alek frowned. He'd grown used to sleeping through the noises of men and machines, but somehow the tiny crackle of dots and dashes from the wireless had woken him. Two weeks of being hunted had altered his senses. "Anything about us?"

Volger shrugged. "The codes have changed again. But there's more chatter than I've ever heard before; the army is preparing for war."

"Maybe they've forgotten me," Alek said. In those first days land dreadnoughts had stalked the hills in every direction, lookouts swarming their spar decks. But lately

the fugitives had seen only an occasional aeroplane buzzing overhead.

"You are not forgotten, Your Highness," Volger said
flatly. "Serbia simply presents an easier target."

"Unlucky for them," Alek said softly.

"Luck had nothing to do with it," Volger muttered.
"The empire has wanted a war with Serbia for years now.
The rest is an excuse."

"An *excuse?*" Alek said, anger rising as he imagined his
murdered parents' faces. But he couldn't argue with Volger's
logic. The dreadnoughts hunting him were German and
Austrian, after all. His family had been destroyed by old
friends, not some hapless gang of Serbian schoolboys. "But
my father always argued for peace."

"And he can argue no longer. Clever, isn't it?"

Alek shook his head. "You horrify me, Volger. I some-
times think you *admire* the people behind this."

"Their plans have a certain elegance—assassinating a
peacemaker to start a war. But they made one very foolish mistake." The man turned and faced him. "They left
you alive."

"I don't matter, not anymore."

Volger switched off the wireless, and the cabin fell into
silence. The flutter of birds filtered down from the rafters
of the barn.

"You matter more than anyone knows, Aleksandar."

"*How?* I have no parents, no real title." Alek looked down at himself, dressed in stolen farmer's clothes and covered with hay. "I haven't even had a proper *bath* in two weeks."

"No, indeed." Volger sniffed. "But your father planned carefully for the coming war."

"What do you mean?"

"When we get to Switzerland, I will explain." Volger switched the wireless on again. "But that won't happen unless we can buy fuel and parts tomorrow. Go wake the men."

Alek raised an eyebrow. "Did you just give me an order, Count?"

"Go wake the men *if you please*, Your Serene Highness."

"I know you're only being insolent to distract me from your little secret, Count. But that doesn't make it any less *annoying.*"

Volger let out a laugh. "I suppose not. But I can't give up my secret yet. I promised your father to wait till the proper time."

Alek's fists tightened. He was growing tired of being treated like this, never told what Volger's plans were until the last moment. Maybe he'd been a child the day his parents had died, but no longer.

In the last two weeks he'd learned how to start a fire, how to replace the engines' glow plugs, how to track their nighttime progress toward Switzerland with a sextant and the stars. He could squeeze the Stormwalker under bridges and into barns, and strip and clean the Spandau machine guns as easily as washing his own clothes— another thing he'd learned to do. Hoffman had even taught him to cook a little, boiling dried meat to soften it, adding the vegetables they'd gathered while trampling some unlucky farmer's field.

But most important, Alek had learned to shut away despair. He hadn't cried since that first day, not once. His misery was locked away in a small, hidden corner of himself. The only time the awful hollowness struck now was when he was alone on watch, while the others were asleep.

And even then Alek practiced the art of keeping his tears inside.

"I'm not a child anymore," he said.

"I know." Volger's voice softened. "But your father asked me to wait, Alek, and I intend to honor his wishes. Go wake the men, and after breakfast we'll have a fencing lesson. You'll need your reflexes sharp for this afternoon's piloting."

Alek stared at Volger another moment, then finally nodded.

He felt the need for a sword in his hand.

"On guard, if you please."

Alek raised his saber and assumed his guard. Volger walked in a slow circle around him, inspecting Alek's stance for what felt like a solid minute.

"More weight on your back foot," the man finally said. "But otherwise acceptable."

Alek shifted his weight, his muscles already beginning to cramp. Long days in the pilot's cabin had ruined his form. This lesson was going to hurt.

Pain was always Count Volger's objective, of course. When Alek had started his training at ten years old, he'd expected swordplay to be exciting. But his first lessons had consisted of standing motionless like this for hours, with Volger taunting him whenever his outstretched arm began to quiver.

At least now, at fifteen, he was allowed to cross swords.

Volger took his own guard.

"Slowly at first. I shall call your parries," Volger said, and began to attack, shouting out the names of defensive movements as he lunged. "*Tierce . . . tierce* again. Now *prime.* That's awful, Alek. Your blade's too far down! Two in *tierce.* Now go back covering. Now *quarte.* Simply dreadful. Again . . ."

The count's attacks continued, but his voice dropped off, relying on Alek to choose his own parries. The swords flashed, and their shuffling feet stirred up dust into the shafts of sunlight lancing through the barn.

It felt odd fencing in farmer's clothes, without servants standing ready to bring water and towels. Mice scrambled underfoot, and the giant Stormwalker watched over them

"PRACTICE."

like some iron god of war. Every few minutes Count Volger called a halt and stared up at the machine, as if hoping to find in its stoic silence the patience to endure Alek's clumsy technique.

Then he would sigh and say, "Again . . ."

Alek felt his focus sharpening as they fought. Unlike in the fencing salon at home, here there were no mirrors along the wall, and Klopp and the other men were too busy checking over the walker's engines to watch. No distractions, just the clear ring of steel and the shuffle of feet.

As the sparring grew more intense, Alek realized they hadn't put on masks yet. He'd always begged to fight without protection, but his parents had never allowed it.

"Why Serbia?" Volger suddenly asked.

Alek dropped his guard. "Pardon me?"

Volger pushed aside Alek's half-ready parry and landed a touch on his wrist.

"What in blazes?" Alek cried out, rubbing his hand. The sporting saber's edge was dull, but could still bruise when it landed on flesh.

"Do not drop your guard until the other man does, Your Highness. Not in time of war."

"But you just asked me . . . ," Alek began, then sighed and raised his sword again. "All right. Continue."

The count began with another flurry of blows, pushing Alek backward. By the rules of saber any contact with the opponent's sword ended a legal attack. But Volger was ignoring every parry, using brute strength to gain his ground.

"Why Serbia?" the count repeated, pushing Alek toward the back wall of the barn.

"Because the Serbs are allied with Russia!" Alek cried.

"Indeed." Volger suddenly ended his attack, turning his back and walking away. "The old alliance of the Slavic peoples."

Alek blinked. Sweat was running into his eyes, and his heart was racing.

Volger took up his stance in the center of the barn. "On guard, sir."

Alek approached warily, his sword up.

Volger attacked again, still ignoring the rules of priority. This wasn't fencing, Alek realized, this was more like . . . *a sword fight.* He let his concentration narrow, his awareness extending down the length of his saber. Like the Stormwalker, the length of steel became an extension of his body.

"And who is most closely allied with Russia?" Volger asked, not even a little breathless.

"Britain," Alek said.

"Not so." Volger's blade slipped inside Alek's guard, whacking his right arm hard.

"Ouch!" Alek dropped his guard and rubbed the

wound. "For heaven's sake, Volger! Are you teaching me fencing or diplomacy?"

Volger smiled. "You are in need of instruction in both, obviously."

"But the British navy command met with the Russians last year! Father said it drove the Germans wild with worry."

"That is not an alliance, Alek. Not yet." Volger raised his sword. "So who is allied with Russia, then?"

"France, I suppose." Alek swallowed. "They have a treaty, right?"

"Correct." Volger paused for a moment, sword point tracing a pattern in the air, then frowned. "Raise your sword, Alek. I won't warn you again; nor shall your enemies."

Alek sighed and took his guard. He felt himself gripping the saber too tightly, and forced his hand to relax. Did Volger think these distractions were useful?

"Focus on my eyes," Volger said. "Not the tip of my sword."

"Speaking of eyes, we aren't wearing masks."

"There are no masks in war."

"There aren't many *sword fights* in war either! Not lately."

Volger raised an eyebrow at this, and Alek felt a moment of triumph. Two could play at this game of being annoying.

The man lunged, and Alek parried, counterattacking for once. His saber's edge missed Volger's arm by a hair.

He pulled back and covered himself.

"So let us review," Volger said, his sword still flashing. "Austria gets revenge on Serbia. Then what happens?"

"To protect Serbia, Russia declares war on Austria."

As Alek spoke, somehow his mind stayed focused on the play of sabers. It was strangely clarifying, wearing no mask. He'd met German officers from the military schools where protection was considered cowardly. Scars stretched across their faces like cruel smiles.

"And then?" Volger said.

"Germany protects Clanker honor by declaring war on Russia."

Volger lunged at Alek's knee, an illegal target. "And then?"

"France makes good its treaty with Russia, and declares war on Germany."

"And then?"

"Who knows?" Alek shouted, thrashing at Volger's saber. He'd lost his footing, he realized—too much of his body was exposed. He turned to correct it. "Britain finds her way in somehow. Darwinists against Clankers."

Volger lunged forward and his saber spun, wrapping around Alek's like a snake and yanking it from his grasp. Metal flashed as the sword soared across the barn, burying itself in the half-rotten wall with a *thunk*.

The wildcount stepped forward and held his saber at Alek's throat.

"And what can we conclude from this lesson, Your Highness?"

Alek glared at the man. "We can conclude, Count Volger, that discussing politics while fencing is idiotic."

Volger smiled. "For most people, perhaps. But some of us are born without the choice. The game of nations is your birthright, Alek. Politics is part of everything you do."

Alek pushed Volger's saber aside. Without a sword in his hand he suddenly felt numb and exhausted, and he didn't have the strength to argue against the obvious. His birth had shaken the Austro-Hungarian throne, and now his parents' death had unsettled the delicate balance of Europe.

"So this war is my responsibility," he said bitterly.

"No, Alek. The Clanker and Darwinist powers would have found a way to fight, sooner or later. But perhaps you can still make your mark."

"How?" Alek asked.

The wildcount did a strange thing then. He took his own saber by the blade and handed it to Alek, pommel first, as if offering it to a victor.

"We shall see, Alek. We shall see."

◦ TEN ◦

He eased the saunters sideways and felt the Storm-walker's right foot shift.

"That's it," Otto Klopp said. "Slowly now."

Alek nudged the controls again, and the walker slid a little farther. It was frustrating, maneuvering in tight quarters like this. One bump of the walker's shoulder could send the whole rotten barn crashing down around them. At least the trembling gauges and levers had begun to make sense. A little more pressure in the knees might help. . . .

With another nudge he'd done it—the viewport was lined up with a ragged gap in the wall of the barn. The late afternoon sun shone into the cabin, the fields stretching out before them. A harvesting combine rumbled along on twelve legs in the distance, a dozen farmers and a four-legged truck following to collect the bundled grain.

Count Volger put a hand on Alek's shoulder. "Wait till they're out of sight."

"Well, obviously," Alek said. With his bruises still throbbing, he'd had enough of Volger's counsel for one day.

The combine made its slow way across the field, finally disappearing behind a low hill. A few workmen straggled behind, black dots on the horizon. Alek soon lost them in the distance, but waited.

Finally Bauer's voice crackled on the intercom, "That's the last one gone, sir."

Corporal Bauer had the uncanny eyesight of an expert gunner. Two weeks ago he'd been on his way to commanding a machine of his own. Master Hoffman had been the Hapsburg Guards' best engineer. But now the two were nothing more than fugitives.

Alek had slowly come to understand everything his men had given up for him: their ranks, families, and futures. If they were caught, the other four would hang as deserters. Prince Aleksandar himself would disappear more quietly, of course, for the good of the empire. The last thing a nation at war needed was uncertainty about who was heir to the throne.

He eased the Stormwalker toward the barn's open doors, using the shuffling step that Klopp had taught him. It erased the machine's massive footprints, along with any other signs that someone had hidden here.

"Ready for your first run, young master?" Klopp asked.

Alek nodded, flexing his fingers. He was nervous, but glad to be piloting in daylight for once, instead of the dead of night.

And really, walker falls weren't so bad. They'd all be bruised and battered, but Master Klopp could get the machine back on its feet again.

As the engines pulsed faster, the smell of their exhaust mixed with dust and hay. Alek eased the machine forward, wood creaking as the walker pushed through the doors and out into the fresh air.

"Smoothly done, young master!" Klopp said.

There was no time to answer. They were in the open now. Alek brought the Stormwalker to its full height, its engines cycling to their maximum. He urged it forward, stretching the metal legs farther with every step. Then came the moment when walking turned to running: both feet in the air at once, the cabin shuddering with every impact against the ground.

Alek heard rye being shredded underfoot. The Stormwalker's trail would be easy to spot from an aeroplane, but by night the harvesting combine would turn back and erase the huge footprints.

He kept his eyes on the goal, a streambed covered with sheltering trees.

This was the fastest he had ever traveled, faster than any horse, even faster than the express train to Berlin. Each ten-meter stride seemed to stretch out over endless seconds, graceful in the vast scale of the machine. The thundering pace felt glorious after long nights spent creeping through the forest.

But as the streambed approached, Alek wondered if the walker was moving *too* fast. How was he supposed to bring them to a halt?

He eased back on the saunters a bit—and suddenly everything went wrong. The right foot planted too soon . . . and the machine began to tip forward.

Alek brought the left leg down, but the walker's momentum carried it forward. He was forced to take another step, like a careening drunk, unable to stop.

"Young master—," Otto began.

"Take it!" Alek shouted.

Klopp seized the saunters and twisted the walker, stretching one leg out, tipping the whole craft back. The pilot's chair spun, and Volger swung wildly from the hand straps overhead, but somehow Klopp stayed glued to the controls.

The Stormwalker skidded onward, one leg outstretched, its front foot ripping through soil and stalks of rye. Dust spilled into the cabin, and Alek glimpsed the streambed hurtling toward them.

Gradually the machine slowed, a last bit of momentum lifting it upright . . . and then it was standing on two legs, hidden among the trees, its huge feet soaking in the stream.

Alek watched dust and torn rye swirl across the viewport. A moment later his hands began to shake.

"Well done, young master!" Klopp said, clapping him on the back.

"But I almost fell!"

"Of course you did!" Klopp laughed. "Everyone falls the first time they try to run."

"Everyone *what?*"

"Everyone falls. But you did the right thing and let me take the controls in time."

Volger flicked sprigs of rye from his jacket. "It seems that humility was the rather tiresome point of today's lesson. Along with making sure we look like proper commoners."

"Humility?" Alek bunched his fists. "You mean you knew I would fall?"

"Of course," Klopp said. "As I said, everyone does at first. But you gave up the saunters in time. That's a lesson too!"

Alek scowled. Klopp was positively beaming at him, as if Alek had just mastered a somersault in a six-legged cutter. He wasn't sure whether to laugh or give the man a good thrashing.

He settled for coughing some of the dust out of his lungs, then taking back the controls. The Stormwalker responded normally. It seemed nothing more important than his pride had been damaged.

"You did better than I expected," Klopp said. "Especially with how top-heavy we are."

"Top-heavy?" Alek asked.

"Ah, well." Klopp looked at Volger sheepishly. "I suppose not really."

Count Volger sighed. "Go ahead, Klopp. If we're going to be teaching His Highness walker acrobatics, I suppose it might help to show him the extra cargo."

Klopp nodded, a wicked smile on his face. He pulled himself from the commander's seat and knelt by a small engineering panel in the floor. "Give me a hand, young master?"

A little curious now, Alek knelt beside him, and together they loosened the hand screws. The panel popped up, and Alek blinked—instead of wires and gears, the opening revealed neat rectangles of dully shining metal, each monogrammed with the Hapsburg seal.

"Are those . . . ?"

"Gold bars," Klopp said happily. "A dozen of them. Almost a quart of a ton in all!"

"God's wounds," Alek breathed.

"The contents of your father's personal safe," Count Volger said. "Entrusted to us as part of your inheritance. We won't lack for money."

"I suppose not." Alek sat back. "So this is your little secret, Count? I must admit I'm impressed."

"This is merely an afterthought." Volger waved a hand, and Klopp began to seal the panel back up. "The real secret is in Switzerland."

"A quarter ton of gold, an *afterthought*?" Alek looked up at the man. "Are you serious?"

Count Volger raised an eyebrow. "I am always serious. Shall we go?"

Alek pulled himself back up into the pilot's chair, wondering what other surprises the wildcount had waiting.

Alek started them down the streambed toward Lienz, the nearest city with any mechanikal industry. The walker desperately needed kerosene and parts, and with a dozen gold bars, they could buy the whole town if need be. The trick was not giving themselves away. A Cyklop Stormwalker was a fairly conspicuous way to travel.

Alek kept the machine in the trees along the stream bank. With the afternoon light already fading, they could steal close enough to reach the city on foot tomorrow.

It was strange to think that in the morning, for the first time in two weeks, Alek would see other people. Not just these four men but an entire town of commoners, none of whom would realize that a prince was walking among them.

He coughed again, and looked down at his dusty disguise of farmer's clothes. Volger had been right—he was as filthy as a peasant now. No one would think he was anything special. Certainly not a boy with a vast fortune in gold.

Klopp beside him was equally grubby, but still wore a pleased smile on his face.

◦ ELEVEN ◦

Even though Mr. Rigby had said not to, Deryn Sharp looked down.

A thousand feet below, the sea was in motion. Huge waves rolled across the surface, the wind tearing white moonlit spray from their peaks. And yet up here, clinging to the *Leviathan*'s flank in the dark, the wind was still. Just like in the airflow diagrams, a layer of calm wrapped around the huge beastie.

Calm or not, Deryn's fingers clutched the rigging tighter as she gazed at the sea. It looked cold and wet down there. And, as Mr. Rigby had pointed out many times over the last fortnight, the water's surface was as hard as stone if you were falling fast enough.

Tiny cilia pulsed and rippled through the ropes, tickling her fingers. Deryn slipped one hand free and pressed her palm against the beast's warmth. The membrane felt taut and healthy, with no whiff of hydrogen leaking out.

"Taking a rest, Mr. Sharp?" called Rigby. "We're only halfway up."

"Just listening, sir," she answered. The older officers said the hum of the membrane could tell you everything about an airship. The *Leviathan*'s skin vibrated with the thrumming of the engines, the shufflings of ballast lizards inside, even the voices of the crew around her.

"*Dawdling*, you mean," the bosun shouted. "This is a combat drill! Get climbing, Mr. Sharp!"

"Yes, sir!" she replied, though there wasn't much point in rushing. The other five middies were still behind her. *They* were the ones dawdling, pausing to clip their safety harnesses to the ratlines every few feet. Deryn climbed free, like the older riggers, except when she was swinging from the airbeast's underside—

Ventral side, she corrected herself—the opposite of dorsal. The Air Service hated regular English. Walls were "bulkheads," the dining room was a "mess," and climbing ropes were "ratlines." The Service even had different words for "left" and "right," which seemed to be going a bit far.

Deryn hooked the heel of her boot into the ratlines and pushed herself up again, the feed bag heavy across her shoulder, sweat running down her back. Her arms weren't as strong as the other middies', but she'd learned to climb with her legs. And maybe she *had* been resting, just a squick.

A message lizard scampered past her, its sucker-feet tugging at the membrane like fingers caught in taffy. It didn't stop to squawk orders at the lowly midshipmen, but flitted past on its way up to the spine. The whole ship was on combat alert, the ratlines swaying with scuttling crew, the night air full of fabricated birds.

In the distance Deryn could make out lights against the dark sea. The H.M.S. *Gorgon* was a Royal Navy ship, a kraken tender that had tonight's practice target in tow.

Mr. Rigby must have seen it too, because he shouted, "Keep moving, you sods! The bats are waiting for their breakfast!"

Deryn gritted her teeth, reached for the next rope—*that's a ratline, you sod!*—and pulled as hard as she could.

The middy's test, of course, had been easy.

Service regulations said the test was supposed to be taken on the ground, but Deryn had begged shamelessly, in order to become a temporary middy on the ship. Her third day aboard the *Leviathan*, the ship's officers had relented. With the towers of Paris drifting past the windows, she'd blazed through a few sextant readings, a dozen strings of signal flags to decode, and map reading exercises that Da had taught her ages ago. Even the sour-faced bosun, Mr. Rigby, had shown a glimmer of admiration.

Since the test, though, Deryn's smugness had faded

a bit. It turned out she *didn't* know everything about airships. Not yet, anyway.

Every day the bosun called the *Leviathan*'s young middies to the ship's wardroom for a lecture. Mostly it was airmanship: navigation, fuel consumption, weather predicting, and endless knots and command whistle tunes to learn. They'd sketched the airship's anatomy so often that Deryn knew its innards as well as she knew the streets of Glasgow. On lucky days it was military history: the battles of Nelson, the theories of Fisher, the tactics of airbeast against surface ships and land forces. Some days they played out tabletop battles against the lifeless zeppelins and aeroplanes of the kaiser.

But Deryn's favorite lectures were when the boffins explained natural philosophy. How old Darwin had figured out how to weave new species from the old, pulling out the tiny threads of life and tangling them together under a microscope. How evolution had squeezed a copy of Deryn's own life chain into every cell of her body. How umpteen different beasties made up the *Leviathan*—from the microscopic hydrogen-farting bacteria in its belly to the great harnessed whale. How the airship's creatures, like the rest of Nature, were always struggling among themselves in messy, snarling equilibrium.

The bosun's lectures were merely a fraction of what she had to cram into her attic. Every time another airship flew past, the middies scrambled to the signals deck to read the messages strung on distant fluttering flags. Six words a minute without error, or you were in for long hours of duty in the gastric regions. Every hour they ran drills to check the *Leviathan's* altitude, firing an air gun and timing the echo from the sea, or dropping a glowing bottle of phosphorescent algae and timing how long till it shattered. Deryn had learned to reckon in a squick how many seconds an object took to plummet any distance from a hundred feet to two miles.

But the strangest thing was doing it all *as a boy*.

Jaspert had been right: Her diddies weren't the tricky part. Water was heavy, so bathing on an airship was done quick with rags and a pail. And the toilets aboard the *Leviathan* ("heads" in Service-speak) were in the dark gastric channel, which carried off clart to turn it into ballast and hydrogen. So hiding her body was easy. . . . It was her *brain* she'd had to shift.

Deryn had always reckoned herself a tomboy, between Jaspert's bullying and Da's balloon training. But running with the other middies was more than just punchups and tying knots—it was like joining a pack of dogs. They jostled and banged for the best seats at the middies' mess table. They taunted each other over signal reading and navigation scores, and whom the officers had complimented that day. They endlessly competed to see who could spit farther, drink rum faster, or belch the loudest.

It was bloody exhausting, being a boy.

Not that all of it was bad. Her airman's uniform was miles better than any girl's clothes. The boots clomped gloriously as she stormed to signals practice or firefighting drills, and the jacket had a dozen pockets, including special compartments for her command whistle and rigging knife. And Deryn didn't mind the constant practice in useful skills like knife throwing, swearing, and not showing pain when punched.

But how did boys keep this up their whole barking *lives?*

Deryn eased the feed bag from her sore shoulders. For once she'd reached the airship's spine ahead of the others, and could take a moment's rest.

"Dawdling again, Mr. Sharp?" a voice called.

Deryn turned to see Midshipman Newkirk climbing into view over the curve of the *Leviathan*, his rubber-soled shoes squeaking. There were no waving cilia up here, just hard dorsal scales for mounting winches and guns.

She called back, "Just waiting for you to catch up, Mr. Newkirk."

It always felt odd calling the other boys "mister." Newkirk still had plooks on his face and hardly knew how to tie his necktie. But middies were supposed to put on airs like proper officers.

When he reached the spine, Newkirk dropped his feed bag and grinned. "Mr. Rigby's still *miles* back."

"Aye," Deryn said. "He can't call us dawdlers now."

They stood there for a moment, panting and taking in the view.

The topside of the airbeast was alive with activity. The ratlines flickered with electric torches and glowworms, and Deryn felt the membrane tremble from distant footsteps. She closed her eyes, trying to *feel* the airship's totality, its hundred species tangling to make one vast organism.

"Barking brilliant up here," Newkirk murmured.

Deryn nodded. These last two weeks she'd volunteered

for open-air duty whenever possible. Being dorsal was *real* flying—the wind in her face, and sky in all directions—as prized as her hours up in Da's balloons.

A squad of duty riggers rushed by, two hydrogen sniffers straining on their leashes as they searched for leaks in the membrane. One snuffled Newkirk's hand as it passed, and he let out a squeak.

The riggers laughed, and Deryn joined in.

"Shall I call a medic, Mr. Newkirk?" she asked.

"I'm fine," he snapped, staring at his hand suspiciously. Newkirk's mum was a Monkey Luddite, and he'd inherited a nervous stomach for fabrications. Why he'd volunteered to serve on a mad bestiary like the *Leviathan* was a flat-out mystery. "I just don't like those six-legged beasties."

"They're nothing to be scared of, Mr. Newkirk."

"Get stuffed, Mr. Sharp," he muttered, hoisting his feed bag. "Come on. Rigby's right behind us now."

Deryn groaned. Her aching muscles could've done with another minute's rest. But she'd laughed at Newkirk, so the endless competition was on again. She hoisted her feed bag and followed him toward the bow.

Barking hard work, being a boy.

∘ TWELVE ∘

As Deryn and Newkirk neared the bow, the bats grew louder, their echolocation chirps rattling like hail on a tin roof.

The other middies were just behind, Mr. Rigby in their midst, urging them to hurry. The bats' feeding had to be timed precisely with the fléchette strike.

Suddenly a shrieking mass of havoc swept out of the darkness—an aerie of strafing hawks, aeroplane nets glimmering in the dark. Newkirk let out a startled cry, his feet tangling together. He tumbled down the slope of the airbeast's flank, his rubber soles squeaking along the membrane. Finally he came to a halt.

Deryn dropped her bag and scuttled after him.

"Barking spiders!" Newkirk cried, his necktie more askew than usual. "Those godless birds attacked us!"

"They did no such thing," Deryn said, offering him a hand up.

"Trouble keeping your feet, gentlemen?" Mr. Rigby called down from the spine. "Perhaps some light on the subject."

He pulled out his command whistle and piped out a few notes, high and raw. As the sound trembled through the membrane, glowworms woke up underfoot. They snaked along just beneath the airbeast's skin, giving off enough pale green light for the crew to see their footing, but not so much that enemy aircraft could spot the *Leviathan* in the sky.

Still, combat drills were supposed to be conducted in darkness. It was a bit embarrassing to need the worms just to *walk*.

Newkirk looked down, shuddering a little. "Don't like those beasties either."

"You don't like *any* beasties," Deryn said.

"Aye, but the crawly ones are the worst."

Deryn and Newkirk climbed back up, now behind the other middies. But the bow was within sight, the bats covering it like iron filings on a magnet. The chirping came from all directions.

"They sound hungry, gentlemen," Mr. Rigby warned. "Be sure they don't take a bite of you!"

Newkirk made a nervous face, and Deryn elbowed him. "Don't be daft. Fléchette bats only eat insects and fruit."

"Aye, and metal *spikes*," he muttered. "That's barking unnatural."

"Only what they're designed to do, Newkirk," Mr. Rigby called. Though human life chains were off-limits for fabrication, the middies often conjectured that the bosun's ears were fabricated. He could hear a discontented murmur in a Force 10 gale.

The bats grew noisier at the sight of the feed bags, jostling for position on the sloping half sphere of the bow. The middies clipped their safety lines together and spread out across the swell of the ship, feed bags at the ready.

"Let's get started, gentlemen," Mr. Rigby shouted. "Throw hard and spread it out!"

Deryn opened her bag and plunged a hand in. Her fingers closed on dried figs, each with a small metal fléchette driven through the center. As she threw, a wave of bats lifted, wings fluttering as fights broke out over the food.

"Don't like these birds," Newkirk muttered.

"They ain't birds, you ninny," Deryn said.

"What else would they be?"

Deryn groaned. "Bats are mammals. Like horses, or you and me."

"Flying mammals!" Newkirk shook his head. "What'll those boffins think of next?"

Deryn rolled her eyes and tossed another handful of food. Newkirk had a habit of sleeping through natural philosophy lectures.

Still, she had to admit it was barking strange, seeing the bats eat those cruel metal fléchettes. But it never seemed to hurt them.

"Make sure they all get some!" Mr. Rigby shouted.

"Aye, it's just like feeding ducks when I was wee," Deryn muttered. "Could never get any bread to the little ones."

She threw harder, but no matter where the figs fell, the bullies always had their way. Survival of the meanest was one thing the boffins couldn't breed out of their creations.

"That's enough!" Mr. Rigby finally shouted. "Overstuffed bats are no good to us!" He turned to face the midshipmen. "And now I've got a little surprise for you sods. Anyone object to staying dorsal?"

The middies let out a cheer. Usually they climbed back down to the gondolas for combat drills. But nothing beat seeing a fléchette strike from topside.

The H.M.S. *Gorgon* was within range now, pulling a target ship behind. The target was an aging schooner that carried no lights, but her sails were a white flutter against the dark sea. The *Gorgon* cut her loose and steamed to safety a mile away. Then sent up a signal flare to show that she was ready to start.

"Out of my way, lads," came a voice from behind them. It was Dr. Busk, the *Leviathan*'s surgeon and head boffin.

In his hand was a compressed air pistol, the only sidearm allowed on a hydrogen breather. He waded in among the bats, their black forms skittering away from his boots.

"Come on!" Deryn grabbed Newkirk's arm and scuttled down the slope of the airbeast's flank for a better view.

"Try not to fall off, gentlemen," Mr. Rigby called.

Deryn ignored him, heading all the way down into the ratlines. It was the bosun's job to take care of middies, but Rigby seemed to think he was their mum.

A message lizard scrambled past Deryn and presented itself to the head boffin.

"You may begin your attack, Dr. Busk," it said in the captain's voice.

Busk nodded—like people always did to message lizards, though it was pointless—and raised his gun.

Deryn hooked an elbow through the ratlines. "Cover your ears, Mr. Newkirk."

"Aye, aye, sir!"

The pistol exploded with a *crack*—the membrane shuddering beside Deryn—and the startled bats rose into the air like a vast black sheet rippling in the wind. They swirled madly, a storm of wings and bright eyes. Newkirk cowered beside her, pulling himself closer to the flank.

"Don't be a ninny," she said. "They're not ready to loose those spikes yet."

"Well, I'd hope not!"

A moment later a searchlight beneath the main gondola flicked on, its beam lancing out across the darkness. The bats headed straight into the light, the blended life threads of moth and mosquito guiding them as true as a compass.

The searchlight filled with their small fluttering forms, like a shaft of sun swirling with dust. Then the beam began to swing from side to side, the horde of bats faithfully tracking it across the sky. They spilled out along its length, closer and closer to the target fluttering on the waves.

The swing of the searchlight was perfectly timed, bringing the great swarm of bats directly over the schooner . . .

. . . and suddenly the light turned blood red.

Deryn heard the shrieks of the bats, the sound reaching her ears above the engines and war cries of the *Leviathan's* crew. Fléchette bats were mortally afraid of the color red—it scared the deadly clart right out of them.

As the spikes fell, the horde began to scatter, exploding into a dozen smaller clouds, the bats swarming back toward their nests aboard the *Leviathan*. At the same time the searchlight dipped toward the target.

The fléchettes were still falling. In their thousands, they shimmered like a metal rain in the crimson spotlight, cutting the schooner's sails to ribbons. Even at this distance Deryn could see the wood of the deck splintering, the masts leaning as their stays and shrouds were sliced through.

"Hah!" Newkirk shouted. "A few like that should teach the Germans a lesson!"

Deryn frowned, imagining for a moment that there were crewmen on that ship. Not a pretty picture. Even an ironclad would lose its deck guns and signal flags, and an army in the field would be savaged by the falling spikes.

"Is *that* why you signed up?" she asked. "Because you hate Germans more than fabricated beasties?"

"No," he said. "The Service was my mum's idea."

"But isn't she a Monkey Luddite?"

"Aye, she thinks fabs are all godless. But she heard somewhere that the air was the safest place in a war." He pointed at the shredded ship. "Not as dangerous as down there."

"That's certain enough," Deryn said, patting the airship's humming skin. "Hey, look . . . *now* we're going to get a show!"

The kraken tender was going to work.

Two spotlights stretched out from the *Gorgon*, flicking through signal colors as they swept across the water, calling up their beast. When the lights reached the schooner, they shifted to a dazzling white, illuminating the damage

"A KRAKEN FINISHES THE JOB."

the *Leviathan*'s bats had done. Hardly anything was left of the sails, and the rigging looked like a tangle of chewed-up shoelaces. The deck was covered with splinters and glittering spikes.

"Blisters!" Newkirk cried. "Look what we . . ."

His voice faded as the first arm of the beast rose from the water.

The huge tentacle swept through the air, a sheet of seawater spilling like rain from its length. The Royal Navy kraken was another of Huxley's fabrications, Deryn had read, made from the life chains of the octopus and giant squid. Its arm uncoiled like a vast, slow whip in the spotlights.

Taking its time, the tentacle curled around the schooner, its suckers clamping tight against the hull. Then it was joined by another arm, and each took one end of the ship. The vessel snapped between them, the awful sound of tearing wood bouncing across the black water to Deryn's ears.

More tentacles uncoiled from the water, wrapping around the ship. Finally the kraken's head rose into view, one huge eye gazing up at the *Leviathan* for a moment before the beastie pulled the schooner beneath the waves.

Soon nothing but flotsam remained above the waves. The guns of the *Gorgon* roared in salute.

"Hmph," Newkirk said. "I suppose that's the ocean navy having the final word. Bum-rags."

"I can't say anyone on that schooner would have been bothered by that kraken," Deryn said. "Being killed a second time doesn't hurt much."

"Aye, it was *us* who did the damage. Barking brilliant, we are!"

The first bats were already fluttering home, which meant it was time for the midshipmen to climb down to get more feed. Deryn flexed her tired muscles. She didn't want to slip and wind up down there with the kraken. The beastie was probably annoyed that its breakfast hadn't contained any tasty crewmen, and Deryn didn't fancy improving its mood.

In fact, watching the fléchette strike had left her shaky. Maybe Newkirk was itching for battle, but she'd joined the Service to fly, not to shred some poor buggers a thousand feet below.

Surely the Germans and their Austrian chums weren't so daft as to start a war just because some aristocrat had been assassinated. The Clankers were like Newkirk's mum. They were afraid of fabricated species, and worshipped their mechanical engines. Did they think their mob of walking contraptions and buzzing aeroplanes could stand against the Darwinist might of Russia, France, and Britain?

Deryn Sharp shook her head, deciding that war talk

was all a load of blether. The Clanker powers couldn't possibly want to fight.

She turned from the scattered wreckage of the schooner and scrambled after Newkirk down the *Leviathan*'s trembling flank.

◦ THIRTEEN ◦

Walking through the town of Lienz, Alek's skin began to crawl.

He'd seen markets like this before, full of bustle and the smells of slaughter and cooking. It might have been charming from an open-air walker or a carriage. But Alek had never visited such a place on foot before.

Steam carts rumbled down the streets, spitting hot clouds of vapor. They carried piles of coal, caged chickens screeching in chorus, and overloaded stacks of produce. Alek kept slipping on potatoes and onions that had spilled onto the cobblestones. Slabs of raw meat swung from long poles that men carried on their shoulders, and pack mules prodded Alek with their loads of sticks and firewood.

But worst of all were the people. In the walker's small cabin he'd grown used to the smell of unwashed bodies. But here in Lienz hundreds of commoners packed the

"THE STREETS OF LIENZ."

Saturday market, bumping into Alek from all directions and treading on his feet without a murmur of apology.

At every stall people yammered about prices, as if obliged to argue over every transaction. Those that weren't bickering stood around discussing trivialities: the summer heat, the strawberry crop, or the health of someone's pig.

Their constant chatter about nothing made a certain sense, he supposed, as nothing important ever happened to common people. But the sheer insignificance of it all was overwhelming.

"Are they always this way?" he asked Volger.

"What way, Alek?"

"So trivial in their conversation." An old woman bumped him, then muttered a curse under her breath. "And rude."

Volger laughed. "Most men's awareness doesn't extend past their dinner plates."

Alek saw a sheet of newsprint fluttering underfoot, half ground into the mud by a carriage wheel. "But surely they know what happened to my parents. And that war is coming. Do you suppose they're really quite anxious, and only pretending not to worry?"

"What I suppose, Your Highness, is that most of them cannot read."

Alek frowned. Father had always given money to the Catholic schools, and supported the idea that every man should be given a vote, regardless of station. But listening to the prattle of the crowd, Alek doubted that commoners could possibly understand affairs of state.

"Here we are, gentlemen," Klopp said.

The mechaniks shop was a solid-looking stone building on the edge of the market square. Its open door led into a cool, mercifully quiet darkness.

"Yes?" a voice called from the shadows. As Alek's eyes adjusted, he saw a man staring up at them from a workbench cluttered with gears and springs. Larger mechaniks lined the walls—axles, pistons, one entire engine hulking in the gloom.

"Need a few parts, is all," Klopp said.

The man looked them up and down, taking in the clothes they'd stolen from a farmer's washing line a few days ago. All three of them were still coated with yesterday's dirt and shredded rye.

The shopkeeper's eyes dropped back to his work. "Not much in the way of farm mechaniks here. Try your luck at Kluge's."

"Here's good enough," Klopp said. He stepped forward and dropped a money purse onto the workbench. It struck the wood with a muffled *chunk*, its sides bulging with coins.

The man raised an eyebrow, then nodded.

Klopp began to list gears and glow plugs and electrikals, the parts of the Stormwalker that had begun to wear after a fortnight of travel. The shopkeeper interrupted with questions now and then, but never took his eyes from the money purse.

As he listened, Alek noticed that Master Klopp's accent had changed. Normally, he spoke in a slow, clear cadence, but now his words blurred and trilled with a common drawl. For a moment Alek thought Klopp was pretending. But then he wondered if this was the man's normal way of speaking. Maybe he put on an accent in front of nobles.

It was strange to think that in three years of training Alek had never heard his tutor's true accent.

When the list was done, the shopkeeper nodded slowly. Then his eyes flicked to Alek. "And perhaps something for the boy?"

He pulled a toy from the clutter. It was a six-legged walker, a model of an eight-hundred-ton land frigate, *Mephisto* class. After winding its spring, the shopkeeper pulled the key from its back. The toy began to walk, jerkily pushing its way through the gears and screws.

The man glanced up, one eyebrow raised.

Two weeks ago Alek would have found the contraption fascinating, but now the jittering toy seemed childish. And it was insufferable that this commoner was calling him a *boy*.

He snorted at the tiny walker. "The pilothouse is all

wrong. If that's meant to be a *Mephisto*, it's too far astern."

The shopkeeper nodded slowly, leaning back with a smile. "Oh, you're quite the young master, aren't you? You'll school me in mechaniks next, I suppose."

Alek's hand went instinctively to his side, where his sword would normally have hung. The man's eyes tracked the gesture.

The room was dead silent for a moment.

Then Volger stepped forward and swept up the money purse. He pulled a gold coin out and slapped it down onto the workbench.

"You didn't see us," he said, his voice edged with steel.

The shopkeeper didn't react, just stared at Alek, as if memorizing his face. Alek stared back at him, hand still on his imaginary sword, ready to issue a challenge. But suddenly Klopp was pulling him toward the door and back out onto the street.

As the dust and sunlight stung his eyes, Alek realized what he'd done. His accent, his bearing . . . The man had *seen* who he was.

"Perhaps our lesson in humility yesterday was insufficient," Volger hissed as they pushed through the crowds, heading toward the stream that would lead back to the hidden walker.

"This is my fault, young master," Klopp said. "I should have warned you not to speak."

"He knew from the first word out of my mouth, didn't he?" Alek said. "I'm a fool."

"We're all three fools." Volger threw a silver coin at a butcher and snatched up two strings of sausages without stopping. "Of course they've warned the Guild of Mechaniks to look out for us!" He swore. "And we brought you straight into the first shop we found, thinking a bit of dirt would hide you."

Alek bit his lip. Father had never allowed him to be photographed or even sketched, and now Alek knew why—in case he would ever need to hide. And yet he'd still given himself away. He'd heard the difference in Klopp's speech. Why couldn't he have kept his own mouth shut?

As they reached the edge of the market, Klopp pulled them to a halt, his nose in the air. "I smell kerosene. We need at least that, and motor oil, or we won't get another kilometer."

"Let's be quick about it, then," Volger said. "My bribe was probably worse than useless." He shoved a coin into Alek's hand and pointed. "See if you can buy a newspaper without starting a duel, Your Highness. We need to know if they've chosen a new heir yet, and how close Europe is to war."

"But stay in sight, young master," Klopp added.

The two men headed toward a stack of fuel cans, leaving Alek alone in the market's crush. He pushed his way through the crowd, gritting his teeth against the jostling.

The newspapers were arrayed on a long bench, their pages weighted down with stones, corners fluttering in the breeze. He looked from one to the next, wondering which to choose. His father had always said that newspapers without pictures were the only ones worth reading.

His eyes fell on a headline: EUROPE'S SOLIDARITY AGAINST SERBIAN PROPAGANDA.

All the papers were like that, confident that the whole world supported Austria-Hungary after what had happened in Sarajevo. But Alek wondered if that were true. Even the people in this small Austrian town didn't seem to care much about his parents' murder.

"What'll you have?" a voice demanded from the other side of the bench.

Alek looked at the coin in his hand. He'd never held money before, except for the Roman silver pieces in his father's collection. This coin was gold, bearing the Hapsburg crest on one side and a portrait of Alek's granduncle on the other—Emperor Franz Joseph. The man who had decreed that Alek would never take the throne.

"How many will this buy?" he asked, trying to sound common.

The newspaper man took the coin and eyed it closely. Then he slipped it into his pocket and smiled as though speaking to an idiot. "Many as you like."

Alek started to demand a proper answer, but the words died on his tongue. Better to act like a fool than sound like a nobleman.

He swallowed his anger and filled his arms with one copy of every paper, even those plastered with photographs of racing horses and ladies' salons. Perhaps Hoffman and Bauer would enjoy them.

As Alek glared at the newspaper man one last time, an unsettling realization overtook him. He spoke French, English, and Hungarian fluently, and always impressed his tutors in Latin and Greek. But Prince Aleksandar of Hohenberg could barely manage the daily language of his own people well enough to buy a newspaper.

◦ FOURTEEN ◦

They trudged along the streambed, the kerosene sloshing with every step, its fumes burning Alek's lungs. With each of them carrying two heavy cans, the trip back to the Stormwalker already seemed much farther than the walk to town this morning.

And yet, thanks to Alek, they'd left behind most of what they needed.

"How long can we last without parts, Klopp?" he asked.

"Until someone lands a shell on us, young master."

"Until something breaks, you mean," Volger said.

Klopp shrugged. "A Cyklop Stormwalker is meant to be part of an army. We have no supply train, no tankers, no repair team."

"Horses would have been better," Volger muttered.

Alek shifted the burden in his grip, the smell of kerosene mixing with the smoked sausages that hung around his neck. His pockets were stuffed with newspapers and fresh fruit. He felt like some vagabond carrying everything he owned.

"Master Klopp?" he said. "While the walker's still in fighting prime, why don't we *take* what we need?"

"And bring the army down on us?" Volger asked.

"They already know where we are," Alek said. "Thanks to my—"

"Listen!" Volger hissed.

Alek came to a halt. . . . He heard nothing but the fuel cans sloshing. He closed his eyes. A low thunder rumbled on the edge of his awareness. Hoofbeats.

"Out of sight!" Volger said.

They scrambled down the banks of the stream into the heavy brush. Alek crouched down, his heart beating hard.

As the sound of hoofbeats grew closer, the baying of hunting dogs joined in.

Alek swallowed—hiding was pointless. Even if the hounds didn't have their scent, sausages and kerosene would make any dog curious.

Volger drew his pistol. "Alek, you're the fastest. Run straight for the walker. Klopp and I will make a stand here."

"But it sounds like a dozen horses!"

"Not too many for a walker. Get *moving*, Your Highness!"

Alek nodded and threw down the sausages. He dashed

into the shallow water, feet slipping on wet stones. The dogs couldn't track him across the stream, and the bank on the other side was flatter and clear of bushes.

As he ran, the sound of horses and dogs drew closer. A pistol shot cracked, and there were shouts and the whinny of a horse.

More shots sounded—the booming reports of rifles. Klopp and Volger were outgunned as well as outnumbered. But at least the horsemen were stopping to fight instead of chasing him. Common soldiers wouldn't know who he was, after all. Maybe they wouldn't bother with a young boy in farmer's clothes.

Alek kept running, not looking back, trying not to imagine bullets slicing through his skin.

The stream ran among the farms, high grass on either side. He could just see the copse of trees where the walker was hidden—half a kilometer away. He lowered his head and ran harder, his focus narrowing to his boots and the stones along the stream bank.

Halfway to the trees an awful sound reached his ears—the hoofbeats of a single horse closing in. Daring a glance back, Alek saw a horseman on the other side of the stream, riding hard. His carbine strap was wound around one arm.

He was ready to fire. . . .

Alek turned away and scrambled up the bank. The

rye in the fields was chest high, tall enough to hide in.

A shot rang out—a geyser of dirt shot up a meter to his right.

He dove into the rye, thrashing away from the stream on hands and knees.

The carbine cracked again, and the bullet sliced past Alek's ear. His instincts screamed to run farther in, but the horseman would see the tall grass moving. Alek froze where he was, panting.

"I missed you on purpose!" a voice called out.

Alek lay there, trying to regain his breath.

"Listen, you're just a boy," the voice continued. "Whatever those other two have done, I'm sure the captain will go easy on you."

Alek heard the horse splash into the stream, in no hurry.

He began to crawl deeper into the rye, careful not to disturb the stalks. His heart was pounding, sweat running into his eyes. He'd never been in a battle like this before—outside the metal skin of the Stormwalker. Volger hadn't let him carry a weapon into town, not even a knife.

His first time in single combat, and he was unarmed.

"Come on, boy. Don't waste my time or I'll thrash you myself!"

Alek came to a halt, realizing his one advantage—this young soldier didn't know whom he was hunting. He was expecting some common ruffian, not a nobleman trained in combat since he was ten years old.

The man wouldn't bargain on a counterattack.

The horse was moving into the rye now; Alek could hear its flanks parting the high stalks. The tall, gaudy plume of the rider's helmet rose into view, and Alek dropped lower. The man was probably standing up in his stirrups to peer down into the grass.

Alek was on the horse's left side, where the rider's saber would be hanging. Not as good as a rifle, but better than nothing.

"Don't waste my time, lad. Show yourself!"

Alek watched the plume of the horseman's helmet, realizing that the curve of its tall feathers betrayed the direction he was facing. Standing up like that, he couldn't be too steady.

Alek crawled closer, staying low, waiting for the right moment . . .

"I'm warning you, boy. Whatever you stole, it's not worth getting shot for!"

He drew closer and closer to the horse, and at last the rider's head turned the other away. Alek rose from the ground and ran a few steps, leaping at the man, grabbing his left arm and pulling hard. The horseman swore—then his carbine fired straight into the air. The explosion of noise startled the horse, which thrashed ahead through the rye, yanking Alek's feet up into the air. Alek held on to the man's arm with one hand, the other grabbing for the saber swinging wildly in its scabbard.

The rider twisted, trying to keep his feet in the stirrups. His elbow smashed down into Alek's face like a hammer. Alek tasted blood, but ignored the pain, his fingers scrambling.

"I'll kill you, boy!" the man shouted, one hand twisted in the reins, the other trying to bring the butt of the rifle down onto Alek's head.

At last Alek's hand closed on the hilt of the saber. He let go of the rider's arm and dropped back to the ground, the steel singing as it drew. He landed beside the still-thrashing horse and spun on one foot, slapping the flat of the sword against the horse's backside.

It reared up on its hind legs, the horseman crying out as he finally tumbled from his perch. The carbine flew from his grasp into the tall grass, and he landed with a heavy thud.

Alek slashed his way through the rye until he stood beside the fallen horseman. He lowered the saber's point to the man's throat.

"Surrender, sir."

The man said nothing.

His eyes were half open, his face pale. He wasn't much older than Alek, his beard wispy, his splayed arms thin. The expression on his face was so still. . . .

Alek took a step back. "Are you hurt, sir?"

Something large and warm nudged him softly from behind—the horse, suddenly calm. Its nuzzle pushed against the back of Alek's neck, sending a cold shiver down his spine.

The man didn't respond.

In the distance, shots rang out. Volger and Klopp needed his help, *now*. Alek turned from the fallen rider and pulled himself up into the saddle. The reins were tangled and twisted, the horse unsteady beneath him.

Alek leaned down and whispered in its ear. "It's all right. Everything's going to be okay."

He prodded his heels into its flanks, and the horse shuddered into motion, leaving its former rider behind in the grass.

The Stormwalker's engines were already rumbling.

The horse didn't hesitate when Alek urged it between the huge steel legs. It must have trained alongside walkers— it was an Austrian horse, after all.

Alek had just killed an Austrian soldier.

He forced the thought away and grabbed the dangling chain ladder, sending the horse clear with a shout and a kick.

Bauer met him at the hatch. "We heard shots and started up, sir."

"Good man," Alek said. "We'll need the cannon loaded too. Volger and Klopp are a kilometer from here, holding off a troop of horses."

"Right away, sir." Bauer offered a hand, and pulled him inside.

As Alek scrambled through the belly and up into the pilot's cabin, more shots sounded in the distance. At least the fight hadn't ended yet.

"Do you need help, sir?" Hoffman asked. He was halfway up through the hatch, a look of concern on his bearded face.

Alek stared at the controls, realizing that he'd never piloted before without Master Klopp sitting beside him. And here he was, about to stride into battle.

"You've never piloted, have you?" Alek asked.

Hoffman shook his head. "I'm just an engineer, sir."

"Well, then, you're better off helping Bauer with the cannon. And both of you strap in tight."

Hoffman smiled, saluting. "You'll do all right, sir."

Alek nodded, turning back to the controls as the hatch swung shut. He flexed his hands.

One step at a time, Klopp always said.

Alek pushed the saunters forward. . . . The walker reared up, valves hissing. One huge foot pushed ahead in the stream, sending spray into the air. Alek took another step, urging the machine faster.

But his power gauges all flickered deep in the green—the engines were still cold.

In a few steps the Stormwalker had climbed the river-bank, up to level ground. Alek gunned the fuel injectors, the engines roaring.

The power gauges began to rise.

He pushed the machine forward, letting its strides grow longer and longer. The furrows began to flash by under-neath, the sound of tearing rye audible above the engines. He felt the moment when the walker shifted into a run, the machine rising up into the air between footfalls.

From the top of each stride he could see the troop of horses ahead. They were spread out across the rye, in search formation.

Alek smiled. Klopp and Volger had also slipped away into the tall grass—that was how they'd held out for so long.

Heads turned, the horsemen wheeling toward the new threat.

The intercom crackled. "Ready to fire."

"Aim over their heads, Bauer. They're Austrians, and Klopp and Volger are somewhere in that grass."

"A warning shot then, sir."

A few of the carbines crackled, and Alek heard a bullet strike metal close by. He realized that the viewport was wide open, with no one to wind it shut.

The young rider he'd killed had missed him on purpose. But these men were aiming to kill.

He changed the walker's stride, pushing outward with the feet so that the machine weaved from left to right. *Running serpentine,* Klopp called this, cutting a path like a snake through the grass.

But the machine's winding path didn't feel as graceful as that.

The cannon boomed below him—then a column of dirt and smoke shot into the air just behind the horsemen. Widening circles rippled through the grass like pond water from a stone, and two horses fell sideways, throwing their riders.

A second later a wave of dirt and sheer force struck Alek through the open viewport, and his hands slipped from the saunters. The walker lurched to one side, wheeling toward the stream. Alek grabbed at the controls, twisting them hard, and the Stormwalker came to, staggering but still upright.

The horsemen had gathered into tight formation, about to retreat. But Alek saw them hesitating, wondering if the walker was out of control. Lurching around like this, it probably looked as intimidating as a drunken chicken. He doubted Bauer could reload the cannon unless he could steady the machine.

Shots crackled again, and something pinged around

"THE CHARGE!"

Alek's ears, a bullet ricocheting around the metal cabin. No point in coming to a halt—it just made him a better target—so Alek leaned low over the controls, heading straight for the troop of horses.

The riders hesitated for another moment, then wheeled about and galloped back toward the stream, deciding not to pit flesh against metal.

"Sir! It's Master Klopp!" Bauer's voice came on the intercom. "Standing up in front of us!"

Alek pulled back on the saunters, just as he had the day before—and again the walker's right foot planted hard, the machine beginning to tip.

But this time he knew what to do. He twisted the walker sideways, thrusting out one steel leg. Dust exploded across the viewport, and the sound of straining gears and tearing grass filled his ears.

Alek felt the machine regain its balance, the momentum of its charge consumed by the skid.

As the walker settled, Alek heard the belly hatch open below. There were shouts, and the clanking of the chain ladder unrolling. Was that Klopp's voice? Volger's?

He wanted to glance down through the cabin hatch, but he stayed at the controls. The dust was clearing before him, and he saw movement in the distance—the flash of helmets and spurs. Perhaps he should fire one of the machine guns into the air, just to keep them in retreat.

"Young master!"

Alek spun around in the pilot's chair. "Klopp! You're all right!"

"Well enough." The man pulled himself up into the cabin. His clothes were torn and bloody.

"Were you hit?"

"Not me. Volger." Klopp fell into the commander's chair, panting. "His shoulder—Hoffman's seeing to it below. But we must go, young master. More will come."

Alek nodded. "Which way?"

"First back to the stream. The kerosene's still there."

"Right. Of course." The dust was clearing in the viewports, and Alek put his shaking hands on the saunters again. He realized that he'd hoped Klopp would take the controls, but the man was still panting, his face bright red.

"Don't worry, Alek. You did well."

Alek swallowed, forcing his hands to push the Stormwalker into a first step. "I almost wrecked it again."

"Exactly: *almost.*" Klopp laughed. "Remember how I said everyone falls the first time they try to run?"

Alek scowled as he planted one giant foot on the riverbank. "I could hardly forget."

"Well, everyone also falls the *second* time they run, young master!" Klopp's laughter turned into coughing, then he spat and cleared his throat. "Except for you, it seems. Lucky for us you're such a Mozart with the saunters."

Alek kept his eyes ahead, not answering. He didn't feel proud, having left that rider behind, lying broken in the grass. The man had been a soldier serving the empire. He couldn't have understood the politics swirling around him any more than those commoners back in Lienz.

But he'd lost his life just the same.

Alek felt himself split into two people, the way he did when he was alone on watch, one part crushing down his despair into its small, hidden place. He blinked away sweat and searched the riverbank for the precious cans of kerosene, hoping that Bauer was watching for horses, and that the cannon was loaded again.

· FIFTEEN ·

Just after morning altitude drills the middies were all at breakfast, chattering about signal scores, the duty roster, and when war would finally come.

Deryn had already finished her eggs and potatoes. She was busy sketching the way the message lizard tubes coiled around the *Leviathan*'s walls and windows. The beasties always poked their heads out as they waited for messages, like foxes in a burrow.

Then suddenly Midshipman Tyndall, who'd been staring dreamily out the windows, shouted, "Look at that!"

The other middies sprang up, scrambling to the port side of the mess. In the distance, across the patchwork of farmlands and villages, the great city of London was rising into view. They shouted to each other about the ironclads moored on the River Thames, the tangle of converging rail lines, and the elephantine draft animals

"BLASÉ ABOUT OLD SIGHTS."

that choked the roads leading to the capital.

Deryn stayed in her seat, taking the opportunity to spear one of Middy Fitzroy's potatoes.

"Haven't you plook-heads seen London before?" she asked, chewing.

"Not from up here," Newkirk said. "The Service never lets us big ships fly over cities."

"Wouldn't want to scare the Monkey Luddites, would we?" Tyndall said, punching Newkirk's shoulder.

Newkirk ignored him. "Look! Is that Saint Paul's?"

"Seen it," Deryn said, stealing a piece of Tyndall's bacon. "I flew over these parts in a Huxley once. An interesting story, that."

"Quit your blethering, Mr. Sharp!" Fitzroy said. "We've heard *that* story enough."

Deryn flicked a piece of potato at Fitzroy's dorsal regions. The boy always assumed superior airs, just because his father was an ocean navy captain.

Feeling the projectile hit home, Fitzroy turned from the view and scowled. "We're the ones who rescued you, remember?"

"What, you sods?" she said. "I don't remember seeing *you* at the winch, Mr. Fitzroy."

"Perhaps not." He smiled and turned back to the view. "But we watched you float past these very windows, swinging from your Huxley like a pair of trinkets."

The other middies laughed, and Deryn sprang up from her chair. "I think you might want to rephrase that, Mr. Fitzroy."

He turned away and gazed serenely out the window. "And I think you might learn to respect your betters, Mr. Sharp."

"*Betters?*" Deryn balled her fists. "Who'd respect a bum-rag like you?"

"Gentlemen!" Mr. Rigby's voice came from the hallway. "Your attention, *please.*"

Deryn snapped to attention with the others, but her glare stayed fixed on Fitzroy. He was stronger than her, but in the two tiny bunk rooms that the middies shared, there were a hundred ways to take revenge.

Then Captain Hobbes and Dr. Busk entered the mess behind Mr. Rigby, and her anger faded. It wasn't often that the master of the *Leviathan*, much less the ship's head boffin, addressed the lowly middies. She exchanged an anxious glance with Newkirk.

"At ease, gentlemen," the captain said, then smiled. "I'm not bringing you news of war. Not today, at least."

Some of the other middies looked disappointed.

A week ago Austria-Hungary had finally declared war on Serbia, vowing to avenge their murdered archduke with an invasion. A few days later Germany had started up with Russia, which meant that France would be next into the fray. War between the Darwinist and Clanker powers was spreading like a vicious rumor, and it didn't seem that Britain could stay out for long.

"You may have noticed London underneath us," the captain continued. "An unusual visit, and that's not the half of it. We'll be setting down in Regent's Park, near His Majesty's London Zoo."

Deryn's eyes widened. Flying over London was bad enough, but coming down in a public park was going to stir the pot for sure. And not just for Monkey Luddites. Even old Darwin himself might have got antsy about a thousand-foot airbeast landing on his picnic.

The captain crossed to the windows and looked down. "Regent's Park is at best a half mile across, a bit more than twice our length. A tricky business, but the risk is a necessary one. We're taking aboard an important guest, a member of the zoo's staff, for transport to Constantinople."

Deryn wondered for a moment if she'd heard right. Constantinople was in the Ottoman Empire, clear on the other side of Europe, and the Ottomans were Clankers. Why in blazes would the *Leviathan* be headed there now?

The airship had spent the last month preparing for war—combat drills every night, and daily musters of the fléchette bats and strafing hawks. They'd even flown within sight of a German dreadnought in the North Sea, just to show that a living airship wasn't scared of any pile of gears and engines.

And now they were headed off on a jaunt to Constantinople?

Dr. Busk spoke up. "Our passenger is a scientist of great renown, who'll be undertaking an important diplomatic mission. We will also be bringing cargo aboard, of a delicate nature. It must be treated with the utmost care."

The captain cleared his throat. "Mr. Rigby and I may have to make a difficult decision about weight."

Deryn took a slow breath. *Weight* . . . so that's what this was about.

The *Leviathan* was "aerostatic," Service-speak for being the same density as the air around it. Maintaining this balance was a fussy business. When rain collected topside, water had to be dumped from the ballast holds. If the ship expanded in the hot sun, hydrogen had to be vented off. And when passengers or extra cargo came aboard, something else had to be taken off—usually something useless.

And there was nothing more useless than a new midshipman.

"I shall be reviewing your signals and navigation scores," the captain was saying. "Mr. Rigby will weigh in on which of you are paying the most attention in lectures. And, of course, any missteps during this landing will be frowned upon. Good day, gentlemen."

He turned and strode from the room, the head boffin leaving with him. There was a moment of silence as the middies absorbed the news. In a few hours some of them might be gone from the *Leviathan* for good.

"All right, lads," Mr. Rigby snapped. "You heard the captain. We're about to land on an improvised airfield, so look smart! They've got a ground crew in from the Scrubs, but no landing master with them. And our passenger is going to need help down there. Mr. Fitzroy and Mr. Sharp, you two are the best with the Huxleys, so you'll head down first. . . ."

As the bosun gave his orders, Deryn looked at the other middies' faces. Fitzroy returned her gaze coolly, and she didn't have to guess what that bum-rag was thinking. She'd been aboard the *Leviathan* barely a month, and it was only by freak chance that she was here at all. Not much better than a stowaway, as far as Fitzroy was concerned.

Deryn glared right back at him. The captain hadn't said anything about who'd been aboard longest. He was looking at airmanship, so he wanted to keep his best men.

And that's exactly what she was, man or not.

Maybe all the competition on the *Leviathan* would serve her well now. Thanks to Da's training, Deryn had always beat the other middies with knots and sextants.

And even Mr. Rigby would admit that her behavior hadn't been *as* rowdy lately, and he'd just complimented her work with the Huxleys.

As long as the landing went brilliantly, there was nothing to worry about at all.

Regent's Park spread out beneath Deryn, its grass thick from the August rains.

Squads of ground men ran across it, shepherding the last few civilians out of the landing area. A thin line of policemen clung to the edges, holding back hundreds of gawkers. The *Leviathan*'s shadow lay across the trees, and the air trembled with the engines' hum.

Deryn was descending fast, aiming for the intersection of two footpaths, where a local chief constable was awaiting orders. A message lizard rode on her shoulder, its sucker-feet tugging at her uniform like the claws of a nervous cat.

"We're almost there, beastie," she said soothingly. She didn't fancy arriving on the ground with a panicked lizard, the captain's landing orders garbled beyond understanding.

Deryn was a bit nervous herself. She'd ridden ascenders a half dozen times since joining the *Leviathan*'s crew—she weighed the least of all the middies, and could always coax her beasts the highest. But that had been on U-boat spotting duty, with the Huxley cabled to the airship. This was the first time she'd free-ballooned since her wild ride as a recruit.

So far, at least, it had been a textbook descent. The airbeast's extra ballast was bringing it down fast, guided by a pair of gliding wings attached to her rig.

Deryn wondered who was so important, to warrant all this trouble. They were ruining a hundred picnics and risking disaster by landing here in the park, and probably scaring the clart out of every Monkey Luddite in London. And all just to get some scientist to Constantinople a bit quicker?

This fellow must be some kind of clever-boots, even for a boffin.

The ground was rushing closer, and Deryn let out a slosh of ballast. Her descent slowed a squick, the spilled water sparkling in the sun as it cascaded down. The message lizard squeezed a little tighter.

"Don't you worry, beastie," Deryn murmured. "It's all under control."

Mr. Rigby had told her to get down fast, with no nonsense. She imagined him watching from above, timing the descent with his stopwatch, pondering who should be cut from the crew.

It didn't seem fair to lose this feeling, not after those two long years of missing Da's balloons. Surely Rigby could see that she'd been *born* to fly.

A crosswind ruffled the Huxley, and as Deryn pulled it back on course, a horrible notion struck her. If she were the unlucky middy, would this be her last time in the air? With war coming, surely they'd stick her on another airship. Maybe even the *Minotaur*, where Jaspert was serving.

But the *Leviathan* felt like part of Deryn now, her first real home since Da's accident. The first place where no one had ever seen her in a skirt, or expected her to mince and curtsy. She couldn't lose her position here just because some boffin needed transportation!

The ground men were running along in the Huxley's shadow, ready to reach up and grab its tentacles. She tipped the gliding wings back to slow the descent, easing the air-beast down into their grasp. There was a jolt as they pulled her to a halt, and the message lizard made a squawk.

"Constable Winthrop?" it babbled.

"Hang on another minute!" she pleaded. The lizard made a tut-tut noise, sounding just like Mr. Rigby when the middies were squabbling. She hoped it wouldn't start jabbering. Message lizards could babble old snatches of conversation when they were nervous. You never knew what embarrassments they'd repeat.

The ground men pulled the Huxley steady and drew it quickly down.

She unstrapped herself from the pilot's rig and saluted

the chief constable. "Midshipman Sharp reporting with the captain's lizard, *sir*."

"That was a smart landing, young man."

"Thank you, sir," Deryn said, wondering how to ask the constable to pass this sentiment on to Mr. Rigby. But the man was already tugging the lizard from her shoulder. The beastie started to babble about landing ropes and wind speeds, rattling off instructions faster than a dozen signalmen.

The constable didn't look as though he understood half of what the lizard was saying, but Fitzroy would be here soon to help. She spotted his ascender landing not far away, and was pleased that she'd beaten him down.

The airship's shadow fell across them then, and men began to scramble in all directions. This was no time to dally. Fitzroy was in charge here; it was Deryn's job to prepare the boffin's cargo for loading.

She saluted the chief constable again, glanced up at the airship looming overhead, and took off for the zoo at a run.

◦ SIXTEEN ◦

His Majesty's London Zoo was squawking like a bag of budgies on fire. Deryn skidded to a halt at the entry gate, stunned by the tumult of hoots and roars and shrieks.

To her right a troop of monkeys clung to the bars of their cage, howling into the air. Past them a netted enclosure was full of agitated birds, a blizzard of plumage and noise. Across a wide moat a giant elephantine stamped the ground nervously, sending tremors through Deryn's boots.

"Barking spiders," she swore softly.

She'd made Jaspert take her to the London Zoo five weeks ago, fresh off the train from Glasgow. But on that visit she'd heard nothing like this ruckus.

Obviously the *Leviathan* had put the beasties in a state.

Deryn wondered how the airship must smell to the natural animals. Like a giant predator coming to gobble them up? Or some long-lost evolutionary cousin? Or did its tangle of fabricated species make them think a whole island was floating past overhead?

"Are you my airman?" a voice called.

Deryn turned to see a woman wearing a long traveling coat, a valise in one hand.

"Pardon me, ma'am?"

"I was promised an airman," the woman said. "And you appear to be in uniform. Or are you simply here to throw peanuts at the monkeys?"

Deryn blinked, then realized that the woman was wearing a black bowler.

"Oh . . . *you're* the boffin?"

The woman raised an eyebrow. "Guilty as charged. But my acquaintances call me Dr. Barlow."

Deryn blushed, bowing a little. "Midshipman Dylan Sharp, at your service."

"So you *are* my airman. Excellent." The woman held out the valise. "If you would be a dear, I'll just fetch my traveling companion."

Deryn took the bag and bowed again. "Of course, ma'am. Sorry to be so thick. It's just that . . . no one told me you were a lady."

Dr. Barlow laughed. "Not to worry, young man. The subject has occasionally been debated."

With that she turned away and disappeared through the gatehouse door, leaving Deryn holding the heavy valise and wondering if she was seeing things. She'd never heard of a lady boffin before—or a female diplomat, for that matter. The only women who tangled with foreign affairs were spies, she'd always reckoned.

But Dr. Barlow didn't quite have the air of a spy. She seemed a bit too loud for a job like that.

"Careful now, gentlemen," her voice boomed from the gatehouse.

Emerging from the door were two young boffins in white coats, carrying a long box between them. The men didn't introduce themselves to Deryn. They were too focused on taking small, cautious steps, as though the box were packed with gunpowder and good china. Sprigs of packing straw poked out between the boards.

No wonder the *Leviathan* was landing smack in the middle of London—this mysterious cargo was too fragile to stick on a horse cart.

Deryn stepped forward to lend a hand, but hesitated when she felt a squick of heat rising from the box.

"Is something *alive* in there?" she asked.

"That's a military secret," said the younger of the two boffins.

Before Deryn could answer, Dr. Barlow burst from the gatehouse, pulled along by the oddest fabricated beastie that Deryn had ever seen.

The creature looked like a sleek tan dog with a long

snout, and tiger stripes on its rump. Straining against the leash, it stretched out to sniff Deryn's offered hand. As she stroked its head, the beastie leaned back on its strong hind legs and hopped once in place.

Did the animal have a squick of *kangaroo* in its life thread?

"Tazza seems to like you," Dr. Barlow said. "Odd. He's usually shy."

"He's very . . . enthusiastic," Deryn said. "But what in blazes is he *for*?"

"For?" Dr. Barlow frowned. "Whatever do you mean, Mr. Sharp?"

"Well, he doesn't look like a hydrogen sniffer. Is he some sort of tigeresque guard dog?"

"Oh, heavens!" The woman laughed. "Tazza isn't fabricated, and he isn't *for* anything. Except that I hate traveling without him."

Deryn pulled her hand away and took a step back. "You mean, that beastie's *natural*?"

"He's a perfectly healthy thylacine." Dr. Barlow reached down to scratch between the bouncing creature's ears. "Commonly known as the Tasmanian tiger. Though we find the comparison to cats a bit infuriating, don't we Tazza?"

The thylacine yawned, its long jaws opening as wide as an alligator's.

Dr. Barlow had to be joking. The creature didn't look natural in the least. And she was taking it along as a *pet*? Tazza looked heavy enough to displace at least one unlucky midshipman.

But it seemed undiplomatic to point that out, so Deryn cleared her throat and said, "Maybe we should get onto the field, ma'am. The ship'll be down soon."

Dr. Barlow gestured to a steamer trunk resting by the gatehouse door. A covered birdcage was sitting on top. "If you'd be so kind, Mr. Sharp."

"Yes, ma'am," Deryn sighed. She tucked the valise under one arm and lifted the birdcage in that hand. The trunk weighed almost as much as she did (another middy gone), but Deryn managed to lift one end and drag it along. The four of them—and Tazza the thylacine—headed back into the park, the boffins carrying the box at a snail's pace.

As they made their way toward the airship, Deryn grumbled under her breath. It was one thing giving up her berth for a renowned boffin on a secret mission, but if some daft beastie named Tazza was going to take her place, the world had gone *completely* barking spiders.

◉   ◉   ◉

Dr. Barlow clicked her tongue. "Your airship looks unhappy."

The *Leviathan* was still about fifty feet up, the captain bringing her down with infinite caution. The cilia on its flanks were rippling, and flocks of fabricated birds roiled across the park, driven from their nesting coves by the airship's twitchiness.

What was the great beastie so nervous about? Deryn glanced up, remembering the squall that had almost ended her Air Service career on the first day. But the sky was cloudless. Maybe it was the gawkers surrounding the field, their bright parasols twirling in the sun.

"My cargo requires a smooth ride, Mr. Sharp."

"It'll be calm once we're off the ground," Deryn said. In one airmanship lecture Mr. Rigby had filled a wineglass to the brim—even during hard turns not a drop had spilled over. "It's just that the airflow gets messy down here."

Dr. Barlow nodded. "Especially in the middle of London, I suppose."

"Aye, ma'am. The streets tangle up the wind, and the big ships get nervous coming down on unfamiliar fields." Deryn said this flatly, not mentioning whose fault the situation was. "You see those wee grassy bits on the ship's flanks? They're called cilia, and they look shivery to me."

"MOORING AT REGENT'S PARK."

"I know what cilia are, Mr. Sharp," the lady boffin said. "I fabricated this particular species, in fact."

Deryn blinked, feeling like a ninny. Lecturing one of the *Leviathan*'s creators on the subject of airflow!

The thylacine was bouncing happily on its hind legs again, its big brown eyes taking in all the activity. Two elephantines waited below the airship, harnessed to a transport wagon and an armored car. The constables could hardly keep the crowd back from the spectacle.

With no mooring mast in the park, ropes stretched in all directions from the *Leviathan*. Deryn frowned, noticing that some of the men clinging to them weren't in Service uniforms. She spotted a few policemen, and even a team of cricketers drafted from games in the park.

"Fitzroy must be daft," she muttered.

"What's the trouble, Mr. Sharp?" Dr. Barlow asked.

"Those men on the ropes, ma'am. If a squall comes up quick, they won't know to let go—and *fast*—or be carried up into the air . . ."

"Where they shall eventually lose their grip," Dr. Barlow said.

"Aye. One strong gust can carry the *Leviathan* up a hundred feet in seconds." It was the first thing they taught ground men: Don't hang on. The trees rippled overhead, sending a shiver through Deryn.

"What would you recommend we do, Mr. Sharp?"

Deryn frowned, wondering if the ship's officers knew what was going on. Most of the untrained men were back at the stern end, out of sight of the bridge. "Well, if we could get word up to the captain, he'll know to get down fast, or cut the ropes if a squall hits."

She scanned the field, looking for Fitzroy, or anyone in charge. But the park was all in chaos, and the chief constable nowhere to be seen.

"Perhaps Clementine can help us," Dr. Barlow said.

"Who?"

Dr. Barlow handed Tazza's leash to Deryn, then reached for the birdcage. She opened the linen cover and reached inside, pulling out a bird with gray feathers and a brilliant red tuft at its tail.

"Good morning, Dr. Barlow," the bird squawked.

"Good morning, dear," she answered. Then she said in a slow, clear voice, "Captain Hobbes, greetings from Dr. Barlow. I have a message from Mr. Sharp: You appear to have some untrained men on your ropes." She looked at Deryn and shrugged. "And . . . I look forward to meeting you, sir. End message."

She gathered the bird closer to her chest, then pushed it toward the airship.

As it swept up and away, Deryn murmured, "What was that?"

"A message parrot," Dr. Barlow said. "Based on the

Congo African Grey. We've been training it especially for this trip. It can read airmen's uniforms and gondola markings, just like a proper Service lizard."

"Training it, ma'am?" Deryn frowned. "But I thought this Constantinople business came up all of a sudden."

"Indeed, things are moving more quickly than expected." Dr. Barlow lay one hand on the mysterious box. "But some of us have been planning this mission for years."

Deryn gave the box another wary glance, then turned to watch the parrot. It flapped through the ropes and guidelines, straight into the open windows of the bridge.

"That's *brilliant*, ma'am. It's like a flying message lizard!"

"They have many of the same life threads," Dr. Barlow said. "In fact, some of us believe that birds share ancestors with the ancient lizards. . . ." Her voice faded as the *Leviathan*'s tanks let loose with a spray of ballast.

The ship rose a little, the men on the ropes skidding along the ground in a losing tug of war against the airship.

"Blisters!" Deryn swore. "Why's he *climbing?*"

"Oh dear," Dr. Barlow said, looking down. "I *do* hope that was Clementine."

Deryn followed her stare to the birdcage. Another hooked gray beak was poking out, gnawing on the bars. "There's two of them?"

The lady boffin nodded. "Winston tends to garble

things, and I can never tell them apart. It's such a bother."

Deryn swallowed, watching as the ballast water rained down on the ground men's heads. It sparkled prettily in the sunlight, but Deryn knew where that ballast came from—it was straight from the gastric channel, clart and all.

The civilians among them thought something had gone wrong. A squad of men in cricketing whites dropped their ropes and covered their heads, retreating from the unexpected rain of smelly water. The ship rose higher as their weight left the ropes, but Deryn saw the hydrogen sniffers on the ship's topside going into a frenzy. The captain was also venting gas.

The ship steadied in the air.

Another spray of ballast came, heavier than the last. The proper ground men, who'd had clart hit their heads a hundred times, hung on. But in a few moments all the untrained men had abandoned their ropes.

"Very clever, your captain," Dr. Barlow said.

"Nothing like a bit of muck to clear things out!" Deryn said happily, then added, "So to speak, ma'am."

Dr. Barlow let out a laugh. "Indeed. I shall enjoy traveling with you, Mr. Sharp."

"Thank you, ma'am." Deryn glanced at the lady boffin's massive pile of luggage. "Perhaps you could mention that to the bosun. You see, the ship's a wee bit overweight."

"I shall," the woman said, taking back her beastie's leash. "We'd like a little cabin boy all our own, wouldn't we, Tazza?"

"Um, that's not really what I . . ." Deryn blethered, starting to explain that midshipmen were officers, practically. They certainly weren't *cabin boys*.

But Dr. Barlow was already leading her thylacine toward the airship, trailed by the other boffins and their mysterious box.

Deryn sighed. At least she'd earned her place aboard the *Leviathan*. And after his blunder with the ropes, that bum-rag Fitzroy might finally get what he deserved. Not bad for one day's work.

Of course, now there was a fresh worry to ponder.

As another female, Dr. Barlow might notice a few odd things the other crewmen hadn't. And she was a clever-boots, with all that science under her bowler. If anyone was going to guess Deryn's little secret, it would be this lady boffin.

"Brilliant," Deryn muttered, taking hold of the heavy trunk and hurrying for the ship.

○ SEVENTEEN ○

The land frigate stood atop a distant rise, its signal flags snapping in the breeze.

"That's a bother," Klopp said, lowering his field glasses. "She's a thousand-tonner, *Wotan* class. A new experimental model. Small enough to make good speed; big enough to pound us into dust."

Alek took the glasses from Klopp and raised them to his eyes.

The *Herkules* wasn't the largest landship they'd seen, but with its eight long legs—arranged like a spider's—it did look nimble. The array of smokestacks suggested a powerful engine bank inside.

"What's she doing here at the Swiss border?" Alek asked. "Isn't there a war on?"

"One might think she was waiting for us," Count Volger said.

"See that crow's nest?" Klopp pointed at a tall mast rising from the frigate's gun deck. Two tiny figures stood on the platform mounted at its top. "That lookout tower isn't standard equipment."

"And the lookouts are facing this way—into Austria," Bauer said. The pilot's cabin was crowded, the other three arranged around Alek like a family portrait. "I doubt they're stationed here to protect us from invasion."

"No, they're here to keep us in," Alek said, lowering the field glasses. "They knew we were headed to Switzerland, thanks to me."

Count Volger shrugged. "Where else would we go?"

Alek supposed he was right. With the war spreading every day, Switzerland was the only country staying neutral—the last place for fugitives and deserters to hide.

But it still didn't seem fair, running straight into this land frigate. They'd been weaving back and forth across Austria for more than a month— creeping through forests for a few hours every night. They'd been hunted, shot at, even dive-bombed by an aeroplane. They'd spent whole days scavenging parts and fuel from farm machines and junkyards, just enough to keep the Stormwalker running. And finally they'd reached a passage to safety, only to find it guarded by a giant metal spider.

It was certain the *Herkules* wasn't going anywhere soon. A command tent was pitched under her engines, where a six-legged cargo walker waited to fetch supplies and fresh crew.

"How far are we from the border?" Alek asked.

"You're looking at it, sir," Bauer said, pointing past the frigate. "Those mountains are in Switzerland."

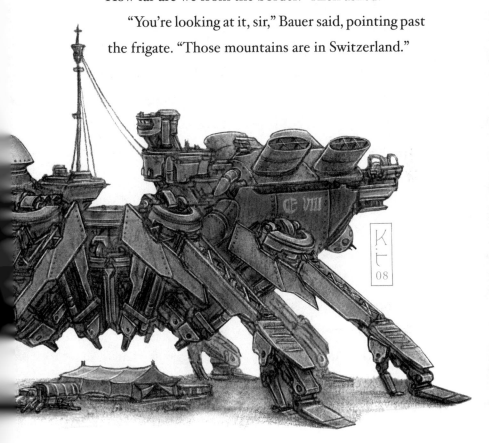

Klopp shook his head. "Might as well be Mars. Back-tracking to another mountain pass will take a week at least."

"We'd never make it," Alek said, flicking the kerosene gauge. The needle shivered at the halfway mark, enough for a few days at most.

Fuel had been hard to come by after Alek's foolishness at Lienz. Horse scouts swept the carriage paths and zeppelins patrolled the skies—all because he'd behaved like a spoiled brat.

But at least Volger had been right about one thing. Prince Aleksandar of Hohenberg had not been forgotten.

"We can't go around them," Alek decided. "So we'll go right through them."

Klopp shook his head. "She's designed for stern chases, young master. Her big guns are in the forward turrets—she can pound us without turning sideways."

"I didn't say we'd *fight* her," Alek said. Klopp and Volger stared at him, and he wondered why they were being so thick. He sighed. "Before this all began, had any of you ever traveled in a walker at night?"

Klopp shrugged. "Too risky. In the Balkan Wars all the walker battles were in broad daylight."

"Exactly," Alek said. "But we've crossed the length of Austria in darkness. We've mastered a skill that no one else even dares to practice."

"*You've* mastered night-walking," Klopp said. "My old eyes can't manage it."

"Nonsense, Klopp. You're still the far better pilot."

The man shook his head. "In daylight, perhaps. But if we're doing any running in the dark, it should be you at the saunters."

Alek frowned. This whole last month he'd assumed old Klopp was letting him pilot for the sake of practice. The idea that he had surpassed his old master of mechaniks was unsettling. "Are you sure?"

"Sure as blazes," Klopp said, clapping Alek on the back. "What do you say, Count? We've given our young Mozart here enough practice in night-walking. Might as well put him to the test!"

They started the engines just after sunset.

The last rays still shone like pearl on the snowy peaks in the distance. But long shadows stretched from the mountains, plunging the pass into darkness.

Alek's hand moved to the control saunters—

Suddenly a pair of searchlights lanced out from the frigate. They swept across the dark expanse—bright knives slicing the night into pieces.

His hands dropped from the controls. "They know we're here."

"Nonsense, young master," Klopp said. "They've realized

by now that we move at night. But two searchlights can't cover the whole border."

Alek hesitated. There were always rumors of German secret weapons: listening devices or machines that peered through fog and darkness with radio waves. "What if they have more than just lights?"

"Then we'll improvise." Klopp smiled.

Alek watched the searchlights carefully. Their paths across the valley seemed to have no pattern. Staying hidden would hinge on pure luck, which didn't seem like enough. This plan had been all his idea; any disaster was on Alek's head alone.

He forced the thought away, remembering his father's favorite line from the poet Goethe: *The dangers of life are infinite, and among them is safety.*

The real hazard was hiding here in Austria. If they tried to avoid any risks, they'd be found sooner or later. He placed his hands on the saunters again.

"Ready?" he said.

"Whenever you are, Alek." Count Volger pulled himself up into the top hatch, resting his feet on the back of the pilot's seat. The toes of his boots tapped Alek's shoulders, both at once—the signal to move ahead.

Alek gripped the control saunters and took a first step.

Volger's boot pressed his left shoulder softly, and Alek nudged the walker leftward. It was annoying, being controlled like a puppet, but from topside the count had a better view.

"Easy now," Klopp said as the walker leaned forward. The path led steeply downhill, into the long, narrow valley that the *Herkules* guarded. "Short steps."

Alek nodded, his grip tightening as the walker skidded down the slope a little.

"Drop the rear anchor, Hoffman," Klopp said into the intercom.

A rattle of unwinding chain came from behind them. Alek felt the tug of the anchor as it cut through roots and undergrowth, dragged along like a child's toy.

"Bothersome, I know," Klopp said. "But this way we won't roll if we fall."

"I'm not going to fall," Alek said, his hands tight on the saunters. With the engines at quarter power, the massive feet moved slowly—like walking in syrup.

The moon was just beginning to rise, and through the viewport Alek could see nothing but a dark confusion of branches. Volger's boots nudged him left and right with no apparent pattern, the walker's feet snagging on roots and underbrush. It was like being led, blindfolded and barefoot, across a room covered with mousetraps.

Finally they reached the valley floor, and Klopp rolled up the anchor. Alek still couldn't see anything but the branches thwacking against the open viewport, scattering leaves across the control panel. He wondered if they were stirring the treetops overhead, like a fish moving below the surface of a pond.

His mind began to buzz with doubts. Perhaps they should have picked a windy night to try this. Or why not wait for a rainstorm? Or the darkness of the new moon?

With a sudden *clang* of boots on metal, Volger dropped into the pilot's cabin.

"Get us down!"

Alek reached for the control panel, but Klopp's hands were faster—a hissing filled the cabin as the walker settled lower in the trees.

Moments later a blinding light swept across them.

The searchlight lingered a few seconds, then drifted into the forest ahead, continuing its lazy path among the trees.

"Get us moving again," Volger said. "They'll look elsewhere now."

"I'm afraid it may be a moment," Klopp said, his eyes on the gauges.

"Our engines are barely running," Alek explained. "Building our knee pressure back up will take time." He leaned back and stretched his fingers, happy for a break. He was starting to wish the frigate would spot them and give chase. A good run would be better than creeping through the dark at quarter speed.

The belly hatch opened, and Hoffman's head emerged.

"Pardon me, sirs. But do you hear that?"

They all listened for a moment, and Alek's ears caught a rushing sound below the engine's rumble.

"A stream?" he asked.

Hoffman grinned. "A noisy one, sir. Noisier than us, anyway."

"Excellent," Alek said, sitting up. "Up to half speed, Master Klopp?"

Klopp listened for another moment, then nodded.

Soon the Stormwalker was splashing down the stream, its engine noise mixing with the rush of water. The moon was higher now, the path shimmering in front of them. Volger was still up top watching for searchlights, but at least he wasn't standing on Alek's shoulders anymore.

The spray from the stream was icy; snow must still have been melting up in the mountains, even now in early August. Alek wondered how long they would have to stay in the Alps. He hoped Volger's mysterious preparations included a cabin with a warm fire.

The ground began to climb. They were nearing the rise where the land frigate stood guard. Alek lowered the engines back to quarter speed, and the Stormwalker became maddeningly lead-footed again. There were no sounds except the calls of night birds, the splashing of giant metal feet, and the babble of the stream.

Then a boot hit the back of his chair with a *thump*.

"Volger! What are you—"

Something flashed in the darkness ahead. Alek froze, the walker pausing halfway through a step. He peered into the darkness.

"Should I shut the engines down?" he whispered.

"Don't!" Klopp said. "If they've spotted us, we'll need power."

Volger swung down from the hatch. "Germans! On foot, a hundred meters ahead. They haven't seen us. Not yet, anyway."

Alek swore softly, his hands flexing on the controls. He wondered which was worse, being spotted or sitting here frozen, like a rabbit waiting for a hawk to swoop. He leaned closer to the viewport, shielding his eyes. Something metal flashed in the darkness, and then he heard a shout.

"I think they just . . . ," he began.

Splashes of water sparkled white in the moonlight— a squad of infantrymen was running across the stream, shouting. One knelt on the bank and raised his rifle.

". . . noticed us," Alek finished as a *crack* rang out. The bullet struck metal somewhere on the walker's body.

"Prepare to fire!" Klopp called through the intercom.

"No!" Alek said as his hands flicked across the controls.

"Alek's right," Count Volger said. "Those rifles might

perk up the frigate's ears, but a cannon shot will remove all doubt. Just go through them."

The engines came to a roar beneath him, and Alek pushed the saunters forward. The Stormwalker's huge feet stretched out, splashing through the shallow water.

They charged up the stream, scattering the Germans like tenpins. A few bullets pinged off the armor as they passed, but Alek didn't bother to order the viewport closed. Vision was more precious than safety.

No stumbles now, no mistakes or they'd all be caught.

The moon had cleared the trees, the water shimmering in their path. A smile grew on Alek's face as he brought the Stormwalker into a run. Let the frigate try and catch them now.

No one could night-walk like him.

⊙ EIGHTEEN ⊙

The flares came first.

They screamed across the sky, burning phosphorous spilling a cold blue light into the darkness. The icy spray from the Stormwalker's footsteps glittered like diamonds scattered in the air.

More flares flew overhead, until the sky glowed with a dozen suns.

Flares and fireworks—not such secret weapons after all.

"Into the forest!" Klopp shouted.

Alek twisted the saunters hard, and the walker climbed the bank of the stream in a single step. It was darker up in the trees, the shadows shifting and dancing as the flares raced overhead.

But there were no more rifle shots, no thud of cannon fire.

"What's happening, Count?" Klopp shouted.

"The frigate is turning," Volger called down. "She looks sluggish."

"Perfect!" Klopp said. "We caught her engines cold."

"But why isn't she firing?" Alek asked, veering the Stormwalker around an outcrop of bare rocks.

"Good question, young master. Perhaps they intend to capture you alive."

Alek raised an eyebrow. "Well, that's reassuring."

The ground became steeper beneath them, the walker's engines straining. Wider spaces opened up among the trees as the slope increased. It made walking easier, but Alek felt exposed in the jittery light of the flares.

"Which way to more cover?" Klopp called up.

Volger lowered himself into the cabin. "It doesn't matter."

"Why not?" Klopp cried.

"The frigate isn't our immediate problem." Volger leaned down next to Alek. "Bring us around. You need to see them. And load that cannon!" he shouted down the belly hatch.

Alek brought the walker into a tight turn.

From up here on the unsheltered slope, he could see the frigate on its hill, the eight legs slowly flexing as it awoke. Its gun turrets had already spun around, but Alek could see why they hadn't fired yet.

Climbing the slope behind them were a half dozen

walkers unlike anything Alek had ever seen. They were four-legged craft, with a galloping stride like metal horses. A single crewman rode half inside each one, his head and shoulders emerging like a centaur's. The scout walkers' single headlights danced through the trees like fireflies.

Their only weapons were small mortar tubes mounted on the rear of the machines. As Alek watched, one blossomed with a cloud of smoke, shooting another flare into the radiant sky.

"Some new kind of scout," Klopp murmured.

"And perfect for tracking the likes of us," Volger said.

Alek frowned. "But those mortars won't even scratch us!"

"They don't have to," Klopp said, "as long as they keep us in sight. The frigate will be moving sooner or later."

"So what do we do?" Alek said, hands clenching the saunters. "Fight them now, while she's still warming up?"

Klopp thought for a moment. "No, keep moving. Maybe you can get us to the border faster than they expect."

Alek turned the walker back around and started up the slope again. He heard Volger preparing the Spandaus. The scout walkers' pilots were only half covered with armor. A few machine-gun bursts might make them think twice about following too closely.

A sudden red glare filled the Stormwalker's cabin, along with a choking wave of smoke. Alek squinted through

the haze—a still-burning flare skittered away across the ground.

He coughed into a fist. "They're shooting *flares* at us now? Are they mad?"

"It *is* a bit pathetic," Klopp said. "But I'll close the view-port."

Alek nodded. The thought of burning phosphorous bouncing around the cabin was unnerving. He hardly needed the viewport open; it was still as bright as day outside.

But one thing was odd. The sky was lit a cold blue, but the flare that had just missed them had burned bright red.

As the viewport cranked closed, another flare rocketed past—also red—missing the Stormwalker by a hair.

Volger started up with one of the machine guns, filling the cabin with the roar of gunfire and still more smoke. Shell casings clattered down onto the metal deck, rolling back and forth underfoot as the walker lurched along.

Another red flare whizzed past, spitting smoke and sparks. Alek's eyes were beginning to sting, and his vision blurred with tears.

"Otto, take over!"

Klopp grabbed the saunters, and Alek searched blindly for his canteen. He drained it onto his face, washing the smoke from his eyes.

A metal *clang* shuddered through the cabin.

"Did you hit something?" Alek asked, blinking the water away.

Klopp shook his head. "Hardly. It's light enough out there!"

Alek frowned, feeling the machine rumble beneath him. The walker's steps were steady on the slope, and the gauges all flickered at normal levels.

Except one—the temperature of the rear exhaust had suddenly jumped.

He stood and pushed the top hatch open.

"Alek!" Volger said, turning from his machine gun. "What are you doing?"

"Something's wrong." He pulled himself up.

Fresh air blew across his face, and the engines' unmuffled roar filled his ears. Keeping his head down, he scanned the forest.

Nothing but trees and undergrowth. Where had the scout craft gone?

Then Alek spotted one in the distance, running away at top speed.

"What the . . . ?" he began, then saw a reddish flicker coming from the rear exhaust ports. He pulled himself a little higher and saw what it was.

A hissing glob of phosphorus was stuck to the engine casing. Still burning, it billowed smoke into the air. Alek lifted his gaze and saw the red column drifting up into the bright sky.

"So much for capturing me alive," he muttered, and dropped back through the hatch.

Count Volger glared at him. "Glad to see you've regained your—"

"Klopp!" Alek shouted. "Run serpentine!"

The master of mechaniks hesitated, then began to weave the Stormwalker through the trees.

"Turn harder, man! That last flare *hit us*. It's stuck to the armor like a mud ball and sending up smoke!" The others just stared at him, and Alek cried, "Those scouts are running off as quickly as they can!"

Awareness finally dawned on Klopp's face. He pulled the walker to the left for a few long strides, then back to the right.

This was why the frigate hadn't fired yet. Its gunners were waiting for the target to be marked and for the scouts to get clear. But now the Stormwalker was in for a thrashing.

Alek looked at the rear exhaust gauge—still hot. That column of red smoke was still rising above the trees.

He turned to Klopp. "Is there any way to put it out?"

"Phosphorous? Water won't work, and it'll burn through anything we try to smother it with. We'll have to wait till it burns out."

"How long?" Volger asked.

"Could be half an hour," Klopp said. "Long enough for them to—"

A rumbling sounded in the distance.

Alek shouted a warning, but Klopp was already twisting the saunters, driving the walker into a hard turn. The machine thrashed through a stand of saplings, and Alek grabbed the hand straps, slipping on the shell casings rolling across the metal deck.

Then a sovereign *boom* rolled through the Stormwalker. The sound shook Alek to his bones, and the world suddenly tipped sideways. He hung from the hand straps, feet swinging in the air.

Klopp's hands never left the controls, and somehow the walker staggered back upright. It swerved, narrowly missing a beech tree. Heavy branches lashed at them, sending an explosion of leaves through the half-closed viewport.

"How long till the next volley?" Volger's voice was dry.

"About forty seconds," Klopp said.

"We have to get that flare off!" Alek shouted. "Give me something to hack at it with!"

Volger shook his head. "It's too dangerous, Your Highness."

Alek had to suppress a hysterical laugh, tearing open the pilot's storage locker. "*Dangerous*, Volger? Compared with letting ourselves be blown to pieces?"

"I'll do it, then," Volger said.

Alek's hand closed on a sword he'd never seen before. He pulled it from the locker—an old cavalry saber, much heavier than the swords they fenced with, perfect for the job.

"I've been climbing on walkers since I was ten, Volger," he said, sticking the scabbard through his belt.

Volger placed his hand on Alek's shoulder. "That sword is two centuries old! Your father—"

"Can't help us," Alek said. "Reload the machine guns in case those scouts come back."

Without waiting for a reply he pulled himself up and out.

Up top, branches slapped at his face, and the machine rocked beneath him like an unbroken horse. Klopp was doing his best serpentine. The hot metal of the engine casing burned Alek's fingers even through his piloting gloves.

The marker flare was stuck among the Stormwalker's exhaust pipes, hissing and spitting, driven brighter by the machine's speed. Red smoke trailed out, spreading as it rose into the brilliant sky.

Alek drew the saber and clutched it with one hand, holding the scabbard with the other. He raised the sword high, then brought the blade down hard.

The flare split open under his blow, but only blazed brighter, like a burning log jabbed with a poker.

Alek raised the sword again and saw flames running along his blade—the fire was clinging to the metal! He

"AN HEIRLOOM SAVES THE HEIR."

swallowed, wondering what would happen if the infernal substance were stuck to someone's skin.

Lights flickered through the trees. Alek looked up and glimpsed the frigate in the distance, smoke pouring from her guns. As he knelt for a firmer handhold, the cannon's rumble followed at the tardy speed of sound.

Long seconds later the shells hit. The shock wave battered his ears, spraying dirt into his face and lifting the walker beneath him.

Alek felt its massive feet hit the ground again, the machine staggering like a newborn colt. He opened his eyes—just in time to duck beneath a tree branch whipping across the walker's head.

Now there was no sound except the ringing in his ears, and his eyes stung with debris and smoke. But he could feel Klopp righting the walker, regaining control.

The frigate would have their range now. Each time they fired, the shells would land closer.

Alek stooped again and raised the saber, hacking at the sticky flare, sending up sparks and angry gouts of smoke. Embers fell from the blade onto his uniform, burning into the leather piloting jacket like hot coals. He smelled his own hair singeing in the heat.

A volley of flares shot past, the retreating scouts taking one last shot at the Stormwalker. Alek ignored the near misses and kept battering at the flame.

Finally a big chunk came free, sticking to his saber like honey on a stick. He waved the blade back and forth in the wind, but that only drove the flare brighter.

Alek swore. The frigate's guns would be loaded again in another few seconds. There was only one thing to do.

He rose into a half crouch, one arm wrapped around an exhaust pipe.

"Sorry, Father," he whispered, and threw the ancient saber as hard as he could into the forest.

He kicked at the last few burning pieces clinging to the Stormwalker's armor, then crawled toward the open hatch.

"Klopp!" he shouted down. "Go straight ahead, as fast as you can!"

Alek glanced back before climbing inside. The ancient sword was still burning back among the trees, sending up red smoke. The gunners on the frigate would think that the Stormwalker had staggered to a halt, or fallen after that last barrage. Hopefully they'd pound the spot a few more times before sending the scouts back in to check.

And by that time the walker would be kilometers away.

As Alek's adrenaline faded, his body began to throb with pain. His hands and knees were bruised and burned, and the leather of his uniform smelled like scorched meat. He hoped Volger had something for burns along with his supply of family heirlooms and pointless secrets.

As Alek lowered himself into the hatchway, Volger's eyes widened, taking in his singed hair and smoldering uniform.

"Are you all right?"

"I'm fine," he said, collapsing into the commander's chair. "Just keep moving."

The mountains were rising taller in the viewport. The border couldn't be far now; the sky up ahead was empty of flares. Soon they'd been in friendly darkness again.

The frigate's guns rumbled again, but the shells hit far behind them, hardly breaking the Stormwalker's stride. The Germans were still firing at his father's sword.

Alek smiled—so much for their secret weapons.

He let his eyes close. After a month of running, finally he could rest. Maybe his life would begin to make sense again, once the Stormwalker had reached safety.

No more surprises for a while.

◉ NINETEEN ◉

"I should like to see your bees, Mr. Sharp."

Deryn looked up tiredly from the sketch pad, putting her pencil aside. Her last watch of the day had just ended—four nervous hours of keeping an eye out for German aircraft—but Dr. Barlow never seemed to sleep. She looked well spruced in traveling coat and bowler hat, and Tazza bounced at the boffin's side, always happy to be exploring the ship.

"*My* bees, ma'am?"

"Don't be tiresome, Mr. Sharp. I meant, of course, the *Leviathan's* bee colonies. Do you always draw while shaving?"

Deryn glanced at her straight razor in its mug, remembering that half her face was covered in lather. She'd been waiting for someone to pass the open cabin door and witness the deception. But after a few minutes she'd given up posing by the mirror. Even copying sketches from the

Manual of Aeronautics's chapter on thermal inversions was more interesting than pretending to shave.

She wiped her face with a towel. "That's the life of a middy, ma'am. Always studying . . . and giving tours to visiting boffins, of course."

"Of course," Dr. Barlow said sweetly. In her two days aboard she'd toured practically every inch of the airship, dragging Newkirk and Deryn from deck to deck, onto the topside, even to the Huxley rookeries in the gut of the whale. There was no fobbing the duty off. Only two middies remained aboard, thanks to the weight of Dr. Barlow's pet thylacine, her numerous outfits, and the mysterious cargo secured in the machine room.

Deryn missed having the others about, if only to share the work of altitude readings and feeding the fléchette bats. The only brilliant thing—besides that bum-rag Fitzroy being gone—was that Deryn and Newkirk each had a private cabin now. Of course, Dr. Barlow's boffin studies didn't seem to have covered the subject of privacy.

"Come on, Tazza," Deryn muttered, taking the beastie's leash as she slipped into the corridor.

She led Dr. Barlow up the aft stairs to the top deck of the gondola. The riggers and sailmakers slept up here, though Deryn couldn't see how they managed. The airbeast's gastric channel filled the air with a smell like rotten onions and cow farts.

The off-duty watch swung in hammocks on either side of the corridor, some of them curled up with their hydrogen sniffers for warmth. The airship was cruising at eight thousand feet, hopefully too high for the German aeroplanes that had been stalking them all day, and the air up here was as cold as a brass monkey's bum.

None of the riggers glanced at Dr. Barlow or the thylacine as they passed. The ship's officers had announced that anyone making a fuss over the lady passenger would be put on report. This was no time for navy superstitions, after all. Germany had declared war on France yesterday and had gone after Belgium today. The rumor was that Britain would be in it tomorrow unless the kaiser put a stop to the whole mess by midnight.

And nobody thought that very likely.

At the gut hatch Deryn took Tazza into her arms and climbed up and out. In the cold, narrow gap between airbeast and gondola, the ventral camouflage cells shone a dull silver, taking on the color of the snowy moonlit peaks below. The Swiss Alps were rising beneath them. The *Leviathan* was a third of the way to the Ottoman Empire, Deryn reckoned.

Tazza scrambled out of her arms and up, curious to explore the strange mix of smells: clart from the gastric channel, the bitter almond of leaking hydrogen, and the salty scent of the airbeast's skin.

Deryn followed the beastie up into the gut, then knelt to lend Dr. Barlow a hand. They paused for a moment in the warm darkness, their eyes adjusting to the dim green light of glowworms.

"I'll take this opportunity to remind you not to smoke, Doctor."

"Very amusing, Mr. Sharp."

Deryn smiled and scratched Tazza's head. Open flames weren't allowed anywhere on the *Leviathan*. Matches and firearms were kept under lock and key, and the airmen's boots had rubber soles to prevent sparks of static. But according to regulations, passengers were to be reminded of the smoking rules whenever the crew thought necessary.

Even if they were fancy-pants boffins and being reminded of the barking obvious happened to annoy them.

Walking forward, Tazza slunk closer to the ground, always a little twitchy inside the whale. The walkway underfoot was aluminum, but the walls of the gastric channel were alive—warm and pulsing with digestion, aglow with worms. The hydrogen bladders overhead were taut and translucent, the whole ship swelling in the thin air of high altitude.

As they approached the bow, a humming sound grew: millions of tiny wings churning the air, drying the nectar gathered that day over France. A little farther and the walls

"IN THE GUTS OF THE SHIP."

were covered with a seething mass of bees, their small round bodies buzzing around Deryn's head, bouncing softly against her face and hands. Tazza let out a low hiss and pressed closer to her legs.

Deryn could appreciate the thylacine's nervousness. Seeing the hives for the first time, she'd assumed they were weapons, like strafing hawks or fléchette bats. But the *Leviathan*'s bees didn't even have stingers. As the ship's head boffin liked to put it, they were simply a method for extracting fuel from nature.

In summer the fields passing beneath the airship were full of flowers, each containing a tiny squick of nectar. The bees gathered that nectar and distilled it into honey, and then the bacteria in the airbeast's gut gobbled that up and farted hydrogen. It was a typical boffin strategy—no point in creating a new system when you could borrow one already fine-tuned by evolution.

A bee came to an inquisitive midair halt in front of Deryn's face. Its body was fuzzy and yellow, its dorsal regions as shiny and black as dress boots, the wings a blur. She squinted, memorizing its shape for sketching later.

"Hello, wee beastie."

"Pardon me, Mr. Sharp?"

Deryn waved away the curious bee and turned. "Anything in particular you wanted to see, ma'am?"

Dr. Barlow was tucking a black veil under her bowler, like a boffin at a funeral. "My grandfather fabricated one of these species. I wanted to taste his handiwork."

Her *grandfather*? Dr. Barlow had to be even younger than she looked.

"You seem surprised, Mr. Sharp. The honey is edible, is it not?"

"Aye, ma'am. Mr. Rigby makes all us middies try some." Fitzroy had made a show of screwing up his face, and Newkirk had looked ready to spew. But the taste was as good as any natural honey, really.

Deryn drew her rigging knife and reached out to the expanse of hexagonal comb, prizing a bit of honey onto its blade. She offered the knife to Dr. Barlow, who loaded a fingertip, then reached under her veil to place it between her lips.

"Hmm. Just like honey."

"Water, mostly," Deryn said. "With a few squicks of carbon for flavor."

Dr. Barlow nodded. "A very sound analysis, Mr. Sharp. But you're frowning."

"Pardon me, ma'am. But did you say your grandfather was a Darwinist? He must have been one of the first."

Dr. Barlow smiled. "He was indeed. And he had rather a fascination with bees, especially how they connected cats and clover."

"*Cats*, ma'am?"

"And clover, yes. He noticed that red clover flowers abundantly near towns but only thinly in the wild." Dr. Barlow rubbed her finger along the knife for another taste. "You see, in England most cats live in towns—and cats eat mice. These same mice, Mr. Sharp, attack the nests of bees for their honey. And red clover cannot grow without bees to pollinate it. Do you follow?"

Deryn raised an eyebrow. "Um, I'm not sure, ma'am."

"But it's very simple. Near towns there are more cats, fewer mice, and thus more bees—resulting in more red clover. My grandfather was good at noticing webs of such relations. You're frowning again, Mr. Sharp."

"It's just that . . . he sounds like a rather eccentric gentleman."

"Some think so." Dr. Barlow chuckled. "But at times eccentrics notice things that others do not. You must sharpen your razor very well."

Deryn swallowed. "My razor, ma'am?"

The lady boffin reached out to hold Deryn by her chin. "Both sides of your face are equally smooth. But didn't I interrupt you halfway through your shave?"

As Dr. Barlow waited for an answer, the buzzing of the hives roared in Deryn's head, and the walkway seemed to tilt beneath her feet. She'd been such a *ninny* to muck about with razors. This was how she'd always been caught out in lies—making things too barking *complicated.*

"I . . . I'm not sure what you mean, ma'am."

"How old are you, Mr. Sharp?"

Deryn blinked. She couldn't speak.

"With a face that smooth, not sixteen," Dr. Barlow continued. "Perhaps fourteen? Or younger?"

A squick of hope began to trickle through Deryn. Had the lady boffin guessed the *wrong secret?* She decided to tell the truth: "Barely fifteen, ma'am."

Dr. Barlow released her chin, giving a shrug. "Well, I'm sure you're not the first boy to come into the Service a bit young. Your secret is safe with me." She handed back the rigging knife. "You see, my grandfather's true realization was this: If you remove one element—the cats, the mice, the bees, the flowers—the entire web is disrupted. An archduke and his wife are murdered, and all of Europe goes to war. A missing piece can be very bad for the puzzle, whether in the natural world, or politics, or here in the belly of an airship. You seem like a fine crewman, Mr. Sharp. I'd hate to lose you."

Deryn nodded slowly, trying to take all of this in. "I'm in agreement with that, ma'am."

"Besides . . ." A hint of a smile played on Dr. Barlow's lips. "Knowing your little secret makes it easier, should I wish to tell you some of mine."

Before Deryn had a chance to wonder what that could

mean, she noticed a distant clanging over the roar of the hives.

"Do you hear that, ma'am?" she said.

"The general alarm?" Dr. Barlow nodded sadly. "I'm afraid so. It would appear that Britain and Germany are finally at war."

° TWENTY °

The Klaxon was ringing in triplets, the signal for an aerial attack.

"I have to run, ma'am," Deryn said quickly. "Can you make it back to your cabin alone?"

"I'd think not, Mr. Sharp. I shall be with my cargo."

"But—but . . . this is an alert," Deryn sputtered. "You can't go to the machine room!"

Dr. Barlow took Tazza's leash from her. "That cargo is more important than your regulations, young man."

"But passengers are supposed to stay—"

"And midshipmen are *supposed* to be sixteen years old." Dr. Barlow waved her hand. "Don't you have some sort of battle station to get to?"

Deryn let out a pained growl, but gave up in disgust and turned away. She'd done her best—the lady boffin could hang herself out the windows if she wanted.

As Deryn ran back toward the main gondola, the aluminum walkway trembled under her feet. The whole crew was scrambling, filling the passageways of the ship. She dodged past a squad of men in gastric suits and reached the gut hatch, dropping halfway through for a peek outside.

The icy wind between gondola and airbeast rumbled with an unfamiliar sound. Not the hum of motivator engines—the angry snarl of Clanker technology. A winged shape caught a flash of moonlight in the distance, an Iron Cross painted on its tail.

The German aeroplanes could fly this high after all.

Deryn dropped the rest of the way down, landing hard enough to bang her teeth together. The middies' battle station was topside with the bats, so she'd need a flight suit to keep from freezing. Deryn's suit was back in her cabin, but the riggers always had spares hanging in their bunk room. She dodged through the press of men and hydrogen sniffers, looking for a suit with a pair of gloves stuffed into the pockets. There wasn't time to find goggles; Dr. Barlow's pigheadedness had delayed her long enough.

As she buttoned the coverall up to her neck, Deryn felt dizzy for a moment. The rush of battle had come too soon after the shock of Dr. Barlow's near discovery. The lady boffin had promised not to tell, but she didn't know the whole story—not yet. With those sharp eyes of hers, she'd *have* to guess the truth eventually.

Deryn took a deep breath and shook her head clear. This wasn't the time to fret about secrets. The war was finally here.

She gave her safety line a yank to test its strength, then headed for the rigging hatches.

There were at least a half dozen flying machines hunting the *Leviathan*. They were hard to count, staying in the distance to keep clear of the strafing hawks and their aeroplane nets.

Deryn was halfway to topside, climbing fast in the freezing wind. Men and fabricated animals swarmed the ratlines, the ropes pressing hard against the membrane with their weight.

She heard the motivator engines change pitch, and the world began to tilt. As the airship rolled, Deryn found herself on the underside again, hanging from the ratlines by two hands. The crewmen around her swung from their safety harnesses, but Deryn's clip dangled unused from her belt.

"Blisters!" she swore, looking up at her aching hands— possibly Mr. Rigby had been right about using safety clips in battle.

She swung her feet, hooking one leg into the ropes to free a hand. The ship rolled harder over, and a message lizard overhead lost its grip. It tumbled past her, shouting random words in a dreadful mix of human voices.

Deryn tore her eyes away from the poor beastie—her fingers had found the safety clip. After snapping it onto a rope, she let herself hang from the harness, resting the burning muscles in her hands.

A roar was building in the air.

From half a mile away a Clanker machine rushed toward her. An engine thundered on each wing, billowing twin trails of smoke. The broad, batlike wings stretched and twisted as the aeroplane came alongside. . . .

Its machine gun erupted, sweeping the flank of the *Leviathan*.

Men and beasties scrambled to escape the path of the bullets. Deryn saw a hydrogen sniffer hit, dancing in agony against the ratlines, then flailing madly as it fell. Glowworms sputtered bright green sparks as they were torn apart beneath the skin.

The aeroplane kept coming, thundering straight toward her. Deryn unclipped her harness and slid down as fast as she could. Bullets rippled through the membrane just overhead, like stones splashing into water. The ropes jerked in her grasp, trembling with the airship's pain.

The gun finally sputtered out, the aeroplane peeling away. But a bright spark flared against the darkness. The gunner had ignited a phosphorous canister. He hoisted it high, the device sparking and smoking as the plane circled back toward the *Leviathan*.

Deryn's hands tightened on the ropes, but there was nowhere to climb. The bitter-almond scent of hydrogen filled her lungs. The entire airship was primed to explode.

But then a searchlight swept into view. An aerie of strafing hawks followed its arc, carrying an aeroplane net. Its glistening strands trailed from the birds' harnesses, binding them together in a web of gossamer.

The hawks turned and wheeled in formation, stretching the glowing lace across the aeroplane's path. . . .

The machine crashed into the net, which wrapped around it, spilling fabricated spider acid from its strands. The acid burned through wings and struts and flesh in seconds. Pieces spun off wildly, the plane's wings folding like scissors in the air.

The Clanker crewmen, the deadly phosphorous canister, and a hundred metal parts tumbled toward the snowy peaks below.

A ragged cheer went up along the airship's flank, fists raised as the machine fell. The riggers were soon at work patching the membrane, but a few men hung unmoving in their harnesses, lifeless or moaning in pain.

Deryn wasn't a medic, and she was supposed to be topside by now, but it took her a long moment to start climbing again and leave the bleeding crewmen behind.

There were more aeroplanes out there, she reminded herself, and the fléchette bats needed feeding.

Topside was covered with crewmen, guns, and sniffers going barmy with the smell of spilled hydrogen.

Deryn stayed off the crowded dorsal ridge, running along the soft membrane to one side. She reckoned the airbeast wouldn't notice one wee middy's footsteps after all those bullets ripping through its side.

The *Leviathan*'s crew was firing back now, air guns chattering from the dorsal ridge and engine pods, searchlights guiding the strafing hawks out into the darkness. But what the ship really needed was more fléchette bats in the air.

When she reached the bow, Newkirk and Rigby were already there, wildly casting handfuls of feed. A few riggers had joined them to make up for the missing middies.

The bosun glared at her, and Deryn spat the words, "Tending to the boffin, sir!"

"Thought as much." He tossed her a feed bag. "They caught us napping, didn't they? Didn't know these blasted Clankers could fly so high!"

Deryn scooped out grain and fléchettes as fast as she could. Most of the bats were already airborne in all the ruckus.

"Get down, lads!" someone cried. "One's coming in!"

An aeroplane was roaring straight toward the bow. Deryn dropped, landing hard on a stray fléchette. The main air gun fired, and she felt the *whoosh* of bolts flying overhead. A host of startled bats streamed up in the bolts' wake.

Deryn glanced up. The air gun had hit home. The aeroplane shuddered, its engine coughing once. Then it twisted in the air and began to spin out of control, crumpling like paper in a giant hand.

Triumphant cries rose up across the airship's topside, but Mr. Rigby didn't pause to cheer. He scrambled to his feet and ran to Newkirk, snapping their safety lines together.

"Come on, Sharp!" he yelled. "Link up! We're going forward."

Deryn jumped up and ran after them, clipping her safety line to Newkirk's. The bosun led them off the dorsal ridge and onto the downward slope of the bow. The last few hundred bats always malingered in the nesting coves, and tonight the *Leviathan* needed all of her beasties in the air.

The bow skin was tougher than the flank, designed for plowing through storm fronts and squalls. Deryn's boots skidded on its hard surface, the heavy feed bag pulling her off balance. She swallowed—ropes and ratlines were few and far apart here on the airbeast's forehead.

The slope grew steeper. Soon Deryn could see all the way down to the blinders stretched across the whale's eyes, shielding them from distractions and the sting of bullets.

Another aeroplane roared beneath them, its machine gun firing at the port engine pod. The sound of shrieking gears rang in the cold air. In answer, two searchlight beams swept to follow the plane, full of dark and fluttering shapes. . . .

Deryn watched with horror. The searchlight crews weren't bothering to turn the beams red, the signal for the bats to release their fléchettes. They were guiding the flock straight into the path of the Clanker aircraft. The bats themselves weren't very heavy, but the metal spikes in their guts were enough to shred the aeroplane. The sickening shrieks of the poor wee creatures carried over the noise of ruined engines and tearing wings.

As Deryn watched the aircraft fall, her feet slipped. The ground was shifting beneath her.

"We're diving, lads!" Mr. Rigby shouted. "Get hold of something!"

Snow-covered mountains tilted into view ahead, and Deryn's stomach twisted. The airship had never dived this fast! Deryn dropped flat, fingers scrabbling for purchase. The feed bag skidded away, spilling figs and fléchettes into the night sky.

She was still sliding . . . *falling*.

Then the safety line jerked, bringing Deryn to a halt. She looked up to see Newkirk and Rigby settled in a nesting cove, bats swirling around their heads.

She pulled herself up into the warmth of the cove. It was full of bat dung and old fléchettes, but there were plenty of handholds, at least.

"Glad you could join us, Mr. Sharp," Newkirk said, grinning like a loon. "This is brilliant, isn't it?"

Deryn frowned. "When did *you* get so brave?"

Before he could answer, the world rolled beneath them again.

"We've lost an engine," Mr. Rigby said.

Deryn closed her eyes, listening to the pulse of the airship. The ship sounded weak. It flew at an odd angle, the airflow turbulent around them.

Clanker aeroplanes still rumbled out there in the darkness—two of them, by the sound—and the *Leviathan*'s searchlight beams looked almost empty of bats. The beasties were uselessly scattered across the night sky, too scared by gunfire and collisions to reform.

"We need more bats in the air!" Mr. Rigby shouted, and swiftly unwound a rope from his belt, replacing the line connecting Deryn and Newkirk with a fifty-foot length. "There's a big cove below us, Sharp. Swing down and see if you can scare up a few more of the little blighters." He shoved his own feed bag into her hands. "Make sure the beasties are stuffed before you boot them out."

"What about me?" Newkirk complained. Battle seemed to agree with him, but Deryn just felt airsick from it all.

"When I've got a longer line on you," Rigby said, still working his ropes. "Don't fancy losing my last two middies."

Deryn climbed over the edge of the cove, trying to ignore the mountain peaks rising steadily toward them. Had the airship lost too much hydrogen to stay aloft?

She forced the thoughts from her head, carefully making her way down toward a dark rift in the airbeast's skin. The growl of a Clanker engine was building in her ears, but Deryn didn't dare look away from her feet and hands.

Only a few more yards . . .

A machine gun erupted behind her, and she pressed flat against the *Leviathan*, closing her eyes and whispering, "Don't worry, beastie. I'll get these bum-rags sorted for you."

Searchlights flashed across her closed eyelids, and the machine roared away, leaving the foul smell of its engine fumes mixed with leaking hydrogen.

Deryn let herself drop the last few feet, her boots barely catching the lip of the cove. She clung to the rope and swung inside, skidding onto her knees.

The cove was empty. Not a single bat remained to take the air.

"Barking spiders," Deryn swore softly.

The floor shifted beneath her, and she turned and looked back out. The horizon tilted. Then the mountains disappeared, replaced by the cold and starry sky. . . . The *Leviathan* was climbing again!

She pulled herself out of the cove. The slope she'd

descended was almost level now that the ship was climbing again. Rigby and Newkirk were out in the open, their harnesses joined by a long rope.

"No luck, sir," she cried up. "I think they're all gone!"

"Come on, then, lads." Mr. Rigby turned and started back up toward the spine. "Let's get off the bow before she dives again."

The three of them spread out to the full length of their safety lines, rousting the last few bats on the way up. Deryn climbed as fast as she could. With the airship twisting and turning like this, being topside didn't seem quite so brilliant anymore.

The last two aeroplanes still skulked in the distance, and Deryn wondered what they were waiting for. A few strafing hawks were in the air, but their nets looked tattered. Only one searchlight was lit—the crew trying to gather the fléchette bats into a single flock.

Up on the spine things had got worse. The forward air gun was being pulled apart by a repair team. Wounded men were everywhere, and the sniffers were in a frenzy from so much spilled hydrogen. The whale's huge harness was frayed with bullet holes.

Deryn knelt beside an injured man, whose hand clutched the leash of a hydrogen sniffer. The beastie whined at her, looking up from its master's pale face. She looked closer. The man was dead.

"CARNAGE ON THE SPINE."

Deryn felt herself start to shake, unsure whether it was the cold or the shock of battle. She'd been aboard only a month, but this was like watching her family dying, her home burning down in front of her.

Then the inevitable roar of Clanker engines built again, and all eyes turned toward the dark sky. The last two aeroplanes were coming in together, hurling themselves against the airship one more time.

Deryn wondered what the crews in those machines were thinking. They'd seen their fellow airmen fall from the sky. Surely they knew they were about to die. What madness made killing the *Leviathan* so important to them?

The lone searchlight swept across their path, and one of the aeroplanes shuddered in the air. The small black shapes of bats tore through its wings and the plane banked hard. An impassive part of Deryn's brain saw how the airflow around the wings had changed, how the plane would soon crumple and fall . . .

She turned away as it burst into flame.

But the noise of the other growling engine still drew closer.

"Blast! She means to ram us!" Mr. Rigby cried, running ahead for a clearer view.

Someone at the front air gun swore. Its compressors had failed again, but other guns fired from farther aft.

Suddenly all the searchlights flared back to life and lanced into the darkness, until the approaching plane glowed like a fireball in the sky.

Tiny black wings fluttered along the searchlight beams, and the aeroplane shuddered and shook as it plowed through the bats. But somehow it kept coming.

A hundred feet away the machine finally twisted in the air. The wings folded, and pieces fluttered in all directions. The gunner's cockpit broke off, his weapon still blazing. The propeller somehow wrenched itself from the engine, spiraling away like a mad insect.

Deryn felt a trembling under her feet, and she pulled off a glove, kneeling to place her palm on the freezing dorsal scales. A low moan shook the airbeast. Bits of the disintegrating plane were tearing into the *Leviathan*, rupturing the membrane. Deryn closed her eyes.

One stray spark would turn them all into a ball of fire.

She heard a cry. Mr. Rigby was staggering away down the slope of the airship's flank, clutching his stomach.

"He's hit!" Newkirk shouted.

Rigby stumbled a few steps, then fell to his knees, bouncing a little on the membrane. Newkirk was running after him, but some squick of instinct held Deryn in place.

The whole ship was tilting forward now, heading back into a steep dive. The smell of hydrogen washed over her.

Mr. Rigby was sliding down the flank—gravity had caught him. His skid turned into a roll.

Deryn took a step forward, then looked down at the rope connecting her to the others. "Barking spiders!"

If the bosun went over the side, he'd drag Newkirk with him. Then Deryn would be snatched away like a fly on the end of a frog's tongue. She looked around for something to clip herself to, but the ratlines at her feet were frayed and stretched.

"Newkirk, *get back here!*"

The boy paused a moment, watching Mr. Rigby slide away. Then he turned back, comprehension dawning on his face. But it was too late—the rope connecting him to Rigby was straightening fast.

Newkirk looked up at her hopelessly, his hand moving to the rigging knife at his belt.

"No!" Deryn cried.

Then she realized what she had to do.

She turned and ran the *other* way, hurtling down the opposite flank of the airship. Dodging crewmen and sniffers as the membrane fell away, Deryn jumped as hard as she could into the night sky. . . .

The *snap* of the rope hit her like a punch in the stomach, the safety harness cutting into her shoulders. She rolled into a ball as her body hit the flank membrane, knocking her breath away.

Deryn bounced to a halt, then found herself skidding back up the flank of the airbeast. Rigby had to have yanked Newkirk off behind him—their combined weight was dragging her back up to the spine!

She grabbed at passing ropes, finally snaring one and bringing herself to a halt. But her safety line pulled harder, the harness squeezing the breath from her lungs.

Then the rope went slack, and Deryn looked up in horror. Had it broken? Had Newkirk cut himself loose?

On the spine a squad of riggers held her line, in a tug of war with something on the other side of the ship. They were pulling Newkirk and the injured bosun back up.

Deryn breathed a sigh of relief, her eyes closing. She

held tight to the ratlines, trusting nothing but her own two hands to keep her from tumbling into the dark sky. But as the ship tipped beneath her again, she looked down and realized that two hands wouldn't be enough.

They were all falling.

The Alps rose toward the ship, the tallest peaks only a few hundred feet below. A blanket of snow covered all but a few dark outcrops of stone, like jagged black teeth waiting patiently for prey.

The wounded *Leviathan* was crashing slowly back to earth.

◦ TWENTY-ONE ◦

The old castle stood on a rugged slope, moonlit snow-drifts piled against its half-ruined walls, the windows dark and gaping. Its battlements glistened with ice in the crystal-cold air, their ragged outlines blending into the rocks behind.

Alek leaned back from the viewport. "What is this place?"

"Do you remember your father's trip to Italy?" Count Volger asked. "To look for a new hunting lodge?"

"Of course I remember," Alek said. "You went with him, and I had four glorious weeks of no fencing lessons."

"A necessary sacrifice. Our real purpose was to buy this pile of old stones."

Aleksandar gazed at the castle with a critical eye—a pile of old stones was right. It looked more like a landslide than a fortress.

"But that was two summers ago, Volger. When did you start planning my escape?"

"The day your father married a commoner."

Alek ignored the slight to his mother; the details of his birthright were meaningless now. "And no one knows about this place?"

"Look around." Count Volger pulled his fur collar tighter. "This castle was abandoned back in the Great Famine."

"Six hundred years ago," Alek said softly, his breath coiling in the moonlight.

"The Alps were warmer then. There was once a thriving town out there." Count Volger pointed at the mountain pass ahead of them, its vast expanse glowing white beneath the almost full moon. "But that glacier swallowed the entire valley centuries ago. It's a wasteland now."

"I'll take a wasteland over another night in this machine," Klopp said, shivering in his furs. "I love my walkers, but I never fancied living in one."

Volger smiled. "This castle contains unexpected comforts, you'll find."

"Anywhere with a fireplace that works," Alek said, placing his cold and tired hands on the controls.

From the inside, the little castle didn't seem so bad.

The roofs under their blanket of snow had been recently repaired. The outer walls were half fallen, but the courtyard stones were solid, holding up under the Stormwalker's weight as it shuffled through the gate. Stacks of firewood lined the interior walls, and the castle's stables were full of provisions: smoked meats, barrels of grain, and neat stacks of military rations.

Alek stared at the endless ranks of cans.

"How long are we staying here?"

"Until this madness ends," Volger said.

"This madness," of course, meant the war. And wars could last for years . . . even decades. Tendrils of snow coiled through the open stable doors and across the floor—and this was the beginning of August.

What would the dead of winter be like?

"Your father and I were very thorough," Volger said, obviously pleased with himself. "We have medicines, furs, a roomful of weapons, and an excellent wine cellar. We'll lack for nothing."

"A bathtub might have been nice," Alek said.

"I believe we have one."

Alek blinked. "Well, that's good news. Perhaps a few servants to heat the water?"

Volger gestured at Bauer, who was already chopping wood. "But you have us, Your Serene Highness."

"You're more like family than servants." Alek shrugged. "All the family I've got, in fact."

"You're still a Hapsburg. Don't forget that."

Alek looked out at the Stormwalker crouched in the courtyard. On its breastplate was his family crest: the double-headed eagle devised of mechanikal parts. As he was growing up, the symbol had always surrounded Alek—on flags, furniture, even the pockets of his nightgown—assuring him of who he was. But now it only filled him with despair.

"Yes, a fine family," he said bitterly. "They disowned me from the start. And five weeks ago my granduncle had my parents killed."

"We can't be certain the emperor was behind that. And as for you . . ." The wildcount paused.

"What is it, Volger?" Alek found himself in no mood

for mysteries. "You promised to tell me all your secrets once we got to Switzerland."

"Yes, but I didn't think we'd make it," Volger said quietly. "Still, I suppose it's time you knew the truth. Come with me."

Alek glanced at the other men, who were hard at work unloading the walker in the dark. Apparently this secret wasn't meant for everyone.

He followed Volger up the stone stairway set against the inner wall, which led to the castle's only tower. It was an unimpressive round parapet jutting out over the cliff, lower than the stable rooftops, but with a commanding view of the valley.

Alek could see why Volger and his father had picked this place. Five men and a Stormwalker could defend it against a small army, if anyone ever found them there. Already the icy wind was blowing loose snow across the walker's giant footprints, gradually erasing the signs that anything had come this way.

Volger looked out across the glacier, his hands deep in his pockets. "May I be frank?"

Alek laughed. "Feel free to put aside your usual tact."

"I shall," Volger said. "When your father decided to marry Sophie, I was one of those who tried to talk him out of it."

"So I have your dismal powers of persuasion to thank for my existence."

"You're very welcome." Volger made a formal bow. "But you have to understand, Alek, we were only trying to prevent the break between your father and his uncle. The heir to an empire can't simply marry anyone he wants. Obviously, your father didn't listen, and the best we could do was a compromise: a left-handed marriage."

"A polite way to put it." The official term was a morganatic marriage, which had always sounded like a disease to Alek.

"But there are ways to adjust such contracts," Volger said.

Alek nodded slowly, remembering his parent's promises. "Father always said that Franz Joseph would give in eventually. He didn't understand how much the emperor hated my mother."

"No, he didn't. But your father understood something more important, that a mere emperor isn't the last word in these matters."

Alek looked at Volger. "What do you mean?"

"On that trip two summers ago we didn't just tour old castles. We went to Rome."

"Are you being obscure on purpose, Count?"

"Are you forgetting your family history, Alek? Before Austria-Hungary existed, who were the Hapsburgs?"

"Rulers of the Holy Roman Empire," Alek dutifully recited. "From 1452 until 1806. But what does that have to do with my parents?"

"Who crowned the Holy Roman Emperors? Whose word invested them with royalty?"

Alek narrowed his eyes. "Are you telling me, Count, that you met with the *pope*?"

"Your father did." Volger pulled a leather scroll case from a pocket of his fur coat. "The result was this dispensation, an adjustment of your parents' marriage. With one condition: that your father keep it a secret until the old emperor passed away."

Alek stared at the scroll case. The leather was beautifully worked, decorated with the crossed keys of the papal seal. But even so, it looked too small to change so much. "You've got to be joking."

"It's signed, witnessed, and sealed with lead. With the power of heaven it names you as your father's heir." Volger smiled. "A bit more impressive than a few gold bars, isn't it?"

"One document gives me an empire? I don't believe you."

"You can read it if you want. Your Latin is better than mine, after all."

Alek turned away, gripping the parapet. A sharp edge of broken stone cut into his fingers. Suddenly he could hardly breathe. "But . . . all this happened two years ago? Why didn't he tell me?"

Volger snorted. "Aleksandar, you don't trust a mere boy with the greatest secret in the empire."

A mere boy . . . The moonlight on the snow was suddenly too bright, and Alek squeezed his eyes shut, his whole life unwinding inside him. He'd always been an impostor in his own house, his father unable to leave him anything, his distant relatives wishing he'd never been born. Even his mother—she was the *cause* of it all. She'd cost him an empire, and somewhere deep down that fact had always stood between them.

How could the abyss that had defined his life disappear so suddenly?

The answer was, it hadn't. The emptiness was still there.

"It's too late," Alek said. "My parents are dead."

"Making you first in line for the throne." The wildcount shrugged. "Your granduncle may not know about this letter, but that doesn't change the law."

"*No one* knows about it!" Alek cried.

"I certainly wish that were true. But you saw how doggedly they've hunted us. The Germans must have found out somehow." Count Volger shook his head slowly. "Rome is filled with spies, I suppose."

Alek took the scroll case, his fist closing tight around

it. "So *this* must be why my parents were . . ." For a moment he wanted to throw it from the battlements.

"That isn't true, Alek. Your father was killed because he was a man of peace, and the Germans wanted war. You are simply a postscript."

Alek took a deep breath, trying to fit himself into this new reality. Everything that had happened in the last two years had to be rethought—all of these plans his father had made, knowing *this*.

Strangely, a small thing troubled him most. "All this time, Volger, you've treated me like . . ."

"The son of a lady-in-waiting?" Volger smiled. "A necessary deception."

"My compliments," Alek said slowly and evenly. "Your contempt was most convincing."

"I am your servant." Volger took one of Alek's hands in both of his and bowed. "And you have proved yourself worthy of your father's name."

Alek pulled away. "So what do we do with this . . . piece of paper? How do we let people know?"

"We don't," Volger said. "We keep your father's promise and say nothing until the emperor dies. He's an old man, Alek."

"But while we hide, this war goes on."

"I'm afraid so."

Alek turned away. The freezing wind still blew against

his face, but he could hardly feel it. He'd spent his whole life wishing for an empire, but he'd never realized the price would be so high. Not just his parents, but the war itself.

He remembered the soldier he'd killed. Over the next years there would be thousands more dead—*tens* of thousands. And he could do nothing but hide here in the snow, clutching this piece of paper.

This frozen wasteland was his kingdom now.

"Alek," Volger said softly, gripping his arm. "Listen . . ."

"I think I've heard enough for one night, Count."

"No, *listen*. Do you hear that?"

Alek glared at the man, then sighed and closed his eyes again. There was the sound of Bauer chopping wood, the moan of the wind, the ticking of the Stormwalker's metal parts still cooling. And somewhere out on the edge of his awareness . . . the rumble of engines.

His eyes sprang open. "Aeroplanes?"

Volger shook his head. "Not at this altitude." He leaned out over the parapets and scanned the valley floor, muttering, "They can't have followed us. They *can't* have."

But Alek was sure the sound came from the air. He squinted into the icy wind, until finally he saw a shape forming in the moonlit sky. But what he saw made no sense at all.

It was *huge*, like a dreadnought flying through the air.

○ TWENTY-TWO ○

"It's a zeppelin!" Alek shouted. "They've found us!"

The wildcount looked up. "An airship, certainly. But that doesn't sound like a zeppelin."

Alek frowned, listening hard. Other noises, tremulous and nonsensical, trickled over the distant hum of engines—squawks, whistles, and squeaks, like a menagerie let loose.

The airship lacked the symmetry of a zeppelin: The front end was larger than the stern, the surface mottled and uneven. Clouds of tiny winged forms fluttered around it, and an unearthly green glow clung to its skin.

Then Alek saw the huge eyes. . . .

"God's wounds," he swore. This wasn't a machine at all, but a Darwinist creation!

He'd seen monsters before, of course—talking lizards in the fashionable parlors of Prague, a draft animal displayed in a traveling circus—but nothing as gigantic as this. It was like one of his war toys come to life, a thousand times larger and more incredible.

"What are Darwinists doing *here?*" he said softly.

Volger pointed. "Running from danger, it would seem."

Alek's eyes followed the gesture, and he saw the jagged trails of bullet holes down the creature's flank, flickering with green light. Men swarmed in the rigging that hung from its sides, some wounded, some making repairs. And alongside them climbed things that *weren't* men.

As the airship passed, almost overhead, Alek half ducked behind the parapets. But the crew seemed too busy to notice anything below them. The ship slowly turned as it settled into the valley, dropping below the level of the mountains on either side.

"Is that godless thing coming *down?*" Alek asked.

"They seem to have no choice."

The vast creature glided away toward the white expanse of glacier—the only place in sight large enough for it to land. Even wounded, it fell as slowly as a feather. Alek held his breath for the long seconds that it remained poised above the snow.

The crash unfolded slowly. White clouds rose up in the skidding airship's wake, its skin rippling like a flag in the wind. Alek saw men thrown from their perches on its back, but it was too far away for their cries to reach him, even through the cold, clear air. The ship kept sliding away, farther and farther, until its dark outline disappeared behind a shroud of white.

"The highest mountains in Europe, and the war reaches us so quickly." Count Volger shook his head. "What an age we live in."

"Do you think they saw us?"

"In all that chaos? I'd think not. And this ruin won't look like much from a distance, even when the sun comes up." The wildcount sighed. "But no cooking fires for a while. And we'll have to set a watch until they leave."

"What if they don't leave?" Alek said. "What if they *can't?*"

"Then they won't last long," Volger said flatly. "There's nothing to eat on the glacier, no shelter, no fuel for a fire. Just ice."

Alek turned to stare at Volger. "But we can't leave ship-wrecked men to die!"

"May I remind you that they're the *enemy*, Alek? Just because the Germans are hunting us doesn't make Darwin-ists our friends. There could be a hundred men aboard that ship! Perhaps enough to take this castle." Volger's voice softened as he peered into the sky. "Let's just hope no res-cue comes for them. Aircraft overhead in daylight would be a disaster."

Alek looked out across the glacier again. The snow thrown up by the crash was settling around the airship, revealing that it lay half on one side, like a beached fish. He wondered if Darwinist creations died from the cold as quickly as natural beasts. Or men.

A *hundred* of them out there . . .

He looked down at the stables below—food enough for a small army. And medicine for the wounded, and furs and firewood to keep them warm.

"We can't sit here and watch them die, Count. Enemies or not."

"Haven't you been listening?" Volger cried. "You're heir to the throne of Austria-Hungary. Your duty is to the empire, not those men out there."

Alek shook his head. "At the moment there isn't much I can do for the empire."

"Not yet. But if you keep yourself alive, soon enough you'll gain the power to stop this madness. Don't forget: The emperor is eighty-three, and war is unkind to old men."

With those last words Volger's voice broke, and suddenly he looked ancient himself, as if the last five weeks had finally caught up with him. Alek swallowed his answer, remembering what Volger had sacrificed—his home, his rank—to be hunted and hounded, to go sleepless listening to wireless chatter. And with safety finally at hand, this obscene creature had fallen from the sky, threatening to wreck years of planning.

No wonder he wanted to ignore the airbeast dying on the snows a few kilometers away.

"Of course, Volger." Alek took his arm and led him down from the cold and windy parapet. "We'll watch and wait."

"They'll probably repair that godless beast," Volger said on the stairs. "And leave us behind without a second glance."

"No doubt."

Halfway across the courtyard, Volger brought Alek to a sudden halt, his expression pained. "We'd help them if we could. But this war could leave the whole continent in ruins. You see that, don't you?"

Alek nodded and led the count into the great hall of the castle, where Bauer was piling wood into the fireplace. Seeing the food laid out and ready to cook, Volger let out a tired sigh and told the other men about the crashed airship—another week without fires, and long, cold watches every night.

But eating in a castle, even a cold one, was still a pleasure after all those meals huddled in the Stormwalker's iron belly. The storerooms held luxuries that none of them had enjoyed for weeks: smoked fish for dinner, dried fruit and canned peaches for dessert. The wine was excellent, and when Alek offered to take the first watch, the others drank to him deeply.

No one talked about rescuing the airmen. Perhaps the

other three assumed that the monstrous creature would fly away again. They hadn't seen the bullet holes in its flanks, or the men hanging wounded and lifeless in the rigging. Instead they talked like soldiers, discussing how to defend the castle against an aerial attack. Bauer and Klopp argued about whether the Stormwalker's cannon could elevate high enough to hit an airship.

Alek listened and watched. He'd slept most of the day, taking the controls only after sunset, when Klopp's old eyes always gave out. It was barely midnight now, and it would be dawn before he needed sleep. But the others were worn down by the day's journey and the freezing cold.

When they had fallen asleep, Alek made his way quietly up to the parapets.

The airship lay in a dark lump on the glacier's featureless white. It looked smaller now, as if slowly deflating. No fires or lamps were visible, just the strange glow he'd noticed earlier. Tiny pinpricks of light moved in the wreckage, like green fireflies buzzing about the giant creature's wounds.

Alek shivered. He'd heard awful stories about the Darwinists' creations: half-breeds of tigers and wolves, mythological monsters brought to life, animals that spoke and even reasoned like humans, but had no souls. He'd been told that when godless beasts were created, the spirits of demons occupied them—pure evil given flesh.

Of course, he'd also been taught that the emperor was wise and kind, that the Austrian people loved him, and that the Germans were his allies.

Alek descended the tower stairs and crept past the sleeping men into the storerooms. The medicine kits were easy to find, eight satchels marked with red crosses. He took three, but didn't weigh himself down with any food. That could come later, if the airship really was grounded for good.

Changing into his commoner disguise, Alek ignored the furs, choosing the most ragged leather coat he could find. From the weapons room he took a Steyr automatic pistol and two eight-round clips. Hardly the sort of weapon a Swiss villager would carry, but Volger was right about one thing—this was still a war, and these Darwinists were the enemy.

Finally he chose a pair of snowshoes. Alek wasn't sure how the contraptions were supposed to help him walk, but Klopp had exalted upon seeing them—something about his mountain campaigns back in the Balkan Wars.

The iron bolt of the castle gate slid silently aside, and the huge door swung open with an easy push. It was so simple to walk out, throwing his hard-won safety to the cold wind. Certainly it felt nobler than hiding here, waiting to inherit an empire.

Half a kilometer out onto the snows Alek realized that he had finally snuck past his old fencing master.

◉　　◉　　◉

The snowshoes looked absurd, like tennis rackets strapped to his boots. But they worked, keeping his feet from breaking through the brittle surface into the powdery snow beneath. His long, sliding steps carried him quickly back along the Stormwalker's footprints, until he was far enough away that his tracks weren't visible from the castle walls.

The smooth, almost featureless glacier was easy going, and in an hour he drew close enough to hear the Darwinists' shouts as they worked on their wounded airship. He climbed up the valley's side, until he reached a ledge overlooking the vast shape.

Alek stood at the edge, astonished by what he saw below.

The wreck looked like a corner of hell bubbling up through the snow. Flocks of winged creatures coiled around hollows in the wilting gasbag. Crewmen moved across the great beast's skin, accompanied by bizarre double-snouted, six-legged dogs that sniffed and pawed at every bullet hole. The green lights he'd seen from the castle covered the creature. They were *crawling*, like glowing maggots on dead meat.

And the stench! Rotten eggs and cabbage, and a salty smell disturbingly close to the fish he'd had for dinner. Alek wondered for a moment if the Germans were right after all. These godless beasts were an insult

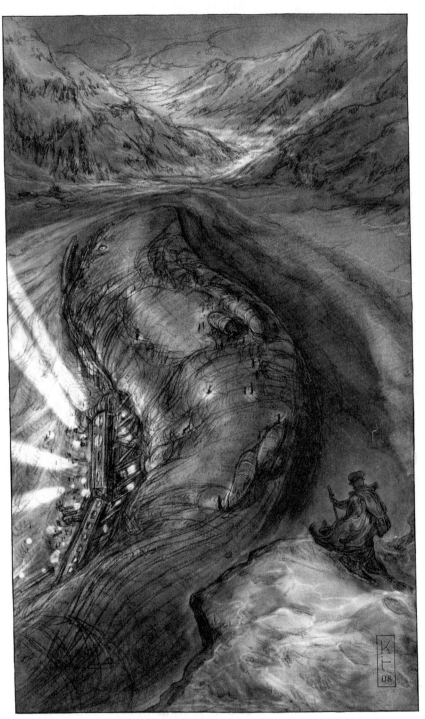

"A VAST FORM STRETCHES OUT."

to nature itself. Perhaps a war was worth ridding the
world of them.

And yet he couldn't take his eyes from the creature.
Even lying wounded it looked so powerful, more like
something from legend than the work of men.

Four searchlights flared to life, illuminating one flank of
the creature. Alek could see now why the beast had rolled
sideways during the crash: The gondolas hanging from its
underside had escaped being flattened against the snow.

Steeling himself, he climbed down to the glacier, heading toward the unlit side of the creature. Only a few men
worked there, though the damage looked just as bad. Drawing nearer, Alek stepped lightly, his snowshoes shushing in
the darkness.

As he stole down the length of the airship, the green
glow seemed to be bleeding out onto the ice. Surely the
beast was dying.

He'd been a fool to think he could help. Perhaps
he should just leave the medicines somewhere and slip
away. . . .

A soft moan came from the shadows.

Alek stole closer to the sound, the air growing warm
around him. His stomach twisted. This was living heat
from the creature's body! Fighting nausea, he went a few
steps nearer, trying not to look at the green lights crawling
beneath the creature's skin.

A young airman lay in the darkness, curled against the beast's flank. His eyes were closed and his nose bloody.

Alek crouched beside him.

The airman was just a boy, with fine features and sandy hair. The collar of his flight suit was caked with blood, and his face looked deathly pale in the soft green light. He had to have been slumped here on the ice for the hours since the crash, the giant creature's warmth keeping him alive.

Alek opened one of the medical satchels, fishing through the bottles for smelling salts and rubbing alcohol.

He waved the salts under the boy's nose.

"Barking spiders!" the boy croaked in a high voice, his eyes fluttering open.

Alek frowned, wondering if he'd heard the words right.

"Are you well?" he ventured in English.

"A bit scrambled in the attic," the boy said, rubbing his head. He sat up slowly, taking in the scene around them, and his glassy eyes widened. "Blisters! We came down hard, didn't we? The poor beastie looks a bloody wreck."

"You're rather bloody yourself," Alek said, twisting open the bottle of rubbing alcohol. He dampened a bandage and held it against the boy's face.

"Ow! Stop that!" The boy pushed the bandage away and sat up straight, his gaze becoming clearer. He looked suspiciously at Alek's snowshoes. "Who are you, anyway?"

"I'm here to help. I live nearby."

"Up *here*? In all this barking snow?"

"Yes." Alek cleared his throat, wondering what to say. He'd always been hopeless at any sort of lying. "In a village, of sorts."

The boy narrowed his eyes. "Wait a wee minute—you talk like a Clanker!"

"Well . . . I suppose I do. We speak a dialect of German in this part of Switzerland."

The boy stared at him another moment, then sighed and rubbed his head. "Right, you're Swiss. The crash must've knocked me silly. For a squick there I thought you were one of those bum-rags who shot us down."

Alek raised an eyebrow. "And then landed here so I could tend to your bloody nose?"

"I *said* it was a wee bit daft," the boy said, yanking the alcohol-soaked bandage from Alek's hand. He pressed it against his nose and winced. "But thanks for your trouble. It's lucky you came along, or my bum would've been frost-bit to blazes!"

Alek raised an eyebrow, wondering if the boy always talked this way, or if he was still groggy from the crash. Even bloody and bruised, he had an odd sort of *swagger*, as if he crash-landed in giant airships every day.

"Yes," Alek said. "A frostbitten bum would've been unfortunate."

The boy smiled. "Give us a lift, would you?"

They grasped hands and pulled each other up, the other boy still unsteady. But when he gained his feet, he bowed triumphantly, pulled off a glove and held out his hand.

"Midshipman Dylan Sharp, at your service."

○ TWENTY-THREE ○

Deryn waited for the strange Swiss boy to shake her hand. After a moment's hesitation he finally reached out.

"My name's Alek," he said. "Pleased to meet you."

Deryn smiled, though her head was aching. The boy was about her age, with reddish-brown hair and sharp, handsome features. His leather coat had once been posh, but it was threadbare now. A twitchiness animated the boy's dark green eyes, as if he were ready to bound away on his ridiculous shoes.

All very odd, Deryn thought.

"Are you sure you're quite all right?" Alek asked. His English was dead proper, even with the Clanker accent.

"Right enough," Deryn said. She stamped feeling back into her feet, wondering when the dizziness was going to go away. Her attic had been scrambled, that was certain. She couldn't recall the exact moment of the crash, only the descent—the snow rising up, the airship rolling over, threatening to crush her if she didn't climb fast enough . . .

Deryn glanced down at her safety line; it was stretched and frayed but still attached to the ratlines. She must have been dragged alongside as the airbeast skidded across the snow. If the ship had rolled over any farther, she'd have wound up a greasy squick beneath the whale.

"A wee bit dizzy, is all," she added, looking up at the bullet-holed membrane. The bitter-almond smell of leaking hydrogen filled her muzzy head. "Not half as bad as this beastie here."

"Yes, your ship looks terrible," Alek said. His eyes were wide, like he'd never seen a fabricated creature before. Maybe that explained his twitchiness. "Do you think you can fix it?"

Deryn stepped back for a better view of the wreck. Hardly anyone was working here on the starboard flank. But up on the spine men were silhouetted against searchlight beams reaching into the sky. The gondolas must have wound up on the other side of the wreck, so the repair work had started over there.

Deryn knew she should be helping them, and finding out what had happened to Newkirk and Mr. Rigby, but her hands felt too weak to climb. The cold had seeped into her bones while she'd lain unconscious.

"Eventually." Her eyes scanned the bleak terrain. "But I wouldn't fancy staying here very long! Maybe your people could help us?"

The boy's eyes widened a bit. "My village is quite far from here. And we don't know anything about airships."

"No, of course not. But this looks like a big job. We'll need lots of rope, maybe machine parts. The engines on this side must be smashed to blazes. You Swiss are good with gears, aren't you?"

"I'm afraid we can't help." Alek pulled a bunch of leather satchels from his shoulder. "But I can give you these. For your wounded men."

He handed the satchels to Deryn. She opened one and peered inside: bandages, scissors, a thermometer in a leather case, and a dozen tiny bottles. Whoever Alek's people were, they knew how to get proper supplies up the mountain.

"Thank you," she said. "But where did you get these?"

"I'm afraid I have to go." The boy took a step backward. "I'm expected home soon."

"Wait, Alek!" she cried, making him jump. Living up here, he probably wasn't used to strangers. But she couldn't let him wriggle away like this. "Just tell me where your village is."

"The other side of the glacier." He made a gesture toward the horizon, in no particular direction. "Quite far away."

Deryn wondered if he was hiding something. Of course, to live in a shivery wasteland like this, you'd have to be a bit cracked in the attic. Or were his people outlaws of some kind?

"Seems like an odd place to have a village," she said carefully.

"Well, it's not what you'd call a *large* village. Just me and . . . my extended family."

Deryn nodded slowly, still smiling. So Alek was changing his story now. Was there a village or wasn't there?

He took another step backward. "Listen, I'm not really supposed to be this far from home. I just happened to be out hiking when I saw your ship come down."

"Out hiking?" Deryn said. "In all this barking snow? At *night?*"

"Yes. I often hike on the glacier at night."

"With *medicine?*"

Alek blinked. "Well, that was because . . ." There was a long pause. "Um, I'm afraid I don't know the word in English."

"The word for what?"

"I just said: I don't *know it!*" He turned from her and began to slide away on his funny oversize shoes. "I have to go now."

Alek's story was clearly a load of blether. And wherever he was from, the ship's officers would want to know about it. She started to follow him, but her foot cracked through the brittle surface, filling her boot with snow.

"Blisters!" she swore, suddenly seeing the point of his big slidey shoes. "Don't go skiting off, Alek! We need you!"

The boy came to a reluctant halt. "Listen. I'll bring you what I can, all right? But you can't tell anyone you saw me. If you come looking for my family, it won't be good. We don't like strangers, and we can be quite dangerous."

"Dangerous?" Deryn asked. They had to be outlaws— or worse. She put a hand into her pocket, feeling for her command whistle.

"Very deadly," Alek said. "So you have to promise not to tell anyone about me! All right?"

He stood there, his green eyes locked with hers. Deryn held her breath, trying to match the intensity of his gaze. Like a stare-off before a fistfight, it made her stomach flutter.

"Do you promise?" he demanded again.

"I can't let you go, Alek," she said softly.

"You . . . what?"

"I have to report you to the ship's officers. They'll want to ask you a few questions."

His eyes widened. "You're going to *interrogate* me?"

"I'm sorry, Alek. But if there's dangerous folks about, it's my duty to tell the officers." She held up the satchels. "You're smugglers or something, aren't you?"

"Smugglers! Don't be absurd," Alek said. "We're perfectly decent people!"

"If you're so decent," Deryn said, "then why've you been telling me a load of yackum?"

"I was just trying to help! And I don't know what *yackum* is!" the boy sputtered, then said something unpleasant in German. He turned around on his giant shoes and headed off into the darkness.

Deryn pulled the command whistle from her pocket. The freezing metal burned her lips as she piped a quick sequence, the notes of an intruder alert ringing in the cold air.

She stuffed the whistle back into her pocket and trudged after him, ignoring the snow collecting in her boots.

"Hold up, Alek! No one's going to hurt you!"

He didn't answer, just kept sliding away. But Deryn heard shouts behind her, and the scrabble of hydrogen sniffers on the ratlines. The beasties jumped like rabbits on fire when you blew an intruder alert.

"Alek, stop! I just want to talk!"

The boy glanced over his shoulder, and his eyes went wide at the sight of the sniffers. He uttered a panicked cry and slowed to a halt, turning to face her again.

Deryn ran harder, hoping to get there before the sniffers did. No point in letting the beasties scare poor Alek to death.

"Just wait there!" she called. "There's no reason to . . ."

Her voice trailed off as she saw what was in Alek's hand—a black pistol, the metal gleaming in the moonlight.

"Are you *daft?*" she cried, breathing in the bitter smell of hydrogen. One spark from a gunshot could ignite the air, turning the ship into a vast fireball.

"Don't come any closer!" Alek said. "And call those . . . *things* off!"

Deryn came to a halt, glancing at the sniffers bounding toward them across the snow. "Aye, I would. But I don't think they'll *listen!*"

The pistol swerved from her to the sniffers, and she saw Alek's jaw tense.

"Don't!" she cried. "You'll set us all aflame!"

But he was raising his arm, aiming at the nearest beastie—

Deryn threw herself forward, smothering the gun with her body. A bullet was nothing compared to catching fire. She grabbed Alek's shoulders and dragged him down into the snow.

Her head went through the brittle ice with a *crack*, sending stars across her vision. Alek landed on top of her, the barrel of the gun jabbing hard into her ribs. She closed her eyes, waiting for an explosion of agony and noise.

He was struggling to free the pistol, so she pulled him harder against her. Ice cut her cheek as their struggle dug them deeper into the snow.

"STRUGGLE ON ICE."

"Let me go!" he cried.

Deryn opened her eyes, glaring straight into his. He froze for a moment—and she spoke in a slow, clear voice.

"Don't. Shoot. The air's full of *hydrogen!*"

"I'm not *trying* to shoot anyone. I'm trying to get away!"

He started struggling again, the pistol jamming harder into her ribs. Deryn let out an *oof*. She wrapped a hand around the gun, trying to push the barrel aside.

A low growl rolled across the snow, and a sniffer thrust its long snout right into Alek's face. He froze again, a look of horror draining the color from his skin. Suddenly the animals were all around them, their hot breath steaming.

"It's okay, beasties," Deryn said in a calm voice. "Just back off a wee bit, please? You're scaring our friend here, and we don't want him pulling the barking *trigger*."

The nearest sniffer cocked its head, letting out a low whine. Deryn heard shouts, crewmen calling off the beasties. Green shadows from wormlamps swung around them.

Alek let out a sigh, his muscles going limp.

"Let go of the gun," she said. "Please?"

"I *can't*," he said. "You're squeezing my fingers."

"Oh." Deryn realized that her hand was still wrapped around his. "Well, if I let go, you won't shoot me, will you?"

"Don't be an idiot," he said. "I would have shot you by now if I'd wanted to."

"You're calling *me* an idiot? You barking ninny! You

almost blew us all up! Don't you know what hydrogen smells like?"

"Of course not," he said, giving her a look of disgust. "What an absurd question."

She glared back at him, but loosened her grip. The boy let the pistol fall aside and stood up, warily facing the men around him. Deryn scrambled to her feet, dusting snow from her flight suit.

"What's going on here?" came a voice from the darkness. It was Mr. Roland, the master rigger.

Deryn saluted. "Midshipman Sharp reporting, sir. I was knocked out in the crash, and when I came to, this boy was here. He gave me these satchels—full of medicines, I think. He lives somewhere hereabouts but won't say where. I was trying to stop him for questioning, and he pulled a gun, sir!"

She knelt and picked up the pistol, proudly handing it to Mr. Roland.

"I managed to disarm him, though."

"You did no such thing," Alek muttered, then turned to Mr. Roland. Suddenly his twitchiness was gone. "I demand you let me go!"

"Do you, now?" Mr. Roland gave Alek a good hard look, then dropped his eyes to the pistol. "Austrian, isn't this?"

Alek nodded. "I suppose so."

Deryn stared at him. Was he a Clanker after all?

"And where did you get it?" Mr. Roland asked.

Alek sighed and crossed his arms. "In Austria. You're all being ridiculous. I only came here to bring you medicines, and you treat me like an *enemy*."

He shouted the last word, and one of the sniffers let out a bark. Alek flinched, looking down at it in horror.

Mr. Roland chuckled. "Well, if you're only here to help, I suppose you've got nothing to worry about. Come with me, young man. We'll get to the bottom of this."

"What about me, sir?" Deryn asked. "I was the one who captured him!"

Mr. Roland gave her a look that all the warrant officers reserved for mere middies, like glancing at something on the bottom of his shoe. "Well, why don't you take those satchels to the boffins. See what they make of them."

Deryn opened her mouth to protest, but the word "boffins" reminded her of Dr. Barlow. Right before the crash she'd been headed for the machine room. Full of widgets and loose parts, it was no place to get bounced around in!

"Aye, sir," Deryn said, and headed back toward the ship at a run.

With a quick apology to the half-deflated airbeast, she grabbed the ratlines and hoisted herself up. Her hands felt shaky and weak, but trudging all the way around the vast creature would take ages—so up and over it was.

She pulled herself higher, forcing questions about the strange boy from her mind.

∘ TWENTY-FOUR ∘

Once over the spine Deryn could see the wreck much better. Men and beasts were everywhere on this flank, four searchlights stretching their shadows to monstrous proportions. The main gondola lay at an angle, half hanging from the harness, half resting in the snow. She scrambled down the ratlines and hit the ground running.

Inside the gondola the decks and bulkheads leaned to starboard, a fun house full of overturned furniture. With the scent of hydrogen everywhere, the oil lamps had been extinguished, leaving the chaos lit with the sickly green of glowworms. Men jostled in the slanting corridors, filling the air with curses and shouted orders.

Deryn dodged and weaved among them, hoping for a glimpse of Newkirk or Mr. Rigby. They'd been dangling from this side of the ship, which had rolled skyward, so they *couldn't* have been crushed. . . .

But the bosun had looked badly wounded. What if he'd been dead before the airship had hit the snow?

Deryn swallowed the thought and kept running. Checking on the boffin was her first responsibility, a duty she was already late for.

She skidded to a halt outside the machine room and flung open the door. The place was a shambles. Boxes of parts had gone tumbling in the crash, leaving the floor covered with metal bits and pieces. They glimmered with the light of a wormlamp hanging aslant from the ceiling.

"Ah, Mr. Sharp," came a voice. "At last you appear."

Deryn sighed—half with relief, half with remembering how tiresome Dr. Barlow could be. She was in a corner of the room, bent over her mysterious box of cargo.

Tazza bounded from the shadows and up to Deryn, bouncing happily on his hind legs. She scratched the beastie's ears.

"Sorry to keep you waiting, ma'am." Deryn indicated the blood-caked collar of her flight suit. "Had a bit of an accident."

"We *all* had an accident, Mr. Sharp. I should think that was obvious. Now could you please lend me a hand?"

Deryn held up the satchels. "Sorry, ma'am, but I'm here to ask you—"

"Time is of the *essence*, Mr. Sharp. I'm afraid your business can wait."

Deryn started to argue, then realized that the top of the cargo box had been pried off. Heat rose from the insides, a few wisps of steam ghosting the freezing air. Straw packing was strewn everywhere—the secret purpose of the trip to Constantinople at last revealed.

"Well, I suppose so," Deryn said. She made her way across the slanted floor, careful not to slip on the hay and rolly bits of metal. Tazza bounced along beside her like he'd been born on the side of a hill.

It took a moment to see into the box's shadows. But as her eyes adjusted, twelve rounded shapes resolved in the soft glow of the wormlamp.

"Ma'am . . . are those *eggs*?"

"Indeed they are, and quite close to hatching." Dr. Barlow scratched Tazza's head and let out a sigh. "Or at least, they were. Most are broken. This wasn't the smooth ride you promised me, Mr. Sharp."

Deryn looked closer, and saw cracks running across the shells, a yellowish liquid seeping out. "I reckon it wasn't. But what are they the eggs *of*?"

"Despite our grim situation, that remains a military secret." Dr. Barlow gestured to the four eggs closest to her. "These seem to be alive, Mr. Sharp. And if they're to stay that way, we'll have to keep them warm."

Deryn raised an eyebrow. "Do you want me to sit on them, ma'am?"

"A delightful image, but no." Dr. Barlow pushed both hands into the straw and withdrew two small jars that shone with a rosy light. They looked like the bottles of phosphorescent algae that the middies dropped for altitude checks.

Dr. Barlow gave the jars a shake, and the glow grew stronger, steam rising in the cold air. She tucked them back into the hay.

"The electrical heater was broken in the crash, but these bacterial warmers should keep the eggs alive for now. The trick is keeping the temperature exactly right, which

won't be easy." She pointed at a mess in one corner of the box—red shivery droplets amid shattered glass. "You'll have to clean up the remains of that thermometer, by the way. Be careful of the mercury; it's quite poisonous."

"Could you use a new one, ma'am?" Deryn dug into one of the satchels Alek had given her. "I happen to have a few with me."

"You have thermometers with you?" The lady boffin blinked. "How very *useful* of you, Mr. Sharp."

"Glad to be of service, ma'am." Deryn handed one over, then opened another of the satchels. "I've got two more, I think."

When Deryn looked up, Dr. Barlow was still staring at the thermometer.

"Does the Air Service generally use Clanker equipment, Mr. Sharp?"

Deryn's eyes widened. Was the lady boffin a barking mind reader now?

"But how did you . . ."

"Again you underestimate my eye for detail." She handed back the thermometer. Deryn took it and stared at both sides. It seemed normal enough to her.

"Note the red line at 36.8 degrees," Dr. Barlow said. "Body temperature in Celsius. And yet in all my interactions with the armed forces they have never used the metric system."

Deryn cleared her throat. "Well, we're not Clankers, are we?"

"Or scientists." Dr. Barlow plucked the thermometer from Deryn's fingers. "So why isn't this red line at 98.6? You don't *seem* like a Clanker spy, Mr. Sharp, unless you're a particularly incompetent one."

Deryn tried not to roll her eyes. "I was going to tell you, ma'am, but you wouldn't let me. There was this strange boy . . . out in the snow. That's where I got these kits."

"A boy? And I suppose he just walked up out of nowhere, bearing thermometers."

"Aye, more or less. When I woke up after the crash, he was standing there."

"I find this story difficult to believe, Mr. Sharp." Dr. Barlow placed a cool palm against Deryn's bruised eye. "Took quite a bump to your head, didn't you?"

"It's not my head, ma'am. It's this whole mountaintop that's dizzy. A boy just came out of nowhere! His name was Alek."

Dr. Barlow shared a dubious look with Tazza. "Mr. Sharp, we both know you're not above a bit of fibbing."

Deryn gaped at the boffin, black affronted. "I may have misled the Service about my . . . *particulars* when I joined up, but that doesn't mean I'd go telling lies for no good reason!"

"Well, if you *are* telling the truth, then this 'Alek' is

possibly quite interesting." Dr. Barlow took the thermometer back again, then gave it a shake and slipped it into the
hay. "Did he say where he lives?"

"Not really." Deryn frowned, trying to remember Alek's
exact words. "He mentioned a village at first, but mostly
talked about his family. I reckon they're outlaws—or maybe
spies. He looked nervous the whole time, as bouncy as Tazza
here. Then he pulled a pistol on me, and was about to blow
us all to pieces! But I wrestled it away from him."

"How fortunate," Dr. Barlow said distractedly, as if
she routinely was saved from a fiery death. She reached
for one of the satchels and arranged its contents on the
slanted floor. "Field dressings, a tourniquet—no, Tazza,
these aren't for sniffing—even a scalpel."

"A bit fancy for some wee village on a mountaintop,"
Deryn said. "Don't you think?"

Dr. Barlow lifted a box, squinting at its label. "And this
is marked with a double-headed eagle—Austrian military
issue."

Deryn's eyes widened. "We're not too far from Austria,
ma'am. But Switzerland's meant to be neutral!"

"Technically, Mr. Sharp, *we* are in violation of that
neutrality." Dr. Barlow turned the scalpel in her hand, and
its blade flashed. "This is an alarming development. But I
trust we'll be taking off soon?"

"I doubt it, ma'am. The ship's a barking mess."

"But surely we can depart once the skin is patched, and make our repairs somewhere warmer? My eggs won't last long in this cold."

Deryn started to say that she wasn't certain, having mostly been unconscious since the crash. But Dr. Barlow didn't look in the mood for blether. And from what Deryn had seen climbing over the wreck, the answer was obvious.

"Not for a few days, ma'am. We've lost half our hydrogen, at least."

"I see," the lady boffin said, sinking down against the side of the cargo box. She pulled Tazza closer, her face pale in the green light of the wormlamp. "Then I'm afraid we may not be leaving at all."

"Don't be daft, ma'am." Deryn remembered the way Mr. Rigby always put it. "This ship isn't some dead Clanker mechanism. It's a living creature. It can make all the hydrogen it wants. I'm more worried about the engines."

"I'm afraid it's not so simple, Mr. Sharp." Dr. Barlow gestured across the slanted room to the porthole. "Have you looked outside?"

"Aye, I've been out there half the night!" Deryn remembered the word the strange boy had used. "It's what they call a *glacier*, ma'am."

"I'm familiar with the concept," Dr. Barlow said. "A great sheet of ice, as dead as the poles themselves. How high in the mountains do you suppose we are?"

"Well, the Clankers hit us at eight thousand feet. And maybe we dropped a thousand or two before we hit the snow . . ."

"Well above the tree line," Dr. Barlow said softly. "My grandfather's bees won't be finding much nectar out there, will they?"

Deryn frowned. She hadn't seen a single living creature out on the snowy waste. Which meant no flowers for the bees, no insects for the bats.

"But what about the hawks and the other raptors, ma'am? They can fly a barking long way to hunt."

Dr. Barlow nodded. "They might find prey in a nearby valley. But the *Leviathan* needs more than a few mice and hares to heal herself. This place is a biological wasteland, empty of everything she needs to survive."

Deryn wanted to argue, but the ship had to eat to get healthy, just like any natural creature. And there wasn't a scrap of food out on that bleak expanse of snow.

"You mean there's nothing we can do?"

"I did *not* say that, Mr. Sharp." Dr. Barlow stood up, pointing at a pile of jars on the slanted floor. "First we shall get these eggs to the proper temperature. Give those warmers a shake."

"Right, ma'am!"

"And then I want to meet this mysterious boy of yours."

◦ TWENTY-FIVE ◦

Alek was miserable, humiliated, and tired. But he was too cold to sleep.

Smashed windows and bullet holes were everywhere in the wounded airship, and icy winds howled down the slanted corridors. Even Alek's cabin, with a locked door and closed porthole, was freezing. Instead of an oil lamp to warm his hands against, the cabin was lit by the same green worms that covered the ship's skin. Dozens were stuffed into a lantern that hung from the ceiling, squirming like glowing lice.

The whole wreck was overrun with godless vermin. The awful six-legged dogs swarmed its wilting gasbag, and flying creatures filled the air. Even here inside the gondola, reptiles of all sizes scuttled along the walls. While the ship's officers had interrogated Alek, a sticky-footed talking lizard had tromped to and fro across the tilted ceiling, repeating random snatches of their conversation.

Not that Alek had said much. The answers to the officers' questions—where he'd come from, why he was here—were beyond their understanding. There was no point telling the Darwinists his real name; they'd never believe he was the son of an archduke. And when he'd tried to tell them how dangerous it was to keep him here, the warnings had sounded like empty, pompous threats.

He'd been such a fool—this vast creature, these people were so alien. It was madness to try to cross the gulf between his world and theirs.

Locked in the cold, dark cabin, Alek wondered if his noble intentions had been a joke from the beginning. As if anyone could carry food for a hundred men across that glacier, every night and in *secret*. Perhaps he'd come here only out of morbid curiosity, drawn like a child to a dead bird on the ground.

Through the cabin's small porthole the black horizon was slowly turning gray. Time was running out.

Otto Klopp would soon come to take the second watch. A quick search would prove that Alek wasn't in the castle, and it wouldn't take much imagination to figure out where he'd gone. Within a few hours Count Volger would be gazing at the grounded airship, drawing his plans and pondering the fact that the heir to the throne of Austria-Hungary was a complete idiot.

Alek set his jaw. At least he'd accomplished *something*.

"A TILTED TALK."

That young airman, Dylan, might have frozen to death if he'd lain in the snow all night. But Alek had saved him from frostbite. Maybe this was how you stayed sane in wartime: a handful of noble deeds amid the chaos.

Of course, Dylan had betrayed him five minutes later. Where was the sanity in that?

Keys jangled in the corridor, and Alek turned from the porthole. The slanted door swung open, and in walked . . .

"*You*," Alek growled.

Dylan smiled at him. "Aye, it's me. I hope you're well."

"No thanks to you, you ungrateful little swine."

"Now *that's* a bit rude. Especially when I've brought you a bit of company." Dylan bowed, sweeping an arm toward the doorway. "May I present Dr. Nora Barlow."

Another person strode into the room, and Alek's eyes widened. Instead of an airman's uniform she wore a gaudy dress and a small black hat, and held the leash of a bizarre doglike creature. What was a *woman* doing on this ship?

"Pleasure to meet you," she said. "Alek, isn't it?"

"At your service." As he bowed, the strange beast nuzzled Alek's hand, and he tried not to flinch. "Are you the ship's doctor? If so, I'm quite unhurt."

The woman laughed. "I'm sure you are. But I'm not a *medical* doctor."

Alek frowned, then realized that her black hat was a

bowler. She was one of the Darwinist fabricators, a practitioner of their ungodly science!

He looked down in horror at the creature snuffling his trouser leg.

"What is this? Why have you brought this beast here?"

"Oh, don't be afraid of Tazza," the woman said. "He's perfectly harmless."

"I'm not telling you anything," Alek said, trying to keep the fear from his voice. "I don't care what this godless animal does to me."

"What, *Tazza*?" Dylan let out a laugh. "I reckon he could lick you to death. And he's perfectly natural, by the way. What they call a thylacine."

Alek glared at the boy. "Then kindly take it *away*."

The Darwinist woman settled herself on a chair at the high end of the tilted cabin, looking down at him imperiously. "I'm sorry if Tazza makes you nervous, but he has nowhere else to go. Your German friends have made rather a mess of our ship."

"I'm not German."

"No, you're Austrian. But the Germans are your allies, are they not?"

Alek didn't answer. The woman was just guessing.

"And what would a young Austrian be doing so high in these mountains?" she continued. "Especially now, in wartime?"

He stared at Dr. Barlow, wondering if it was worth trying to reason with her. Though she was a woman, she was also a scientist, and the Darwinists worshipped science. She might have power on this ship.

"It doesn't matter why I'm here," he said, trying to use his father's tone of command. "What matters is that you have to let me go."

"And why is that?"

"Because if you don't, my family will come to get me. And believe me, *you don't want that!*"

Dr. Barlow narrowed her eyes. The ship's officers had only laughed at his threats. But she was listening to him.

"So your family knows where you are," she said. "Did they send you here?"

He shook his head. "No. But they'll guess, soon enough. You don't have much time to let me go."

"Ah . . . time is of the essence." The woman smiled. "So your family lives nearby?"

Alek frowned. He hadn't meant to give that away.

"Then I suppose we must find them, and quickly." She turned to Dylan. "What do you suggest, Mr. Sharp?"

The young airman shrugged. "I suppose we could follow his tracks backward in the snow. Maybe bring a present for his ma, so there are no hard feelings."

Alek shot the boy a cold look. It was one thing to be betrayed, but quite another to be mocked. "I was careful with my tracks. And if you do manage to find my family, you'll only get yourselves shot. They hate strangers."

"What unsociable people," Dr. Barlow said. "And yet they hired English tutors of the highest caliber for you."

Alek turned back to the porthole and took a deep breath. Once again his speech and manner were giving him away. It was *infuriating*.

The woman continued, amused that he was upset. "I suppose we shall have to use other means, Mr. Sharp. Shall we introduce Alek to the young Huxleys?"

"The Huxleys?" A smile spread across Dylan's face. "That's a brilliant idea, ma'am!"

Alek stiffened. "Who are they?"

"A Huxley isn't a *who*, you ninny," Dylan said. "It's more of a *what*, being mostly made of jellyfish."

Alek glared at the boy, certain he was being mocked again.

They led him through the ship, a busy warren of slanted corridors and strange smells. The other crewmen hardly glanced at Alek as they passed, and his only guards were Dr. Barlow and Dylan, who looked as skinny as a rail. It was all rather insulting. Maybe the creature Tazza was more dangerous than they'd admitted.

Of course, running was pointless. Even if he found his way out of the ship, his captors had taken his snowshoes, and he was already half frozen. He wouldn't last an hour on the glacier.

They went up a spiral staircase that was tilted, like the rest of the ship, at a precarious angle. The smells grew stranger as they climbed. Tazza began to sniff the air, hopping on his hind legs along the slanted floor. Dylan came to a halt beneath a hatch in the ceiling and stooped to gather the beast into his arms. He climbed up through the hatchway, disappearing into darkness overhead.

As Alek followed, he sensed a huge space opening up around him.

His eyes adjusted slowly. The high, curved walls were a mottled translucent pink, and a segmented white arch stretched overhead, the air heavy with unfamiliar smells. Alek realized how warm he was, and the truth hit him.

"God's wounds," he murmured.

"Brilliant, isn't it?" Dylan asked.

"Brilliant?" Alek's throat closed on the word, a sharp taste in his mouth. The segmented arches around him were a giant spine! "This is . . . disgusting. We're *inside* an animal!"

Suddenly the tilted walkway beneath his feet felt slippery and unstable.

Dylan laughed, turning to help Dr. Barlow up through the hatch. "Aye, but the skins of your zeppelins are made of cattle gut. That's like being inside an animal, isn't it? And so's wearing a leather jacket!"

"But this one's alive!" Alek sputtered.

"True," Dylan said, heading down the metal walkway with Tazza. "And being inside a dead animal is much more awful, if you think about it. You Clankers really are an odd bunch."

Alek didn't bother answering this nonsense. He was too busy staring at his feet and staying in the exact center of the walkway. It was tilted more than the rest of the wrecked ship, and the thought of slipping off and actually touching the pinkish innards of this godless monster was too awful to bear.

"Sorry about the smell," Dylan said, "but this is the beastie's digestive tract."

"Digestive tract? Are you taking me to be *eaten?*"

Dylan laughed. "We could probably use your hydrogen!"

"Now, now, Mr. Sharp. Don't give me any ideas," Dr. Barlow said. "I simply want to show Alek how easily we can find his family."

"Aye," Dylan said. "And there's a Huxley now!"

Alek squinted into the gloom. He saw a tangle of ropes ahead of them. They stirred slowly back and forth, like willow branches in a breeze.

"Look higher, you daft git!" Dylan said.

Alek forced his eyes to follow the swaying ropes up the awful pink walls. A shape floated there in the gloom, bulbous and indistinct.

"Oi, *beastie!*" Dylan cried, and one of the ropes seemed to move in response, curling like a cat's tail.

They weren't ropes at all. . . .

Alek swallowed. "What *is* that thing?"

"Have you not been listening?" Dylan said. "It's a Huxley, a sort of jellyfish full of hydrogen. Looks like it's had a growth spurt too. Watch this!"

He dashed toward the dangling ropes—*or tentacles?*—and grabbed a handful, pulling his feet up to swing along the catwalk. The other tentacles curled and flailed, but Dylan climbed higher, pulling the bulbous object down toward himself. Alek could see its piebald skin all too clearly now. It was covered with bulges—like blisters, or the warts on a frog's skin.

And yet, despite his horror, Alek found himself fascinated by the alien grace of the tendrils. The beast was like something from the deep ocean, or a dream. Watching it left him half disgusted and half hypnotized.

Tazza ran beneath Dylan as he swung, nipping at his boots and barking. The boy laughed, still climbing, dragging the swollen creature down until he was almost touching its horrid skin.

Finally he let go, landing with a *clang* on the metal walkway. The angry tentacles slithered around him as the creature shot back into the upper reaches of the beast's innards.

"That one's getting strong," Dr. Barlow said. "It'll be ready soon."

"Ready for what?" Alek asked softly.

"To carry me." Dylan smiled. "The big ones can take an airman up a mile! We've got a few adult Huxleys living deeper in."

Alek stared up at the creature. *A mile* . . . more than a kilometer and a half. From that height they'd easily spot the castle's rectangular shape, or even glimpse the Stormwalker standing in the courtyard.

"I see you understand, Alek," Dr. Barlow said. "We'll find your family soon enough. Perhaps you should save us the bother."

Alek took a slow breath. "Why should I help you?"

"You already tried to help us," she replied. "And, yes, I know you've been treated abominably in return. But you can't blame us for being suspicious. There is a war on, after all."

"So why make more enemies than you've already got?"

"Because we need your help—your family's help. Without it we may all die."

Alek stared hard into the woman's eyes. She was completely serious.

"You can't fix the ship, can you?"

Dr. Barlow shook her head slowly, and Alek turned away.

If the Darwinists really were stuck here, the only way to save them was to give up the castle and all its stores. It was that or let them starve. But could he trade his own men's safety, maybe even the future of his empire, for a hundred lives?

He needed to talk to Volger.

"Let me go," he said. "And I'll see what we can do."

"Perhaps if *you* took us to your home?" Dr. Barlow said. "Under flag of truce, to prevent any unpleasantness."

Alek thought for a moment, then nodded. They were going to find the castle anyway. "All right. But we don't have much time."

"I shall talk to the captain." She snapped for Tazza. "Mr. Sharp, I believe you have duties in the machine room."

"Aye, ma'am," Dylan said. "But what about Alek? Shall I lock him up again?"

Dr. Barlow looked at Alek. *"Bella gerant alii?"*

Alek nodded again. "This isn't my war to wage."

The woman gave him a smile, and turned to lead Tazza away. "I think we can trust Alek not to run amok, Mr. Sharp. Feel free to take him to the machine room with you. He's a very well brought-up boy."

She and Tazza disappeared into the gloom, the dangling tentacles of the Huxleys swirling in their wake.

"You understood what she said?" Dylan asked. "That bit in boffin-speak?"

Alek rolled his eyes. "It's called Latin, you simpleton. *Bella gerant alii* means 'Let others wage war.' She was saying we don't have to fight each other."

"You know Latin?" Dylan laughed. "You're barking posh, aren't you?"

Alek frowned, realizing his mistake. "What I am is stupid."

Dr. Barlow was still testing him, trying to figure out who and what he really was. No smuggler's son or mountain villager would have understood Latin, but he'd answered her without blinking.

The strange thing was, the phrase she'd uttered was part of an old saying about the Hapsburgs, how they'd gained more lands by marriage than war. Was she a mind reader as well as a scientist?

The sooner he was away from these Darwinists, the better.

· TWENTY-SIX ·

As they walked back toward the hatchway, Dylan said, "The lady boffin must think you're something special."

Alek looked at him. "What do you mean?"

"That machine room is supposed to be off-limits." Dylan leaned closer, whispering, "There's something barking odd in there."

Alek didn't answer, wondering what could possibly qualify as *odd* in this menagerie of abominations. In the last few hours he'd seen enough uncanny creatures for a lifetime.

"But I suppose it's all right," Dylan continued. "Seeing as how you've decided to help us."

"No thanks to you."

Dylan came to a halt. "What's that supposed to mean?"

"If it were just you stranded on this glacier, I wouldn't lift a finger."

"Well, that's a bit rude!"

"A bit *rude?*" Alek sputtered. "I brought you medicines. I saved you from . . . frostbitten bum. And when I asked you to keep quiet, you set those awful dogs on me!"

"Aye," Dylan said. "But you were running off."

"I had to go home!"

"Well, *I* had to stop you." Dylan folded his arms. "I took an oath to the Air Service, and to King George, to protect this ship. So I couldn't go making promises to some intruder I'd just met, could I?"

Alek looked away, his anger suddenly exhausted. "Well, I suppose you were doing your duty."

"Aye, I suppose so too." Dylan turned with a huff and started walking again. "And I was *going* to thank you for not shooting me."

"You're most welcome."

"And special thanks for not burning up the whole ship. Including yourself, you daft bum-rag."

"I didn't *know* the air was full of hydrogen."

"Couldn't you smell it?" Dylan laughed. "Those fancy tutors didn't teach you much useful, did they?"

Alek didn't argue—among the things he'd learned from his tutors was how to ignore insults. Instead he asked, "So is that hydrogen I'm smelling now?"

"Not in here," Dylan said. "The digestive tract has regular air, except for a wee bit of extra methane. That's why it smells like cow farts."

"My education continues," Alek said with a sigh.

Dylan gestured up at the pink curved walls. "See those puffy bits between the ribs? Those are hydrogen bladders. And the whole top half of the whale is full of the stuff. What you're seeing is just the gut—a wee sliver. The beastie's two hundred feet from top to bottom!"

More than sixty meters—Alek felt a bit unsteady on his feet.

"Makes you feel like a tick on a dog, doesn't it?" Dylan said, opening the hatch. He hooked his boots around the ladder's edges and slid down, hitting the deck with a thump.

"A charming image," Alek muttered, feeling a shiver of relief as he climbed back down into the gondola. It was good to have a sturdy deck under his feet again, even if it was tilted, and walls that were solid instead of membranes and bladders. "But I prefer machines, I'm afraid."

"Machines!" Dylan cried. "Barking useless. Give me fabricated species any day."

"Really?" Alek said. "Have your scientists bred anything that can run as fast as a train?"

"No, but have you Clankers ever made a train that can hunt for its own food, or heal itself, or *reproduce?*"

"Reproduce?" Alek laughed. For a moment he imagined a litter of baby train cars populating a railroad yard, which led his mind to other aspects of the mating process. "Of course not. What a repulsive idea."

"And trains need tracks to run," Dylan said, ticking off points on his fingers. "An elephantine can move across any sort of terrain."

"So can walkers."

"Walkers are rubbish compared to real beasties! Clumsy as a drunk monkey, and they can't even get up when they fall!"

Alek snorted, though that last part was true of the bigger dreadnoughts. "Well, if your 'beasties' are so wonder-

ful, then how did the Germans shoot you down? With *machines.*"

Dylan gave him a dark look, pulling off a glove. His bare hand curled into a fist. "Ten to one, and all of them went down too. And I'll bet they didn't land as softly."

Alek realized he'd said too much. Dylan probably knew crewmen who'd been wounded, or even killed, in the crash. For a moment Alek wondered if the boy was going to punch him.

But Dylan simply spat on the floor and turned to stalk away.

"Wait," Alek called. "I'm sorry."

The boy stopped but didn't turn around. "Sorry about what?"

"That your ship's so badly hurt. And for saying I'd let you starve."

"Come on," Dylan said gruffly. "We've got eggs to tend to."

Alek blinked, then hurried to follow. *Eggs?*

They made their way to a small room on the gondola's middle deck. It was a mess—machine parts strewn across the floor, along with broken glass and sprigs of hay. It felt oddly warm in here, with a smell like . . .

"Is that brimstone?" Alek asked.

"The scientific name is sulfur. See here?" Dylan led

him to a large box in a corner, which steamed with heat in the cold air. "Eggs have loads of sulfur in them, and most of these are broken, thanks to your German pals."

Alek blinked in the gloom. The rounded shapes before him looked exactly like . . . giant eggs.

"What sort of monstrous creature laid these?"

"They weren't laid, but made in a laboratory. When you create a new beastie, they have to stew for a while. The life threads are in there, building the beasties out of egg muck."

Alek looked down with distaste. "It all sounds very ungodly."

Dylan laughed. "The same thing happened when your ma carried you. Every living creature's got life threads, a whole instruction set in every cell of your body."

This was clearly pure rubbish, but Alek didn't dare argue. The last thing he wanted was more disgusting details. Still, he couldn't take his eyes off the gently steaming eggs.

"But what's going to come out of these?"

Dylan shrugged. "The lady boffin's not telling."

The boy slipped his hand into the hay where the giant eggs were nestled, and pulled out a thermometer. He squinted at it, swore softly at the darkness, then drew a tin pipe from his pocket and blew a few notes.

The room grew brighter, and Alek noticed a cluster

of the glowing worms hanging from the ceiling by his head. He took a step away from them. "What are those things?"

Dylan looked up from his work. "What? Glowworms?"

Alek nodded. "An appropriate name, I suppose. Haven't you Darwinists discovered *fire* yet?"

"Get stuffed," Dylan said. "We use oil lamps, but until the ship's all patched, it's too barking dangerous. What do they use on zeppelins, *candles?*"

"Don't be absurd. I imagine they have electrical lights."

Dylan snorted. "Waste of energy. Bioluminescence worms make light from any kind of food. They can even eat soil, like an earthworm."

Alek eyed the cluster of worms uneasily. "And you *whistle* at them?"

"Aye." Dylan brandished the pipe. "I can command most of the ship's beasties with this."

"Yes, I remember you whistling up those . . . spider-dogs?"

Dylan laughed. "Hydrogen sniffers. They patrol the skin for leaks—and chase down the occasional intruder. Sorry if they scared you."

"They didn't scare—," Alek started, but then he noticed a pile of satchels on the floor. They were the ones he'd brought, the first-aid kits.

He knelt and opened one up. It was still full.

"Oh, right." Dylan turned back to the eggs, looking sheepish. "We haven't got those to the sick bay yet."

"I can see that."

"Well, Dr. Barlow had to check them first!" Dylan cleared his throat. "Then she wanted to see you straightaway."

Alek sighed, closing the satchel again. "Bringing medicine was probably a pointless gesture. No doubt you Darwinists heal people with . . . *leeches* or something."

"Not that I know of." Dylan laughed. "Of course, we do use bread mold to stop infections."

"I certainly hope you're kidding."

"I never lie!" Dylan said, standing up from his work. "Listen, Alek, these eggs are warm as toast. Let's take those kits to the surgeons now. I'm sure they'll find a use for them."

Alek raised an eyebrow. "And you're not just humoring me?"

"Well, I'd also like to look for the bosun. He got shot right before the crash, and I don't know if he made it. Him and a mate of mine were dangling from a rope when we went down."

Alek nodded. "All right."

"And coming here was hardly a pointless gesture," Dylan said. "After all, you saved my bum from frostbite."

◉   ◉   ◉

As they made their way toward the sick bay, Alek noticed that the corridors and stairways felt less dizzying.

"The ship isn't as slanted, is it?" he asked.

"They're adjusting the harness," Dylan said. "A bit each hour, so as not to disturb the whale. I've heard we should be level by dawn."

"Dawn," Alek muttered. By then Volger would be launching whatever plans he'd made. "How long is that from now?"

Dylan pulled a watch from his pocket. "Half an hour? But it may be a while before the sun comes over the mountains."

"Just half an hour?" Alek fumed. "Do you think the captain will listen to Dr. Barlow?"

Dylan shrugged. "She's a fancy-boots, even for a boffin."

"And what does *that* mean, exactly?"

"It means she's barking important. We set down in Regent's Park just to pick her up. She'll make the old man listen."

"Good." They passed a row of portholes, and Alek looked out at the brightening sky. "My family will be here soon."

Dylan rolled his eyes. "You're quite up yourself, aren't you?"

"Pardon me?"

"You think quite highly of yourself," Dylan explained slowly, as if talking to an idiot. "Like you're something special."

Alek looked at the boy, wondering what to say. It was pointless to explain that, in fact, he *was* something special—the heir to an empire of fifty million souls. Dylan had no way of understanding what that meant.

"I suppose I've had an unusual upbringing."

"You're an only child, I'd guess."

"Well . . . yes."

"Hah! I knew it," Dylan crowed. "So you think your family are going to throw themselves against a hundred men in a warship, just to get *you* back?"

Alek nodded, saying simply, "They are."

"Barking spiders!" Dylan shook his head and laughed. "Your parents must spoil you rotten."

Alek turned away, starting down the corridor again. "I suppose they did."

"They *did*?" Dylan ran a few steps to catch up. "Hang on, are your parents dead?"

Alek's answer caught in his throat, and he realized something strange. His mother and father had died more than a month ago, but this part—telling someone about it—was new. The Stormwalker's crew had known before he had, after all.

He didn't dare speak. Even after all this time, saying

the words aloud risked his losing control of the emptiness inside.

All he could do was nod.

Bizarrely, Dylan smiled at him. "My da's gone too! It's pure dead horrible, isn't it?"

"Yes, it is. I'm sorry."

"At least my mum's still alive." The boy shrugged. "I've had to give her the slip, though. She didn't understand me wanting to be a soldier."

Alek frowned. "What mother wouldn't want a soldier for a son?"

Dylan bit his lip, then shrugged again. "It's a wee bit complicated. My da would've understood, though. . . ."

His voice trailed off as they passed through a wide room with a long table at its center, a cold wind sweeping in through a large shattered window. Dylan paused and stood there a moment, watching the sky turn a metallic rosy gray. The silence felt heavy to Alek, and he wished for the hundredth time that he'd inherited his father's gift for saying the right thing.

Finally he cleared his throat. "I'm glad I didn't shoot you, Dylan."

"Aye, me too," the boy said simply, and turned away. "Now let's get those kits to the surgeon and see about Mr. Rigby."

Alek followed, hoping that Mr. Rigby, whoever he might be, was still alive.

• TWENTY-SEVEN •

Thirty minutes later Deryn was up on the spine, strapping herself into the pilot's rig of the *Leviathan*'s biggest Huxley. She was exhausted and half frozen, but for the first time since the wreck things felt under control.

She and Alek had found Mr. Rigby in the sick bay, alive and well and shouting orders from his bed. A bullet had passed clear through him, somehow missing all the important bits. According to the ship's surgeon he'd be back on duty in a week.

A message lizard had found them there, relaying the captain's plan in Dr. Barlow's voice: A well-armed party would escort Alek home under flag of truce, but not until a Huxley had gone up for a good look. So Alek was stuck on egg-watching duty and Deryn was here on the spine, ready to ascend.

She tightened the rig across her shoulders, glancing up

at the Huxley. The beastie looked healthy, its membrane taut in the thin mountain air.

Good for a mile of altitude at least. If Alek's family lived anywhere in this valley, Deryn would spot them in a squick.

"Mr. Sharp!" a voice called from halfway down the flank. It was Newkirk, smiling as he climbed toward her. "It's true—you're alive!"

"Of course I am!" Deryn called back, cracking a smile. Mr. Rigby had told her Newkirk was unhurt, but it was good to see him with her own eyes.

He ran the rest of the way up, carrying a pair of field glasses in one hand. "The navigator sends these with his compliments. They're his best pair, so don't break them."

Deryn frowned at the maker's mark on the leather case: Zeiss Optik. Everyone said Clanker binoculars were the best, but it was annoying to be reminded of it. At least Alek wasn't here to make some stuck-up remark. Orphan or not, she'd had enough of his Clanker arrogance for one day, and the sun wasn't even up yet.

"Mr. Rigby and I were beginning to think you'd fallen off before the crash," Newkirk said. "I'm happy to see you were just dawdling."

"Get stuffed," Deryn said. "If it weren't for me, you'd both be wee splotches in the snow. And I haven't been dawdling. I've been escorting important prisoners about the ship."

"Aye, I've heard about your mad boy." Newkirk narrowed his eyes. "Is it true he says an army of abominable snowmen are coming to his rescue?"

Deryn chuckled. "Aye, his attic's a wee bit scrambled. But he's not that bad, I suppose."

Seeing Mr. Rigby with his shirt cut open around the wound, Deryn had realized how lucky she'd been. If Alek hadn't woken her up, it might have been *her* laid out on a bed in sick bay. And even if it had only been a squick of frostbite, the surgeons might've stripped off her uniform . . . and seen exactly what was hidden beneath.

She owed the boy for that, Deryn reckoned.

A whistle sounded, and the two fell silent.

On the glacier below, all hands were assembling, sheltered by the huge crescent of the airbeast's bulk. The captain was going to address the crew at first light.

To the east the sun was just cresting the mountains, bringing a squick of warmth to the air. The *Leviathan's* membrane was already turning black, ready to absorb the heat of the day.

"I hope the captain's got good news," Newkirk said. "Don't want to be stuck on this iceberg too long."

"It's a glacier," Deryn said. "And the lady boffin seems to think we might be."

There was a stir among the men below, and attention was called as the captain came out onto the snow.

"The last patch went on at six a.m. this morning," he announced. "The *Leviathan* is airtight once again!"

The riggers arrayed along the spine raised a cheer, and the two middies joined them.

"Dr. Busk has checked her insides, and the beast seems healthy enough," the captain continued. "What's more, our Clanker friends hardly dented the gondolas. There may be a lot of broken windows, but our instruments are in fine shape. Only the motivator engines need serious repairs."

Deryn glanced down at the port engine pod, riddled with bullet holes and leaking black oil onto the snow. The tail engines looked bad as well. The Germans had focused most of their fire on the mechanical parts of the ship—typical Clanker thinking. The starboard pod lay beneath the whale, of course, smashed against the glacier.

"We'll need two working engines to control the ship," the captain said. "At least we have no shortage of parts." He paused. "So our greatest test will be reinflating the ship."

Here it comes, Deryn thought.

"Unfortunately, we don't have enough hydrogen."

An uncertain murmur spread through the crew. The wee beasties in the whale's gut *made* hydrogen, after all, the same way people breathed out carbon dioxide. Even after a long winter's hibernation the ship always swelled back to her old size within a few days.

"THE CAPTAIN ADDRESSES THE CREW."

It was normally so simple that everyone had missed the obvious—hydrogen didn't come from out of the blue. It came from the airship's bees and birds.

The head boffin stepped forward.

"The Alps were once the bedrock of an ancient sea," he said. "But now these peaks are the highest in Europe, not fit for man or beast. If you look around, you'll see no insects, plants, or small prey for our flocks. For the moment our fabs are living off the ship's stores. As long as they remain alive, the ship will process their excreta and slowly refill her hydrogen cells."

"Excreta?" Newkirk whispered.

"That's boffin-talk for 'clart,'" Deryn replied, and Newkirk snorted a laugh.

"But when the *Leviathan* was designed," Dr. Busk continued, "none of us imagined landing in a place so bleak. And I'm afraid that the equations are indisputable: All the hydrogen in our ship's stores isn't enough to lift us into the air."

Another murmur spread through the crew. They were getting the picture now.

"Some of you may be wondering," Dr. Busk said with half a smile, "why we don't simply take hydrogen from the snow around us."

Deryn frowned. She'd been wondering no such thing, but it seemed like a fair question. Snow was just water, after all—hydrogen and oxygen. It'd always seemed a bit suspect to her, that two gasses mixed up made a liquid, but the boffins were dead certain on the issue.

"Unfortunately, separating water into its elements requires energy, and energy requires food. The ecosystem that is our home depends on sustenance from nature to repair itself." Dr. Busk's gaze swept across the glacier. "And in this awful place, nature herself is empty."

As the captain stepped forward again, Deryn heard no sound but the wind in the rigging and the panting of hydrogen sniffers. The crew had gone dead silent.

"Early this morning we loosed a pair of homing terns to carry our position to the Admiralty," the captain said. "No doubt one of our sister ships will reach us soon enough, provided the war doesn't get in the way."

A chuckle rose up from the crew, and Deryn began to feel a squick of hope. Maybe things weren't as bleak as Dr. Barlow thought.

"But mounting a rescue mission for a hundred men in wartime may take weeks." The captain paused, and the head boffin beside him looked grim. "We don't have much food in our stores—a little more than a week at half rations. Longer if we use the other resources at our disposal."

Deryn raised an eyebrow. *What* other resources? The head boffin had just said there was nothing on the glacier.

The captain drew himself up taller. "And my first responsibility is to you, the men of my crew."

The *men*—not the fabricated creatures. Did he mean taking the beasties' food? But surely the captain wasn't saying . . .

"To save ourselves we may have to let the *Leviathan* die."

"Barking spiders!" Newkirk hissed.

"It won't come to that," Deryn said, pulling the Clanker field glasses from his hands. "My mad boy's going to help us."

"What?" Newkirk asked.

"Tell the men at the winch to give me some rope," she said. "I'm ready to go up."

"Don't you think it's a bit rude," Newkirk whispered, "taking off while the captain's talking?"

Deryn looked out across the glacier—nothing but blank white snow, turning brilliant as the sun rose. But somewhere out there were people who knew how to survive in this awful place. And the captain *had* said to go up at first light. . . .

"Quit your dawdling, Mr. Newkirk."

The boy sighed. "All right, your admiralship. Will you be wanting a message lizard?"

"Aye, I'll call one," Deryn said. "But fetch me some semaphore flags."

As Newkirk went for the flags, Deryn took out her command whistle, blowing for a message lizard. A few heads turned in the crowd below, but she ignored them.

Soon a lizard crested the wilting airbag and scuttled toward her along the spine. Deryn snapped her fingers, and it climbed up her flight suit, nestling on her shoulder like a parrot.

"Stay warm, beastie," she said.

The winch had started to turn, a length of slack rope coiling down the airbeast's flank. Newkirk handed her the semaphore flags and stood ready at the tether line.

Deryn gave him a thumbs-up, and he let the knot spill.

The air became clearer as she rose.

Down near the surface, icy particles flurried on the constant wind, swirling across the glacier like a freezing sandstorm. But up here, above the haze of airborne snow, the whole valley spread out below her. Mountains rose on either side, covered under a patchy blanket of white. The strata of the ancient seabed jutted up through the snow in a broken sawtooth pattern.

Deryn pulled the field glasses from their case. Where to start?

First she scanned the perimeter of the wreck, looking for fresh tracks in the snow. Several spindly trails led away from the ship and back, where crewman had snuck off to smoke a pipe or relieve themselves. But one set was wider and shuffly looking—Alek's funny shoes at work.

Deryn followed the tracks away from the wreck. They wandered back and forth, crossing exposed rock whenever possible. Alek had been clever, trying to confuse anyone trying to follow him home. But he hadn't reckoned on someone tracking him from the sky.

By the time the footprints had faded into the distance, she was certain he'd come from the east, where Austria lay.

The sun was fully up now, making the white snow glare. But Deryn was glad for the warmth. Her eyes were watering from the cold, and the message lizard clenched her shoulder like a vise. Fabricated lizards weren't properly cold blooded, but freezing air slowed them down.

"Hang on there, beastie. I'll have a mission for you soon."

Deryn swept her glasses back and forth across the eastern end of the valley, looking for anything out of place. And suddenly she saw them . . . tracks of some kind.

But they weren't human. They were huge, as if a giant had shuffled through the snow. What had Newkirk said about abominable snowmen?

The tracks led to an outcrop of rocks, or what looked like rocks. As Deryn stared, the shapes of broken walls came into focus, along with stone buildings huddled around an open courtyard.

"Blisters!" she swore. No wonder Alek talked so posh. He lived in a barking *castle*.

But she still hadn't found whatever had made those tracks. The courtyard was empty, the stables too small to hold anything so massive. Deryn slowly scanned the structure until she found the gate in the castle walls. . . . It was open.

Her hands shaking a little, she followed the tracks away from the castle again, and saw what she'd missed the first time. Another set branched off, heading toward the wrecked airship.

And these tracks were fresh.

Deryn remembered her argument with Alek about animals and machines. He'd mentioned walkers, hadn't he? Those crude Clanker imitations of beasties. But what sort of barking mad family had its own walker?

Deryn swept her gaze across the snow faster now, until a glint of metal flashed across her vision. She blinked, backtracking until . . .

"Blisters!"

The machine bounded across the snow, shimmering with heat in the cold, like a monstrous, angry teakettle on two legs. The ugly snout of a cannon thrust from its belly, and two machine guns sprouted like ears from its head.

It was running straight for the *Leviathan*.

She pulled the semaphore flags from her belt, waving

them hard. A light flashed in response from the airship's spine—Newkirk was watching.

Deryn whipped the flags through the letters, spelling out . . .

E-N-E-M-Y—A-P-P-R-O-A-C-H-I-N-G—D-U-E—E-A-S-T

She squinted, watching for confirmation from below. The light flashed in answer: W-H-A-T—M-A-N-N-E-R-?

W-A-L-K-E-R—T-W-O—L-E-G-S, she answered.

Another confirmation flashed, but that was all. They'd be scrambling now, trying to mount some defense against an armored attack. But what could the *Leviathan*'s crew do against an armored walker? An airship was defenseless on the ground.

They needed more details. She raised the glasses to her face again, trying to read the markings on the machine.

"Alek, you *bum-rag!*" she cried. Two steel plates hung down to protect the walker's legs, both painted with the Iron Cross. And a double-headed eagle was painted on its breastplate. Alek was no more Swiss than he was made of blue cheese!

"Beastie, wake up," Deryn snapped. She took a breath to steady herself, then said in a slow, clear voice, "Alert, alert. Regards to the *Leviathan* from Midshipman Sharp. The approaching walker is Austrian. Two legs, one cannon, type uncertain. It must be Alek's—that boy we caught—

family on their way. Maybe he can talk to them. . . ."

Deryn paused for a moment, wondering what else to say. She could think of only one way to stop the machine, and it was too complicated to cram into a lizard's drafty wee attic.

"End message," she said, and gave the beastie a shove. It scuttled away down the ascender's rope.

As she watched its progress, Deryn let out a soft groan. Away from her body heat the freezing air was slowing it down. The beastie would take long minutes to deliver the message.

She peered across the glacier again, using only her naked eyes. A tiny flash of metal winked at her from the snow, closer to the airship every second. The charging walker was going to arrive before the lizard.

Alek was the key to stopping the machine, but in all the ruckus would anyone think of him?

The only way to make sure was to go down herself.

◉ TWENTY-EIGHT ◉

This was Deryn's first sliding escape.

She'd studied the diagrams in the *Manual of Aeronautics*, of course, and every middy in the Service wanted an excuse to try one. But you weren't allowed to *practice* sliding escapes.

Too barking dangerous, weren't they?

Her first problem was the angle of the cable stretching down to the airship. Right now it was much too steep; she'd wind up a splotch in the snow. The *Manual* said that forty-five degrees was best. To get there the Huxley needed to lose altitude—fast.

"Oi, beastie!" she yelled up. "I think I'll light a match down here!"

One tentacle coiled serenely in the breeze, but otherwise the airbeast didn't react. Deryn growled with frustration. Had she found the one Huxley in the Service that couldn't be spooked?

"Bum-rag!" she called, bouncing in the saddle. "I've gone insane, and I'm keen to set myself on fire!"

More tentacles coiled, and Deryn saw the venting gills softly ruffle. The Huxley was spilling hydrogen, but not fast enough.

She kicked her legs to swing herself back and forth, yanking on the straps that connected her harness to the airbeast. "Get down, you daft creature!"

Finally the smell of hydrogen filled her nose, and Deryn felt the Huxley descending. The tether line looked less steep every second, like the string of a falling kite.

Now came the tricky part—reconfiguring the pilot's harness into an escape rig.

Still yelling at the beast, Deryn began to take apart the harness. She loosened the straps around her shoulders, wriggling one arm free, then the other. As the belt around her waist unbuckled, the first wave of dizziness hit. Nothing was keeping her in the saddle now except her own sense of balance.

Deryn realized she'd been awake almost twenty-four hours—if you didn't count lying unconscious in the snow, which was hardly quality sleep. Probably not the best time for risky maneuvers . . .

She stared at the undone straps and buckles, trying to remember how they went back together. How was she meant to reassemble them while clinging to her perch?

Sighing, Deryn decided to use both hands—even if that meant she was one Huxley twitch away from a long fall.

"Forget what I was saying earlier, beastie," she murmured. "Let's just float calmly, shall we?"

The tentacles stayed coiled around her, but at least the creature was still descending. The tether line had almost reached forty-five degrees.

After a long minute's fiddling, the escape rig looked right—the buckles forming a sort of carabiner in the center. Deryn gave the contraption a jerk between her hands, and it held firm.

Now came the scary part.

She clenched the rig between her teeth and pulled herself up with both hands. As her bum left the saddle, a fresh wave of dizziness hit. But a moment later Deryn was standing in a half crouch, her rubber-soled boots gripping the curved leather seat.

She reached up and clipped the buckles onto the tether line, then took one end of the strap in each hand, winding the leather several times around her wrists.

Deryn glanced down at the glacier. "Blisters!"

While she'd been getting ready, the walker had closed almost half the distance to the airship. Worse, the tether line had gotten *steeper*. The wind was tugging the Huxley higher. At this angle she'd slide down the rope much too fast. The *Manual* was full of gruesome tales about pilots who'd made that mistake.

Deryn stood to her full height, her head inches from the Huxley's membrane.

"Boo!" she cried.

The airbeast shivered all over, venting a bitter-smelling wash of hydrogen right into her face. The saddle jerked beneath Deryn, and her boots slipped from the worn leather . . .

A fraction of a second later the straps around her wrists snapped, yanking her shoulders hard. And she found herself sliding down toward the massive bulk of the airship below.

She felt nothing but a roar in her ears, like staring into a headwind on the spine. Tears streamed from her face, freezing to her cheeks, but Deryn found herself letting out a wild, exultant scream.

This was *real* flying, better than airships or ascenders or hot-air balloons, like an eagle zooming down toward its prey.

For a few terrifying seconds the angle grew steeper, but the *Manual* had predicted that. It was the Huxley springing up behind Deryn as her weight slid away from it.

She glanced up at the rig. The metal buckles were giving off an audible *hiss* and a squick of smoke from the

"EMERGENCY ZIP LINE."

friction. But she was moving too quickly to burn through the rope. Everything was going perfectly.

As long as another gust of wind didn't pull the Huxley higher . . .

The airship grew in front of her. The crew were already scrambling, a muddle of tiny dots swarming on the snow. That was good. She didn't have time to make a formal report. She had to get to the machine room and back out before the walker arrived . . .

But what was *that*? From out of nowhere a small shape had appeared on the rope ahead—a tangle, or some imperfection in the cable. At this speed, running into a knot could break her wrists—or even worse, snap the leather of the rig.

Then Deryn realized what it was: the message lizard, still making its plodding way down toward the ship.

"Out of the way, lizarrrrrrd!" she screamed.

At the last moment the beastie heard her—and leapt straight into the air! Deryn whipped past it, spinning herself around to look back. The lizard came down onto the rope, wrapping its sticky feet around the cable and shrieking random warnings as Deryn zipped away.

"Sorry, beastie!" she cried, then spun back toward the airship.

It was coming at her so *fast*.

She tried to slow herself, letting her legs dangle to

catch the air. At least the membrane was squishy and half deflated. The flank was seconds away now, sniffers and riggers scrambling to get out of her way. Deryn let the straps around her wrists unwind . . .

At the last second she dropped.

The membrane crumpled around her with a *whump*. For a moment she was buried in the warm, smothering embrace of the airbeast's skin, breathless and dazed.

She rolled over to face upward, her ears still ringing with the impact, and found herself nose-to-nose with a curious hydrogen sniffer.

"Ow," Deryn told it. "That *hurt*."

The beastie sniffed her and let out a concerned bark—apparently the impact had popped open a leak.

Hands reached down and pulled her up, setting Deryn onto her feet.

"You all right there, lad?"

"Aye, thanks," she said, looking around for an officer. But none had appeared to demand a report. The riggers were in motion all around her, the crew scattering below. "Is it in sight yet?"

"You mean that contraption?" The rigger turned and looked across the snow. On the horizon a squick of a reflection pulsed in a steady pattern, matching the rhythm of the walker's stride. "They say it's a big one."

"Aye, it is," Deryn said, and headed down.

◉   ◉   ◉

Dashing across the membrane on shaky legs, she hoped
that Alek was still with the eggs. Would he guess what the
ringing battle Klaxon meant and try to escape? Or, with
the enemy approaching, would some daft officer decide to
lock him up again?

The faster she found him, the better.

Spotting a tangle of ratlines draped across the main
gondola, Deryn didn't bother using a gangway. She climbed
down the ropes, swinging into the gondola through a
smashed window. Shards of broken glass tugged at her
flight suit, but the suit's thick leather snapped them from
the frame, her boots skidding as she landed.

There was no chaos inside, just controlled urgency. A
troop of men ran past, carrying small arms. A chorus of
command whistles sounded, calling for the hawk tenders
to assemble.

But air guns and aeroplane nets against an armored
walker? They wouldn't stand a chance.

The machine room was just down the corridor. She
headed toward it, then burst through the door at a run.

"Mr. Sharp!" Dr. Barlow said from the darkness. "What's
all the fuss out there?"

A moment later Deryn's eyes adjusted—there he was,
kneeling by the cargo box.

"Alek!" she cried. "It's your family!"

He stood, letting out a sigh. "As I expected."

"They've sent an emissary?" Dr. Barlow asked.

"They've sent a barking war machine!" Ignoring the boffin's expression, Deryn grabbed Alek's arm and pulled him out the door.

Once she'd dragged him into the corridor, he began to run under his own power. She led him toward the lower deck.

"I thought Volger might take a direct approach," he said as they scrambled down the stairs.

"Speaking of direct, how come you didn't mention that your family had a barking *walker?*"

"Would you have believed me?"

"I'm *still* not sure I believe it!"

On the lower deck, Deryn ran for the gondola's main door. But when they reached the gangway, it was already occupied by a line of crewmen carrying heavy crates. The words "high explosives" brought Deryn to a skidding halt.

"Don't want to bump into these fellows. Aerial bombs."

Alek's eyes widened. "What are they going to drop them from?"

"A Huxley, maybe? Just what we need to start that walker of yours shooting!" She pulled him away. "Come on, we'll jump out a window."

At the middies' mess the broken window they'd passed that morning still hadn't been repaired. Deryn jumped up onto the ledge, but paused. With the gondola at this angle the drop was a bit farther than she'd expected.

Alek climbed up beside her, looking down dubiously.

"The snow's dead soft," Deryn said, trying to convince herself. "It's an easy jump!"

"After you, then," Alek said.

"No chance." Deryn grabbed his arm, and off they went.

It wasn't so bad. The snow compacted beneath them with a muffled *crunch*, like being whacked with a big freezing pillow.

Alek rose to his feet, glaring. "You pushed me!"

"More of a *pull*, really." She pointed across the snow. "No time to dawdle."

The walker was almost here.

As they ran, Deryn could feel the machine's footsteps rumbling beneath her now, and the roar of its engines shaking the air. Its huge feet thrashed the snow, raising white clouds in its wake.

"At least they aren't shooting yet."

"They're well within range," Alek said. "But they don't want me getting hurt."

"That's what I'm counting on." She pulled him across the snow, past the crewmen arrayed to defend the ship.

Deryn could see now what the captain was planning. A second ascender was in the air—Newkirk aboard, clutching an aerial bomb in his arms. More bombs lay half buried in the snow ahead, wires running to them. If the walker stumbled too close to one, maybe they could blast it off its feet.

As she and Alek ran through the defenses, someone called after them. But Deryn pretended not to hear. She had to get Alek out in front before the shooting started.

"Do you reckon they can see us yet?" she asked.

"Let's make sure." Alek slowed, waving his arms.

The walker thundered toward them for another few seconds, then suddenly tipped backward. Deryn thought for a moment that it was going to fall. But then one steel leg stretched out in front, plowing through the snow and bringing the machine to a sliding halt, an icy cloud drifting up around it.

"Nicely done, Klopp," Alek murmured, and turned to Deryn. "They see us."

"Brilliant! Oh, and sorry about this." Deryn grabbed Alek's arm, drew her rigging knife, and pressed it against his throat.

"What are you—," he started, but the words choked off as cold metal touched his flesh.

"Don't struggle, you ninny!" she hissed. "Do you want your head cut off? I'm just making sure no one gets hurt."

"I fail to see your *logic!*" Alek growled at her, but he stopped struggling.

As she stared up at the huge machine, Deryn put a

"NEGOTIATIONS AND COLLATERAL."

defiant scowl on her face. The walker stood there, utterly motionless, as if transformed into a vast iron statue.

"Hey, in there!" she yelled. "Don't move or I'll spill your friend's guts!"

"If you do that," Alek pointed out, "they'll simply blow you to pieces."

"Don't be daft," she whispered. "I'm not *really* going to . . ."

Her voice trailed off as the machine's head began to move. Two sets of steel teeth slowly opened, revealing a pair of faces inside.

"Hah!" Deryn said. "They can see us for sure now."

Alek sighed. "Yes, but what do you expect them to do? Surrender to the superior force of your *knife*?"

"Well . . ." Deryn frowned. "I hadn't really thought past this bit."

Alek looked at her. "You really are a ninny, aren't you?"

"Me, a ninny?" Deryn cried. "I've just saved us all from getting blown up!"

"You don't really think they would have . . . ," Alek started, then let out a disgusted sigh. "Just yell for Volger to come down, under flag of truce. He'll know what to do."

Deryn thought this sounded sensible, whoever Volger was. She took a deep breath and shouted, "Attention, Clankers! Send down Volger, under truce."

There was a long wait. Deryn glanced up, and saw Newkirk and his ascender drifting uselessly over the airship. The wind had died. She just hoped he had a good grip on his aerial bomb.

Behind them the airship's crew was silent, the wind almost still. The only sounds were ticks and pops from the war machine as its engines cooled. She wondered if the officers would be upset about this idea of hers. No one had ordered her to use Alek as a hostage.

Of course, no one had ordered her *not* to either.

A soft metal groan pulled her eyes back to the walker, her grip on Alek tightening. Some sort of hatch was swinging open between the walker's legs. A ladder made of chains spilled down from it, jangling wildly for a moment, the sun flashing from its steel rungs.

A man climbed down then, slowly and carefully. Deryn noticed a sword swinging under his fur coat.

"Is that Volger?" she whispered.

Alek nodded. "I just hope your captain honors the truce."

"Aye, me too," Deryn said. One shot from that cannon could still destroy the *Leviathan* where it lay.

These negotiations had to work.

⬡ TWENTY-NINE ⬡

Count Volger made his way toward them, the expression on his face unreadable.

Alek swallowed. Under the circumstances, Volger was unlikely to give him the tongue-lashing he deserved. But it was humiliating enough, standing here, held hostage by a mere boy.

Volger stopped a few meters away, his eyes moving warily between the airship's crew in the distance and the blade at Alek's throat.

"Don't worry about this young fool," Alek said in German. "He's only playing at threatening me."

Volger glanced at Dylan. "I can see that. Unfortunately, those men behind you are deadly serious. I doubt we can make it back to the Stormwalker before they pick us off."

"No, but I think these people can be bargained with."

"Hey, you two!" Dylan snapped. "Stop that Clanker-talk!"

Count Volger gave the boy a bored look, then continued in German, "Are you certain he doesn't speak our language?"

"I very much doubt it," Alek said.

"Well, then," Volger said. "Let's pretend that I don't know English. We might learn something interesting if the Darwinists think I can't understand them."

Alek smiled—Volger was already taking control of the situation.

"What are you two saying?" Dylan demanded, tightening his grip.

Alek turned to face him, switching to English. "My friend doesn't speak your language, I'm afraid. He wants to meet with your captain."

The boy looked hard at Volger, then jerked his head toward the airship. "All right, let's go. But no funny business."

Alek coughed politely. "If I promise to avoid funny business, could you perhaps remove this knife from my throat?"

Dylan's eyes widened. "Oh, aye. Sorry about that."

The cold steel left his flesh, and Alek touched his neck and looked down at his hand. No blood.

"I used the dull edge, you daft git," Dylan whispered.

"Much appreciated," Alek said. "And I suppose that was quick thinking, getting me down here."

"Aye, it was," Dylan said, smiling. "Pure dead brilliant, me. I just hope the officers don't give me a good kicking for thinking for myself."

Alek sighed, wondering if he'd ever understand Dylan's peculiar way of speaking. But at least no one was shooting yet.

Maybe the boy wasn't such a fool after all.

The captain met them in a salon that took up the whole width of the airship. Now that oil lamps were lit and the gondola was almost level, the airship seemed less bizarre, even luxurious. The ceiling arches reminded Alek of vines curving overhead, and though his chair felt solid, it seemed to weigh nothing. Did the Darwinists fabricate trees as well as animals? The table was decorated with a pattern that seemed woven into the grain of the wood itself.

Volger's eyes were wide as he scanned the room. Alek realized that the two of them were probably the first Austrians ever aboard one of the big hydrogen breathers.

Seven people sat around the table: Volger and Alek, Dr. Barlow and a bowler-hatted male scientist, the captain, and two of his officers.

"I hope you won't mind coffee," the captain said as they were served. "It's a bit early for brandy, and cigars are strictly forbidden."

"And there *is* a lady present," Dr. Barlow said with a smile.

"Well, of course," the captain muttered, clearing his throat and giving her a tiny bow. The two didn't seem entirely friendly with each other.

"Coffee is more than welcome," Alek said. "I haven't slept much."

"It has been a long night for us all," the captain agreed.

Alek made a show of translating what had been said so

far. Volger smiled and nodded as he listened, as if hearing everything for the first time.

Then he asked, "Do you think any of them speak our language?"

When Alek glanced around the table, none of the Darwinists volunteered an answer. But Alek murmured, "The lady has excellent Latin. Perhaps she knows other languages as well?"

Volger gave a slight nod, his gaze resting for a moment on Dr. Barlow's bowler hat. "Then let us be careful."

Alek nodded, and turned back to the *Leviathan*'s captain.

"Well, then," the captain said. "Let me start by apologizing for any rough treatment. In wartime we have to suspect the worst of an intruder."

"No harm done," Alek said, reflecting on how apologies always came easier when you had a cannon pointed at someone.

"But I must admit, we're still confused about who you are." The captain cleared his throat. "That is an Austrian Stormwalker, is it not?"

"And carrying the Hapsburg seal," Dr. Barlow said.

As Alek translated for Volger, he remembered Klopp's plans to disguise the palace guard walker. But somehow a fresh coat of paint had never seemed terribly important while they'd been running for their lives.

"Explain that we're political opponents of the emperor," Volger said. "And that he's seized the war as an opportunity to get rid of his enemies. We aren't deserters. We had no choice but to run."

As Alek translated this into English, he marveled at Volger's quick thinking. The explanation was not only believable; it bordered on the truth.

"But who exactly *are* you?" Dr. Barlow asked when he was done. "Household retainers? Or are you Hapsburgs yourselves?"

Alek paused for a moment, wondering what the Darwinists would do if he told them he was the grandnephew of the emperor. Take him back to England as a war prize? Publish the story of his escape as propaganda?

He turned to Volger. "What should we tell them, Count?"

"It might be wise," the man said in a hard whisper, "not to address me by rank."

Alek froze for a moment, glancing at Dr. Barlow. Either she hadn't heard the word "count" or she was too clever to show it. Or maybe she didn't speak German after all.

"Tell them we prefer not to discuss such a thing with foreigners," Volger continued. "Suffice it to say that we are neutral in this war. We certainly have no grudge against a shipwrecked crew."

Alek translated this carefully, thankful he'd been practicing his English with Dylan.

"Most mysterious," Dr. Barlow said.

"But certainly hopeful." The male scientist leaned forward. "Perhaps you can help us. What we need is quite simple: food. Lots of it."

"Just food?" Alek frowned.

"This is hardly some dead Clanker machine," the man said pompously, as if repeating a catechism. "The ship can heal herself, if we can just feed her enough."

Alek turned to Volger and shrugged. "He says all they need is food."

"Well, then. We'll give it to them."

"We will?" Alek asked. "But just yesterday you—"

"Your foolishness has given me a chance to reconsider," Volger said. "As we planned our attack this morning, they sent carrier birds aloft. Calling for rescue, no doubt. And worse, the Germans might be looking for them."

"So the sooner they leave this valley, the better," Alek said, feeling his humiliation fade a bit. If his reckless trip across the snow had forced Volger to help the airship's crew, perhaps he'd done the right thing after all.

"Besides," Volger said, "they'll want us to trade something for you, my annoying, useless young friend."

Alek glared at Volger, who smiled placidly back at him. He was only playing down Alek's importance, of course, in case Dr. Barlow could understand them. But Volger hardly had to *relish* it so much.

Alek gathered himself, then said in English, "We're happy to give you food. What kind does your ship need?"

"Raw meat and fruit are best," Dr. Barlow said. "Anything a bird would eat. Sugar and honey are useful for our bees, and we can dissolve starches, like flour, in the gastric channel."

"But how much?" he asked.

"Six or seven tons in all."

Alek raised an eyebrow, trying to remember what an

English ton was. Almost a thousand kilograms? God's wounds, this was a hungry beast.

"I'm afraid we have no . . . honey. But lots of sugar, meat, and flour. Will dried fruit do?"

Dr. Barlow nodded. "Our bats are very happy with dried fruit."

Bats? Alek shuddered a bit as he translated for Volger.

"Your little expedition is getting expensive, Alek," the wildcount said. "But we can spare it. And in return we'll take you away from here—now."

Alek faced the captain. "We'll trade you the food for my freedom."

The man frowned. "We'll be happy to send you home, of course. Once we have the food in hand."

"I'm afraid you'll have to release me now." Alek glanced at Volger. "My family will stand for nothing less."

Dr. Barlow was smiling. "Their concern for you is touching, Alek. But there is one problem. Once you're no longer our guest, that walker could easily destroy us."

"I suppose so," Alek said. He turned to Volger and said in German, "They want to keep me as insurance."

"Offer them a trade. Me for you."

"I can't let you do that, Volger. This is all *my* fault!"

"It would be difficult to argue with that," Volger said. "But we'll need two skilled pilots to move that much food."

Alek frowned. He suspected that the real reason was

to keep him safe for the throne of Austria-Hungary. But it was true—old Klopp couldn't drive a laden Stormwalker back and forth in this cold, not alone. And, of course, here was the real reason Volger was pretending not to speak English. He wanted to spy on the unsuspecting Darwinists while he was their hostage.

"All right, then. I'll tell them we want a swap."

Volger held up a hand. "Perhaps we should drive a harder bargain. If we hold one of them hostage, they might be more inclined to return me in working order."

Alek smiled. He'd been ordered around by the Darwinists all night. It was time to return the favor.

"Volger will stay in my place," he said. "And we shall require a . . . guest in return. Perhaps you, Captain?"

"I should think not," one of the officers said. "The captain is needed here."

"As are all my officers and crew," the captain said. "This is a wounded ship. I'm afraid we don't have anyone to spare."

Alek folded his arms. "Then I'm afraid we have no food to spare."

The table was silent for a moment, the Darwinists glaring at Alek while Count Volger looked on placidly, pretending not to understand.

"Well, the answer is obvious," Dr. Barlow finally said. "I shall go."

"What?" the captain sputtered. "Don't be absurd!"

"I am rarely absurd, Captain," Dr. Barlow said archly, then began to count off points on her finger. "Firstly, I shall hardly be making any repairs. Secondly, I know what food the *Leviathan*'s creatures can and cannot eat."

"As do I!" the other scientist said.

"But you are the ship's surgeon," Dr. Barlow said. "Whereas I am hopeless as a nurse. Clearly I am the right choice."

As the officers began to argue with her, Alek leaned closer to Volger.

"She'll get her way," he said. "For some reason she's quite important here."

"That makes her an ideal hostage, I suppose."

"Not really," Alek muttered. Neither Klopp nor the other men spoke any English. He'd have to deal with Dr. Barlow on his own.

"Do you think she'll be trouble?" Volger asked.

"I suppose I can handle one woman," Alek said, sighing. "As long as she doesn't bring that wretched beast of hers."

THIRTY

Tazza seemed to enjoy riding in the Stormwalker.

The beast scrambled about the floor of the pilot's cabin, pawing for spent cartridges that had rolled into crevices and corners. Soon bored with that, it sniffed the emergency ration locker, then watched Alek's feet on the pedals and growled. It was quite annoying.

"This machine has a peculiar stride," Dr. Barlow said from the commander's chair. Her gaze stayed fixed on Alek's hands as he drove, which was unsettling. "Is it based on any particular animal?"

"I've no idea," Alek said, wishing that Klopp could answer her questions. He'd retreated down to the gunners' station, horrified by the presence of a woman in his Stormwalker. Or maybe he was afraid of Tazza.

"It walks a bit like a bird," Dr. Barlow said.

"Aye, a great iron rooster!" Dylan added.

Alek sighed, wishing he'd negotiated a more equal exchange of hostages. It seemed unfair that Dr. Barlow should bring an entourage with her—a beast, an assistant, and a trunk full of luggage. Back at the airship Volger didn't even have a change of socks.

Alek shut out their questions, focusing on the controls. The Stormwalker was negotiating the rocky slope leading up to the castle, and he didn't want to stumble in front of the Darwinists.

Dr. Barlow leaned forward as the crumbling walls came into view. "How rustic."

"It *is* meant to be hidden," Alek mumbled.

"Disrepair as camouflage? Ingenious."

Alek slowed the walker as the gate drew nearer, but grazed the iron hinges with its right shoulder. He winced as a metal screech rang through the cabin, Tazza matching the noise with a piercing whine.

"Bit tight, isn't it?" Dylan remarked. "If you're going to stroll about in this monstrosity, you should get a bigger door!"

Alek squeezed the saunters tighter as he brought the walker to a halt, but he managed to hold his tongue.

"There must be quite a lot of you," Dr. Barlow exclaimed.

"Just five," Alek said, opening the stable doors wider. "But we're well provisioned." He didn't mention that this was only one of many storerooms.

"How convenient." Dr. Barlow unhooked Tazza's leash from his collar, and the beast trotted deeper into the gloom, sniffing every box and barrel along the way. "But you couldn't have brought all this in your machine."

"We didn't," Alek said simply. "It was waiting here, just in case."

The woman tutted sadly. "Long-standing family squabbles can be most tiresome."

Alek didn't answer, gritting his teeth. Every word out of his mouth only betrayed more information.

He wondered if the Darwinists had already guessed who he was. The assassination was still front-page news, and the rift between his father and the emperor was no secret. Luckily, the Austrian papers had never revealed that Alek was missing. The government seemed to want his disappearance kept quiet, at least until it could be made permanent.

Dylan appeared at the stable door and gave a low whistle.

"Is this your pantry?" The boy laughed. "It's a wonder you're not fatter."

"Let us not question good fortune, Mr. Sharp," Dr. Barlow said, as if she hadn't been full of questions herself a moment ago. She handed Dylan a notepad and safety pen, then began to move among the crates and sacks, reading the labels and calling out her results to be written down.

After a moment of watching her effortlessly translate the labels, Alek cleared his throat. "Your German is quite good, Dr. Barlow."

"Why, thank you."

"I'm surprised you didn't have a chat with Volger," he said.

She turned to him and smiled innocently. "German is such an important language in the sciences, so I've learned to read it. But conversation is another matter."

Alek wondered if that were true, or whether she'd understood them perfectly. "Well, I'm glad you think our science is worth reading."

She shrugged. "We borrow as much from your engineering as you do from ours."

"Us, borrow from Darwinists?" Alek snorted. "How absurd."

"Aye, it's true," Dylan spoke up from across the room. "Mr. Rigby says you Clankers wouldn't have invented walking machines without our example to follow."

"Of course we would have!" Alek said, though the connection had never occurred to him. How else would a war machine get around? On *treads*, like an old-fashioned farm tractor?

What a preposterous idea.

As the two Darwinists returned to their work, Alek's fuming turned to annoyance with himself. If he hadn't let slip his discovery that Dr. Barlow understood German, perhaps Volger could have concocted some way to mislead her.

But then he sighed, depressed at how often his thoughts turned to deception now. After all, Dr. Barlow had only done what Volger was doing with the Darwinists, pretending not to speak their language to spy on them.

It was odd, really, how alike those two were.

Alek shuddered at the thought, then went to help Klopp and the others prepare the Stormwalker. The sooner the Darwinists were gone, the sooner all this skullduggery could end.

"Can your contraption really pull all that?" Dylan asked.

Alek looked at the sledge, which was piled high with barrels, crates, and sacks—eight thousand kilograms in all. Plus the weight of Tazza, who sat atop the mountain of food,

catching the sun's last rays. There was no chance of starting before dark, but they'd be ready at dawn tomorrow.

"Master Klopp says it should slide easily on the snow. The trick is not breaking the chains."

"Well, it's not a bad job," Dylan said. The boy was sketching the Stormwalker and its load, capturing the walker's lines with swift, sure strokes. "I'll have to admit you Clankers are clever-boots with machines."

"Thank you," Alek said, though making the sledge had been simple enough. They'd taken one door off the castle gate and laid it flat, adding two iron bars for runners. The tricky part was securing the sledge to the Stormwalker. At the moment Klopp was halfway up a ladder, reinforcing the walker's anchor ring with the sputtering flame of a welding torch.

"But isn't it a bother?" Dylan asked. "Making a machine to do something that animals are better at?"

"Better?" Alek said. "I doubt one of your fabricated creatures could pull this load."

"I reckon an elephantine could drag that, easy." Dylan pointed up at Klopp. "And you wouldn't have to oil its gears every few minutes."

"Master Klopp's only being careful," Alek said. "Metal can be brittle in this cold."

"That's exactly what I mean. Mammothines *love* the cold!"

Alek recalled seeing photos of a mammothine—a huge, shaggy sort of Siberian elephant, the first extinct creature that the Darwinists had brought back. "But don't they fall over and die in the heat?"

"That's a Clanker lie!" Dylan exclaimed, then shrugged. "They're fine, unless you take them south of Glasgow."

Alek laughed, though he was never quite sure when

Dylan was joking. The boy had sharp wits, despite his rough manner of talking. He'd been very clever about tying cargo onto the sledge, and had hit it off with Bauer and Hoffman in an easy way that Alek had never managed—without speaking a word of German.

Alek might have trained in combat and tactics his whole life, but Dylan was a *real* soldier. He swore with an effortless extravagance, and during lunch had thrown a knife three meters and hit an apple square in its heart. He was skinnier than most boys his age, but could work alongside men and be treated as their equal. Even his lingering black eye from the crash had a piratical swagger to it.

In a way Dylan was the sort of boy Alek would have wanted to be, if he hadn't been born the son of an archduke.

"Well, don't worry," Alek said, clapping a hand on Dylan's shoulder. "The Stormwalker can carry all the food your airbeast needs. Though I can't see how one creature could eat all this."

"Don't be daft. The *Leviathan* isn't one creature," Dylan said. "It's a whole tangle of beasties—what they call an *ecosystem*."

Alek nodded slowly. "Did I hear Dr. Barlow say something about bats?"

"Aye, the fléchette bats. You should see those wee beasties at work."

"Fléchette? Like 'dart' in French?"

"That sounds right," Dylan said. "The bats gobble up these metal spikes, then release them over the enemy."

"They eat spikes," Alek said slowly. "And then . . . *release* them?"

Dylan stifled a laugh. "Aye, in the usual way."

Alek blinked. The boy couldn't possibly be saying what Alek thought he was. Perhaps it was another of his peculiar jokes.

"Well, I'm glad we're at peace, so your bats won't be, um . . . *releasing* their fléchettes on us."

Dylan nodded, a serious look on his face. "I'm glad too, Alek. Everyone says that Clankers only care about their machines. But you're not like that."

"Well, of course not."

"It was dead brave, coming across that ice alone."

Alek cleared his throat. "Anyone would have done the same."

"That's a load of blether. You got in trouble for helping us, didn't you?"

"I can't argue with that."

Dylan held out his hand. "Well, it was barking decent of you."

"Thank you, sir." Alek took the boy's hand and shook. "And it was decent of you to save me from a fiery death."

"That doesn't count," Dylan said. "It would've been my fiery death as well!"

Alek laughed. "I appreciate it nonetheless—as long as you promise not to hold me at knifepoint again."

"I promise," Dylan said, but his face stayed serious. "It must have been rough, having to run away from home."

"It was," Alek said, then looked at the boy suspiciously. "Did Dr. Barlow ask you to find out who I am?"

"The boffin doesn't need *my* help." Dylan snorted. "She already reckons you must be quite important."

"Because of this castle? Because they came for me in a walker?"

Dylan shook his head. "Because they traded a barking *count* for you."

Alek swore softly. Dr. Barlow had understood perfectly when he'd called Volger by his title. And that wasn't the only foolish thing he'd let slip.

"Can I trust you, Dylan? To keep a secret."

The boy looked at him askance. "Not if it's a danger to the ship."

"Of course not. It's just that . . . Do you mind not telling Dr. Barlow what I said about being an orphan?" Alek paused, wondering if simply asking this would give him away. "If she knows that, she'll figure out who I am. And then there might be trouble between us again."

Dylan stared at Alek a moment, then nodded solemnly. "I can keep that secret. Your family's no business of ours."

"Thank you." As they shook hands again, Alek felt

a burden lift, knowing that Dylan would keep his word. After a month of being betrayed—by his family, his country's allies, and his own government—it was a relief to trust someone.

He shivered and stamped his feet. "Shall we get out of this cold?"

"Aye. A hot cup of tea would be brilliant."

"We can build a fire!" Alek said, realizing that there was no need to hide their smoke anymore. Another good thing about helping the Darwinists—he could have a warm bath and a hot meal for the first time in weeks.

Dinner was an extravagant affair, but bathing was better.

First Bauer packed the tub with snow, then melted it with pots of boiling water. The resulting bath was deliciously hot, and for the first time in a month removed the engine grease from under Alek's fingernails. With a lady present, Klopp, Bauer, and Hoffman all shaved, and Dylan complained loudly that he hadn't brought his razor, though the boy hardly seemed to need it.

Dr. Barlow, of course, was disinclined to bathe in a castle full of men. But when Dylan didn't take advantage of the bathtub either, Alek wondered if hot water flowed freely aboard the Darwinists' airship.

Hoffman thawed a lamb over the fire, while Master Klopp and Bauer cooked a vast pot of potatoes in chicken broth, onions, and black pepper. The feast went on past dark, despite how exhausted they all were.

It was refreshing to have a lady at the table. As Alek had suspected, Dr. Barlow's spoken German was quite fluent. And Dylan somehow managed to make the other men laugh with only the words he'd picked up in one day.

As the night drew on, Alek began to wonder when next he would see an unfamiliar face. After hiding for five weeks, he'd already half forgotten what it was like to meet a new person, or to make a new friend.

What if he were stuck in this castle for years?

The next morning Alek's first steps were slow ones.

The sledge wouldn't budge at first, like a dog refusing to take a walk. But finally its runners cracked their overnight coat of ice and began to scrape along the courtyard stones.

As the Stormwalker neared the gate, Alek wondered if the sledge behind them was straight.

Master Klopp read his mind. "Perhaps I should watch out the hatch, like Volger."

"No offense, Klopp," Alek said, "but you're a bit too sturdy to stand on my shoulders."

The master of mechaniks shrugged, looking relieved.

"Perhaps Mr. Sharp can help," Dr. Barlow suggested in German. She was sitting in the commander's chair again, Tazza at her feet.

Alek agreed, and soon Dylan was halfway up through the hatch, facing backward, his boots settled on Alek's shoulders.

"At least we know the sledge fits through the door," Klopp muttered. "Since it *is* the door."

After a few bumps and scrapes they were out on the open ice. But dragging the sledge was still like walking through molasses. Every step set the engines groaning. Annoyingly, Dylan stayed up top, his boots bouncing on Alek's shoulders.

"Be ready to speed up a bit," Klopp said as they reached the slope leading down from the castle. "We don't want our cargo sliding into us from behind."

Alek nodded, grasping the saunters tighter. Going down the hill, the sledge would build up its own momentum.

With a metal *clang* Dylan dropped back down into the cabin.

"They're here!"

They all looked at him, speechless.

"To rescue us!" he shouted. "Two airships, coming over the mountains ahead!"

Alek brought the Stormwalker to a quick halt, looking at Klopp. "Cut us loose. We need to get Volger back!"

"But they'll think we're attacking."

"Wait a moment, both of you," Dr. Barlow said.

"According to the captain the Air Service shouldn't be here for a week!"

Master Klopp didn't answer, leaning forward and raising his glasses to his eyes. His gaze swept the sky a moment, then fixed on a single spot, a frown growing on his face.

Alek squinted out the viewport and saw them—two dots just above the horizon. He silenced the walker, listening for the sound of the airship's engines across the snow.

"Not airbeasts," Klopp said simply. "They're the kaiser's zeppelins, coming for the kill."

THIRTY-ONE

Deryn listened to the old mechanic arguing with Alek.

She didn't have to speak Clanker to know what they were saying—she'd heard the word "zeppelin" come from Klopp's mouth. So it wasn't rescuers coming . . .

It was barking Germans!

She reckoned Klopp wanted to slink back to the castle and let the zeppelins do their work. The airships wouldn't have spotted the Stormwalker yet. So once the *Leviathan* was destroyed, Alek and his friends could go back into hiding.

Dr. Barlow was about to join the argument, but Deryn silenced her with a hand on one shoulder, knowing exactly what to say.

"Your friend Volger's out there, Alek. Because he traded himself for you!"

"I *know* that," Alek said. "But it seems Volger planned

for this. He made Klopp promise to keep me hidden if the Germans came."

Deryn sighed. That count was a shifty one.

Alek switched back to Clanker-talk, ordering Klopp to disconnect the walker from the sledge. It was odd how many words in German were almost the same as in English, once you'd got your ear in. For once, though, Alek wasn't getting his way. The old man folded his arms, and kept saying *nein* and *nicht*, which any dafty could tell were Clanker for "no."

And it was obvious Bauer and Hoffman would obey Klopp, not Alek, however important the boy was back in Clanker-land. Without their help the Stormwalker was stuck here, like a dog tied to a stake.

Deryn drew her rigging knife, but reckoned that holding it to Alek's throat wouldn't work twice. Besides, she'd promised not to.

But it was time for this squabble to end.

With the hilt of the knife she thumped Klopp hard on his pointy helmet. It slipped down over his eyes, squelching his latest argument.

She turned to Alek. "Give me an axe."

Deryn was down the chain ladder in a squick, the axe thrust through her safety harness. The snow was deep here on the slope, filling her boots with murderous cold as she trudged up to the sledge.

She'd watched Klopp rig this contraption, so she knew its weakness. The ends of the chain were welded to two iron posts on the front of the sledge, the chain's length threaded through a steel ring at the Stormwalker's waist. If she cut either end, the chain would slide through the ring and out, freeing the walker.

But it was massive, each link as big as Deryn's hand. She chose the right side of the sledge. The welding looked hasty there, the wood of the sledge dotted with globs of metal. She scooped up snow in her gloved hands and packed it around a link of chain. Hopefully Alek was right and the freezing cold would make the metal brittle.

"All right, then," she said, raising the axe. "Break!"

Her first swing bounced limply back. The chain was too slack to take the force of the blow.

"We don't have *time* for this!" she cried, glancing at the horizon. The two airships were close enough for her to see their markings now—Iron Crosses on their tail fins, their skins silvery in the morning sun.

"Mr. Sharp!" called Dr. Barlow, her head sticking up from the Stormwalker's hatch. "Anything we can do?"

"Aye," Deryn shouted. "Pull it tight!"

Dr. Barlow disappeared, and a moment later the Stormwalker's engines surged. It took a shuffling step ahead, the chain snapping taut. The sledge shifted a bit beside Deryn as she packed more snow.

Her next swing hit the unyielding metal hard, sending a nasty shock up her arms. She knelt to look closer: The blow had left a notch in one of the metal links, and another in the axe. But the chain wasn't split.

"Blisters."

"Anything?" Dr. Barlow called.

Deryn didn't answer, swinging again as hard as she could. The axe bounced from her hands—she leapt back as it spun through the air, landing a few yards away.

"Careful, Mr. Sharp!" the lady boffin admonished.

Deryn ignored her, peering closer. One link of the chain showed a tiny fracture, too narrow for another link to slip through.

But under enough force the metal might bend.

She called up to the Stormwalker, "Tell Alek to pull—as hard as he can!"

Dr. Barlow nodded, and soon the Stormwalker began to roar again. The machine shifted from foot to foot, digging itself deeper into the snow. Sparks glimmered as its metal feet scraped bare stone below. The sledge crept forward a bit, nudging at Deryn's knee like some huge dim beastie trying to get her attention.

The broken link was bending, the fissure stretching wider with every surge of the walker's engines. Deryn took a wary step back. The chain was going to lash out like a giant metal bullwhip when it finally pulled free.

She scanned the horizon. The two airships had split apart to come at their prey from opposite directions. The sky rippled as the *Leviathan*'s flocks took to the air. But the whale itself lay motionless on the ground, helpless to escape the Clankers' approach.

"Blister this!" Deryn trudged to where the axe had fallen and pulled it from the snow. One good wallop anywhere along the chain would pull that barking link open.

She grabbed a loose cargo strap to brace herself, listening to the surges of the Stormwalker for a moment. When she had its rhythm in her head, Deryn raised the axe in one hand, and brought it down just as the engines hit the peak of their roar. . . .

The chain split, whipping away too fast to see. As the suddenly freed walker staggered ahead, the links threaded through the metal ring at its waist, rattling like a Maxim gun. The loose end flailed for a few seconds, snapping wildly about the walker's head and driving the startled lady boffin back inside.

But the chain was still attached to the left side of the sledge . . . and as the loose end slipped through the steel ring on the Stormwalker, the whole length flung itself *back at Deryn.*

She dove into the snow, and heard the metal whipping past overhead. It smacked against the cargo on the

"BREAKING THE LINE."

sledge, slashing through sacks of flour—a spray of white dust filled the air.

The chain dropped to the snow and slithered away, meekly following the staggering walker, its energy finally expended.

Deryn stood up, coughing out the dry taste of inhaled flour.

Something was nudging at her knee. . . .

The sledge was pushing her insistently, its speed building. But what was pulling it? Then she realized what had happened. The last jerk of the chain had got it started down the slope.

"Oh, that's brilliant!" Deryn said, scrambling aboard the sledge. The *shush* of runners on the snow grew louder as she spat more flour from her mouth.

Before her the Stormwalker had come to a halt, facing away. Alek was waiting for her to climb back up the ladder.

The sledge was headed straight for the walker's legs!

Standing up unsteadily on a bag of dried apricots, Deryn cupped her hands and yelled, "Dr. Barlow!"

No answer came, and no one poked their head from the hatchway. What were they doing in there? Playing Parcheesi?

The sledge was still building speed.

"Dr. Barlow!" she screamed again.

Finally a black bowler emerged from the hatch. Deryn

waved her arms, trying to indicate the sledge, movement, and the general notion of destruction. The boffin's eyes widened as she saw their recently freed cargo bearing down on them.

She disappeared again.

"About time," Deryn said, crossing her arms.

It was lucky she'd scrambled aboard. The sledge was building momentum every second, already sliding faster than Deryn could have run in this snow. She grabbed the loose strap again, not wanting to fall and wind up a greasy spot in the sledge's tracks.

The Stormwalker was finally moving again, taking a ponderous step forward. The machine wavered a bit, like a dim-witted beastie wondering whether to run from some predator.

Deryn frowned, hoping that they wouldn't scamper off for the battle without her. But Alek didn't seem like the type to leave one of his crew behind.

Dr. Barlow popped up again, and the walker's engines roared to life. She was shouting down into the cabin, guiding Alek in some boffin-inspired strategy.

But the sledge was still catching up, building speed faster than the Stormwalker on the ice-crusted snow. Deryn looked up at the cargo towering over her. If the two giant objects collided, she was going to be right in the middle of it.

"Get going!" she cried, climbing higher on the pile.

The Stormwalker drew closer and closer, and Deryn realized that Dr. Barlow had gone barking mad. She wasn't even *trying* to get out of the way. The walker was keeping a steady pace, just a squick slower than the sledge.

She pantomimed confusion for Dr. Barlow, and the lady boffin made climbing gestures in reply.

Deryn frowned, then saw the ladder hanging from the Stormwalker's belly hatch. It flailed in the air as the machine ran, trailing behind like some daft child's broken kite string.

"Oh, you're not thinking I should grab on to *that*," she muttered. The ladder was all chains and metal rungs— heavy enough to knock a tooth out!

Deryn crossed her arms. She could climb up into the walker once the sledge came to a halt, couldn't she? Of course, the quicker she got aboard, the sooner they could go help the *Leviathan*.

Across the ice, the Clanker airships were making their first pass. Machine guns flickered from their gondolas, a cloud of fléchette bats swirling around them. She could see how small the zeppelins were now—barely two hundred yards long. But the *Leviathan* was almost helpless beneath them, her flocks hungry and battered from last night's battle.

"No barking choice, I suppose," she muttered.

The Stormwalker drew nearer, so close that its giant feet were kicking snow back into her face. But the ladder flailed just out of reach. Deryn edged to the front end of the sledge, balanced precariously on a barrel of sugar. Still, she couldn't reach it. She was going to have to jump.

Deryn readied herself, flexing her hands and trying to see some pattern in the ladder's thrashing.

Finally she leapt into the air . . .

Her fingers closed around a metal rung, and she found herself swinging forward between the walker's legs. The engine noise was deafening. Gears and pistons clanked and gnashed about her, and a pair of exhaust pipes hissed hot black smoke into her face. Her grip was jolted with every giant step, her feet swinging wildly. The ladder twisted in the air, whirling Deryn like a drop spindle.

She thrashed her feet until one boot caught a lower rung, anchoring the ladder—the world stopped gyrating.

Glancing up, she saw Bauer and Hoffman peering down from the darkness of the belly hatch. Bauer's hand was out. All she had to do was climb a few meters.

As if *that* were easy.

Deryn reached up to grab the next rung. The metal was jaggy, gripping her gloves with little teeth. She pulled herself grimly upward, trying to ignore the spikes arrayed around the hatch.

"CLAMBERING UP INTO THE GEARS."

Finally she was close enough to reach up and take Bauer's hand. Hoffman grabbed hold, and the two of them pulled her inside in a squick.

"Willkommen an Bord," Bauer said with a smile, meaning "Welcome aboard," of course.

Blisters, but Clanker-talk was easy.

∘ THIRTY-TWO ∘

"You're white as a ghost!" Dr. Barlow said.

"It's only flour." Deryn pulled herself the rest of the way into the pilot's cabin with a groan. Her hands ached from clinging to the flailing ladder, and the muscles in her arms were howling. Her heart still beat like a hammer.

"Flour?" Dr. Barlow said. "How odd."

"Well done, Dylan!" Alek was twisting at the controls. "I've never seen anyone come aboard a walker that way!"

"I wouldn't recommend it." She plonked down on the lurching cabin floor, panting hard. Tazza crept over to nuzzle her hand, then sneezed out a snootful of flour.

Within moments Deryn felt dizzy from the walker's motion. The trip out to the castle had been bad enough—the screech of metal against metal, the smell of oil and exhaust, and the endless, murderous noise of the engines. But at full trot, riding in the walker was like being shaken in a tin snuffbox. No wonder the Clankers wore those silly helmets; it was all Deryn could do to keep her head from banging against a wall.

Klopp, who was peering out the viewport through field glasses, said something in German to Alek.

"I thought *he* wasn't helping," Deryn muttered.

"That was when we could hide," Dr. Barlow said. "Now that the Germans have certainly seen us, he's changed his tune. If we don't shoot both of those zeppelins down, they'll report about our Austrian friends."

"Well, he might have made up his mind a bit faster." Deryn looked down at her aching hands. "I could've used some help cutting that chain."

Dr. Barlow patted her shoulder. "You did well, Mr. Sharp."

Deryn shrugged off the compliment and stood up. She'd had enough of being bounced about blindly. Grabbing on to two hand straps that hung from the ceiling, she pulled herself up and out the top hatch.

The cold hit her full in the face. It was like being on the spine of the airship in a storm, the horizon lurching around her with every step.

Deryn squinted into the eyeball-freezing wind. The zeppelins were skimming low, dragging ropes along the ground. Men slid down them, landing in the snow with guns and equipment on their backs.

But why bother? If they wanted to destroy the *Leviathan*, they could stay up high and use phosphorous bombs.

She dropped back inside. "They're putting men down."

"Those are Kondor Z-50s," Alek said. "They carry commandoes instead of heavy weapons."

"It seems their objective is to capture our ship," Dr. Barlow said.

"Blisters!" Deryn swore. A live hydrogen breather in the Clankers' hands would be a disaster; they'd learn everything there was to know about the great ship's weaknesses. "But aren't they afraid of *us*?"

"They'll have anti-walker guns aboard," Alek said grimly. "They can't fire them from the air. But from the ground, they'll give us a fight."

Deryn swallowed. It was bad enough, riding in this contraption. But the thought of being broiled alive by some armor-piercing shell made her ill.

"We need your help again, Dylan."

She stared at Alek. "Do you want me to *drive* this barking contraption now?"

"No," he said. "But tell me, do you know how to fire a Spandau machine gun?"

Deryn knew no such thing, but she'd fired an air gun plenty of times.

This was quite different, of course. Like everything

else made by Clankers, it was ten times louder, shakier, and more cantankerous than it looked. When she gave the trigger a test squeeze, it rattled like a piston in her hands. Bullet casings spewed from its side, bouncing from the cabin wall in a hot metal hail.

"Cripes!" she swore. "How do you hit anything with this?"

"Simply point it in the general direction," Dr. Barlow said. "What the Clankers lack in finesse they make up for with blanket ruination."

Deryn leaned forward, squinting out the tiny peephole. All she could see was snow and sky bouncing along. She felt claustrophobic and half blind. It was the opposite of watching from the *Leviathan*'s spine, with the battle spread out below like the pieces on a chessboard.

She glanced over at Klopp, who was manning the other machine gun. Instead of looking out, he was waiting for Alek to tell him when to fire.

"Stuff this. I'll be back in a squick," Deryn said, pulling herself up through the hatch again.

Both Kondors had dropped commandoes now. One group was storming toward the *Leviathan*, their zeppelin supporting them with machine-gun fire. The other bunch was assembling some sort of artillery, a long-barreled field gun that was pointed straight at the Stormwalker.

"Oh, blisters," she said.

"DIE ANTI-WANDERPANZER TRUPPEN."

The Clankers worked swiftly, and a moment later the gun's muzzle erupted with flame. The walker twisted beneath her, throwing her hard against the side of the hatch. She barely kept from falling back through, her feet flailing below.

For a moment Deryn thought they'd been hit. But then she felt the shell whiz by, her ears popping as its passed. The Stormwalker staggered into a long turn, finally regaining its balance on the snow.

Alek was either barking *brilliant* at the controls, or he was completely mad. They were headed straight for the anti-walker gun, lurching back and forth across its sights while the crew desperately reloaded.

Deryn dropped back inside and took her machine gun, aiming it low. She reckoned they'd be among the Germans in another five seconds, if they hadn't already been blown to blazes.

"Get ready!" Alek shouted.

Deryn didn't wait, and squeezed the trigger. The gun jumped and rattled in her hands, spewing death in all directions. A few dark shapes slipped past her peephole, but she had no idea whether they were men or rocks or the anti-walker gun.

A metal *clank* shook the cabin, and suddenly the world was staggering to port. Deryn was thrown from her gun, her feet slipping on spent casings rolling across the floor.

She landed on something soft, which turned out to be Dr. Barlow and Tazza huddled in the corner.

"Sorry, ma'am!" she cried.

"Not to worry," the lady boffin said. "You really are quite insubstantial."

"I think we hit it!" Alek said, still twisting at the controls.

Deryn scrambled to her feet and pulled herself up and out the hatch again. Behind them the anti-walker gun lay wrecked in their giant footprints—overturned, the barrel bent. Its crew were scattered, a few motionless, the white snow about them flecked with vivid red.

"You stomped it, Alek!" she shouted down, her voice hoarse.

She spun around to face forward. The Stormwalker was headed for the other group of commandoes now. They were hunkered down in the snow, an aerie of strafing hawks skimming over them, razor talons glimmering in the sun.

A few of the commandoes turned and saw the walker coming at them, and Deryn wondered if she should drop down to fire her murderous weapon again. But then the Stormwalker shook beneath her. A cloud of smoke spewed from its belly, billowing over Deryn and filling her mouth with an acrid taste.

Her eyes stung, but she forced them open as the shell hit. It exploded among the commandoes, throwing men in all directions.

"Barking spiders," she murmured.

When the smoke and snow flurries subsided, nothing moved except a few strafing hawks flapping back toward the *Leviathan*. Deryn glanced back at the field gun. The remaining crew were running away, a Kondor coming down to skim them from the ice.

The Clankers were in retreat!

But where was that *other* zeppelin?

She scanned the horizon—nothing. Then a shadow flickered on the snow, due west, and Deryn looked straight up. The airship was directly overhead, its bomb racks bristling. A cloud of fléchette bats swirled farther up, and she saw a concussion shell arcing its way from the *Leviathan*, its big harmless *boom* about to scare the clart right out of them.

She grabbed the hatch handle and dropped, pulling it shut behind her.

"Bombs coming!" she cried. "And barking fléchettes as well!"

"Vision to quarter," Alek said calmly, and Klopp started turning a crank over at his side of the cabin. Deryn saw an identical one beside her, and wondered which way it was meant to go.

As her hand reached out for it, the world exploded. . . .

A blinding flash lit the cabin, followed by a peal of thunder that threw Deryn off her feet again. The floor was tipping, everything sliding to starboard. The shriek of gears and Tazza howling filtered into her half-deafened ears, and her shoulder struck metal as the whole cabin lurched once—hard.

Then an avalanche of snow was pouring in through the viewport, a rush of cold and sudden silence burying her . . .

○ THIRTY-THREE ○

Alek tried to move, but his arms were pinned, wrapped in a freezing embrace of snow.

He struggled for a moment, then realized he was still strapped into the pilot's seat. As he opened the buckles and slipped from the chair, the world seemed to reorient itself.

The viewport was sideways, like the vertical slit of a cat's eye.

Now that he thought of it, the whole cabin was sideways. The starboard wall was now the floor, and the hand straps all hung helter-skelter.

Alek blinked, unable to believe it. He'd wrecked the walker.

The cabin was dark—the lights had failed—and strangely silent. The engines must have shut down automatically in the fall. Alek heard breathing beside him.

"Klopp," he said, "are you all right?"

"I think so, but something's . . ." The man lifted one arm. Tazza crawled out from beneath it with a plaintive whine, then shook himself, spraying snow across the cabin.

"Do stop that, Tazza," Dr. Barlow's voice came from the darkness.

"Are you all right, ma'am?" Alek asked.

"I am, but Mr. Sharp appears to be hurt."

Alek crawled closer. Dylan lay with his head in Dr. Barlow's lap, his eyes closed. A fresh cut stretched across his forehead, blood running into his black eye from the crash. His thin features were pale behind the bruising.

Alek swallowed. This was *his* fault—he'd been at the controls.

"Help me find some bandages, Klopp."

Shoveling snow aside, they managed to get the storage locker open. Klopp pulled out two first-aid kits and handed one to Alek.

"I'll see to Mr. Sharp," Dr. Barlow said, taking the kit from him. "I'm not as hopeless a nurse as I pretend."

Alek nodded and turned to help Klopp with the belly hatch, which was now in the wall of the upended cabin. The mechanism resisted for a moment, then opened with an angry metal screech.

Hoffman, strapped sideways into the gunner's chair,

called out that he and Bauer were bumped and bruised, but whole. Alek breathed a sigh of relief. At least he hadn't killed anyone.

He turned to Klopp. "I'm sorry I fell."

The man let out a snort. "Took you long enough, young master. Now we can finally call you a proper pilot."

"What?"

"You think I've never wrecked a walker?" Klopp laughed. "It's all part of learning the craft, young master."

Alek blinked, not sure if the man was kidding.

A metal *plink* rang through the cabin. Klopp looked up as another, then more, followed, like a hailstorm slowly building.

"Fléchettes," Dr. Barlow said.

"Let's hope they get those zeppelins," Klopp said softly. "Otherwise Count Volger will be very unhappy with us."

"I'll take a look outside," Alek said. "We might be able to stand up and rejoin the fight."

Klopp shook his head. "Not likely, young master. Stay here till the battle's over."

"That sounds like wise advise," Dr. Barlow said in German.

But the rain of fléchettes was tapering off, and Alek heard the sound of airship engines close by.

"I have to see what's going on," he said. "We've still got a working machine gun!"

"STANDING FIRM."

Klopp tried to argue, but Alek ignored him, shoveling a few handfuls of snow aside and shimmying out the viewport.

The sunlit snow was blinding for a moment, except for the dark crater left by the zeppelin's aerial bomb. Almost a direct hit. The Stormwalker's trail of footprints went straight into the blackened hole, then zigzagged to where the machine lay in a crumpled heap.

Alek flexed his hands, remembering his struggle to keep the walker upright. He'd almost done it. But *almost* meant nothing now. The engine casing was cracked; hot oil steamed out onto the snow. One giant metal leg was twisted wrong. The machine couldn't possibly stand again.

He tore his eyes away, scanning the sky. The Kondor that had bombed them was barely a hundred meters away. It was flying just above the snow, its gasbag fluttering, full of holes from the fléchette attack.

Shouts came from up on its topside. Two airmen had seen him, and were swinging a machine gun around.

Then Alek realized where he was standing—right in front of the walker's breastplate, the Hapsburg coat of arms proclaiming exactly who and what he was . . .

An utter fool.

Before he could move, the Kondor's machine gun erupted. Bullets rang from the walker's steel hull and kicked up snow around his feet. Alek froze, waiting for hot metal to rip through his flesh.

But then the air began to crinkle around the zeppelin. The dazzling flash of the machine gun was spreading, shimmering down the airship's flanks. Too late, the German airmen realized what was happening. The gun fell silent.

But the flame was a living thing now, dancing in the hydrogen spilled from the torn skin. The Kondor dropped, its gondola thudding against the snow. The gasbag crumpled, squeezing more hydrogen from the holes, and a hundred fiery geysers erupted.

Alek squinted and covered his face. The whole airship glowed from within as it rose up, carried back into the sky by its own heat. The aluminum skeleton inside was melting. The Kondor twisted, then broke in the middle, a huge mushroom of fire bellowing from the split.

And then the two halves were swirling downward again.

They seemed to hit the ground gently, but the snow shrieked and hissed as melted metal and burning hydrogen turned it to steam. White clouds billowed around the two halves of wreckage, and Alek heard awful cries over the roar of flame.

"You Clankers really should use air guns."

Alek turned. "Dylan! Are you all right?"

"AS THE KONDOR BURNS."

"Aye, you know me," the boy said. His forehead was bandaged, his eyes bright as he watched the inferno. "A bit of smelling salts and I'm back on my feet." He smiled, then swayed a bit.

Alek put an arm around the boy's shoulders to steady him, but their eyes were drawn to the dying airship again.

"Horrible, isn't it?" Alek whispered.

"Too much like my nightmares." Dylan looked around. "Look, the other one's scampering."

Alek turned. The second zeppelin was in the distance, headed away. A few of the *Leviathan*'s larger hawks were giving chase, harrying the crew on its back. But soon it had slipped over the mountains, making for the floating hangars on Lake Constance.

"We beat them," Dylan said with a weary smile.

"Maybe. But now they know where we are."

Alek looked at the Stormwalker again—broken and silent, except for a hiss where hot oil was leaking onto the snow. If Klopp couldn't fix it, the Germans would have two prizes waiting when they returned: the wounded *Leviathan* and the missing prince of Hohenberg.

"When they come back," he said, "they'll bring more than a pair of Kondors."

"Aye, maybe." Dylan clapped his shoulder. "But don't worry, Alek. We'll be ready for them."

"Perhaps the Darwinists can help us," Klopp said.

Alek looked up from the engine hatch, where he was passing tools to Hoffman. The transmission wasn't as bad as he'd expected. Every drop of oil was spilled, but none of the gears had cracked.

The real problem was standing up again. One of the walker's knees was twisted. It might have the strength to walk, but scrambling to its feet was a different matter.

Alek shook his head. "I doubt they have any creatures strong enough to lift a walker."

"They have one," Klopp said, gazing at the vast bulk of the airship. "When that godforsaken beast goes up, we can run cables to the Stormwalker. Like lifting a puppet on strings."

"A thirty-five-ton puppet?" Alek wished that Dr. Barlow were still here; she would know the *Leviathan*'s lifting capacity. But she and Dylan had headed off to check her precious eggs.

"Why not?" Klopp said, looking back at the castle. "They've got all the food they could ask for."

Across the glacier the Stormwalker's abandoned cargo was swarming with birds. The Darwinists had sent a work party to chop open the boxes and barrels, and hungry flocks had soon descended.

The *Leviathan*'s creatures seemed to know there was no time to lose.

"Young master?" Hoffman said quietly. "Here comes trouble."

Alek looked up and saw a figure in a fur coat coming across the snow. He felt his mouth go dry.

Count Volger wore a cold expression. One hand was clenched around the pommel of his sword.

"Do you know what you've done to us?" he said.

Alek's mouth opened, but nothing came out.

"It was my—," Klopp started.

"Be silent." Volger held up a hand. "Yes, you should have knocked this young idiot on the head to keep him out of sight. But I want to hear *his* explanation, not yours."

"In point of fact they knocked *me* on the head," Klopp mumbled, heading off to help Bauer.

Alek drew himself up. "It was the right choice, Count. Shooting down both of those zeppelins was our only chance to stay hidden." He pointed at the charred remains across the snow. "We got *one* of them, after all."

"Yes, bravo," Volger said, acid in his voice. "I witnessed your brilliant strategy of standing in front of its guns."

Alek took a slow breath. "Count Volger, you will kindly keep a civil tone."

"You abandon your post, you ignore your own safety, and now this!" Volger pointed at the broken walker, his hand quivering with anger and disgust. "And you're telling me to be *civil*? Don't you realize that the Germans will be back soon, and you've left us with no way to escape!"

"It was a risk I was willing to take."

Volger's voice dropped. "It's one thing to risk yourself, Alek, but what about the lives of your men? What do you think will happen to *them* when the Germans come?"

Alek glanced at the spot where Klopp had been standing, but the other three men had found work for themselves out of sight.

"Klopp says we can repair the walker."

"I may be a cavalry officer, Alek, but I can see that this machine won't stand on its own."

"No. But the Darwinists can pull us upright, once they reinflate the airship."

"Forget your new friends," Volger said bitterly. "After this last attack their ship is beyond repair."

"But the zeppelins hardly touched it."

"Only because they wanted to capture the airbeast alive," Count Volger said. "So they focused their fire on the mechaniks. From what I've overheard, the engines are shot to pieces—impossible to fix."

Alek peered at the giant black shape splayed across the snow, the birds whirling overhead. "But they're reinflating the ship. They must be planning something."

"That's why I'm here," Volger said. "They're going up without engines, like a hot-air balloon. An east wind will carry them over France. It should work, as long as that wind arrives before the Germans do."

Alek looked at the Stormwalker, despairing. Maybe they could still pull the walker upright . . . but the *Leviathan* would never have enough control to set the walker on its feet.

Volger took a step closer, the anger fading from his face. Suddenly he looked exhausted. "It's up to you to decide, Alek, if you want to surrender."

"Surrender?" Alek said. "But the Germans would hang me."

"No—to the Darwinists. Tell them who and what you are, and I'm sure they'll take you with them. You'll be a prisoner, but you'll be safe. Perhaps they'll win this war. And then, if you've been obedient, they might install you on the throne of Austria-Hungary, a friendly puppet emperor to keep the peace."

Alek took a step backward in the snow. Volger *couldn't* be saying this. It was one thing to stay hidden—no one expected a fifteen-year-old to fight on the front lines. But surrendering to the enemy?

He'd be remembered as a traitor for all time.

"There must be another choice."

"Of course. You can stay here and fight when the Germans come. And die with the rest of us."

Alek shook his head. It made no sense, Volger talking

like this. The man *always* had a strategy, some plan to bend the world to his will. He couldn't be giving up.

"You needn't decide yet, Alek," Volger said. "We have a day or so before the Germans return. You might have a long life in front of you, if you surrender." He shrugged again. "But I'm done with giving you advice."

With that, the man turned and walked away.

THIRTY-FOUR

Alek took a deep breath and knocked on the door.

Dylan opened it, frowning when he saw Alek.

"You look barking awful."

"I've come to see Dr. Barlow," Alek said.

The young airman opened the door of the machine room wider. "She'll be back soon. But she's in a foul mood, I'm afraid."

"I know about your engine trouble," Alek said. He'd decided not to hide that Count Volger had been spying on them. For his plan to work he and the Darwinists had to trust each other.

Dylan pointed at the box of mysterious eggs. "Aye, and on top of the engines, that barking idiot Newkirk didn't keep these warm enough last night. But it's all *my* fault, of course, as far as the boffin is concerned."

Alek looked down at the box—only three eggs were left.

"That's too bad."

"The mission's stuffed anyway." Dylan pulled a thermometer from the box and checked it. "With no engines we'll be lucky to make it back to France."

"That's what I've come about," Alek said. "Our walker's also finished."

"Are you sure?" Dylan gestured at the drawers that filled the room. "We could give you any spare parts you need. They're useless to us."

"We need more than parts, I'm afraid," Alek said. "We can't stand the walker back upright."

"Barking machines!" Dylan exclaimed. "Didn't I tell you? I've never seen a beastie that couldn't get up on its own. Well, except a turtle. And one of my auntie's cats."

Alek raised an eyebrow. "And I'm sure your auntie's cat would have survived that aerial bomb."

"You'd be surprised. He's quite fat." Dylan's eyes lit up. "Why don't you come with us?"

"That's the problem," Alek said. "I don't think the others will, not if it means surrendering to the French. But if we could sneak away when you land, then maybe . . ."

Maybe he could convince his men to save themselves. And perhaps he could salvage a little of Volger's respect.

Dylan was nodding. "We'll be crash-landing in some random spot, so I doubt there'll be an honor guard there to greet us. Mind you, it's a dodgy business, free-ballooning in a hydrogen breather. Anything could happen."

"What are your chances?"

"Not so bad." Dylan shrugged. "One time I flew a Huxley halfway across England—and all by myself!"

"Really?" Alek said. For a boy, Dylan seemed to have had the most extraordinary adventures. For a moment Alek wished he could forget his birthright and become just like him, a common soldier without land or title.

"It was my first day in the Service," Dylan began, "and an unexpected storm came up, one of the worst London's *ever* seen. Tore up whole buildings from the ground, including—"

The door suddenly flew open and Dr. Barlow swept in, wielding a map case and a furious expression.

"The captain is a fool," she announced. "This ship is full of idiots!"

Dylan saluted. "But the eggs are warm as toast, ma'am."

"Well, that's reassuring, though meaningless under the circumstances. Back to France he wants to go!" Dr. Barlow spun the map case in her hands, then looked up distractedly. "Ah, Alek. I hope your walking machine is in better shape than this benighted airship."

He bowed. "I'm afraid not, Doctor. Master Klopp doesn't think we can get it standing again."

"Is it as bad as that?"

"I'm afraid so. In fact, I'm here to ask if we can come with you." Alek looked at his boots. "If you can manage the weight of five extra men, we'd be in your debt."

Dr. Barlow tapped the map case against her palm. "Lift won't be a problem. We're exhausting our own food as well as yours, giving everything to the animals." She stared out the window. "And our crew is smaller than it once was."

Alek nodded. He'd seen the shrouded bodies outside, and the men laboring to bury them in the iron-hard ice beneath the snow.

"But France isn't neutral territory," she said. "You'll be taken prisoner."

"That's the favor I've come to ask." Alek took a deep breath. "You'll be coming down in some random spot, Dylan says. We could slip away the moment you land."

"And no one the wiser," Dylan added.

Dr. Barlow nodded slowly. "It might work. And we certainly owe you a debt, Alek. But I'm afraid it's not up to me."

"Are you saying the captain won't look the other way?" Alek said.

"The captain is an idiot," she repeated bitterly. "He refuses to complete our mission. He won't even try! If one can free-balloon to France, surely the Ottoman Empire is possible. It's simply a question of catching the right wind." She waved the map case. "The air currents of the Mediterranean are hardly a mystery!"

"Might be a *bit* tricky, ma'am," Dylan said, and cleared his throat. "And technically our destination is still a military secret."

Dr. Barlow glared at the eggs. "An utterly *meaningless* one, at this point."

Alek frowned, wondering why the *Leviathan* was headed to the Ottoman Empire. The Ottomans were devoutly anti-Darwinist, thanks to their Muslim faith. They'd been enemies with Russia for centuries, and the sultan and the kaiser were old friends. Volger always said that sooner or later the Ottomans would join forces with Germany and Austria-Hungary.

"That's neutral territory, isn't it?" he said carefully.

"For the moment." Dr. Barlow sighed. "Of course that may change soon, which is why this delay is a disaster. Years of work, wasted."

Alek listened to her fume, puzzling over this new development. The Ottoman Empire was the perfect place to disappear. It was a vast and impoverished realm, where a few gold coins could go a long way. There were German agents in abundance there, but at least he wouldn't be taken prisoner the moment he arrived.

"If you don't mind telling me, Dr. Barlow, was your mission one of peace or war?"

She held his gaze a moment. "I can't babble all our secrets to you, Alek. But it should be obvious that I am a scientist, not a soldier."

"And a diplomat?"

Dr. Barlow smiled. "We all do our duty."

Alek glanced at the box again. What the eggs could have to do with diplomacy was beyond him. But what mattered was that Dr. Barlow would risk anything to get them to the Ottoman Empire. . . .

Which gave Alek a bold idea.

"What if I could give you engines, Dr. Barlow?"

She raised an eyebrow. "Pardon me?"

"The Stormwalker has two powerful engines," he said. "Both in good working order."

There was a moment of silence, and then Dr. Barlow turned to Dylan. "Is such a thing possible, Mr. Sharp?"

The boy looked dubious. "I'm sure they've got enough power, ma'am. But they're barking heavy! And that Clanker machinery is a fiddle. Making it work could take ages, and we're a bit pressed for time."

Alek shook his head. "Your crew wouldn't have to do much. Klopp is the best master of mechaniks in Austria, handpicked by my father. He and Hoffman kept that Stormwalker running for five weeks on a handful of parts. I would imagine they can get a pair of propellers spinning."

"Aye, maybe," Dylan said. "But there's a bit more to it than just spinning the props."

"Then your engineers can help us." Alek turned to Dr. Barlow. "What about it? Your mission can go forward, and my men and I can escape to a friendly power."

"But there is one problem," the woman said. "We'll be dependent on you."

Alek blinked—he hadn't thought of that. Control of the engines meant control of the airship.

"We could train your engineers as we go," he said. "Please believe me, I enter into this alliance in good faith."

"I trust you, Alek," she said. "But you're just a boy. How can I be sure your word holds with your men?"

"Because I'm . . . ," Alek started, then took a slow breath. "They'll do what I say. They traded a count for me, remember?"

"I remember," she said. "But if I'm going to bargain with you, Alek, I need to know who you really are."

"I . . . I can't tell you that."

"Let me make this easy, then. The best master of mechaniks in all of Austria was part of your father's household?"

Alek nodded slowly.

"And you say you've been on the run for five weeks," she continued. "So your journey began roughly June twenty-eighth?"

Alek froze. Dr. Barlow had named the night that Volger

and Klopp had come for him in his bedroom—the night his parents had died. She must have suspected already, after all the clues he'd let slip. And he'd just handed her the final pieces of the puzzle.

He tried to deny it, but suddenly he couldn't speak. Keeping his despair a secret had made it easier to control, but now the emptiness was rising up in him again.

Dr. Barlow reached out and took his hand. "I'm so sorry, Alek. That must have been awful. So the rumors are true? It was the Germans?"

He turned away, unable to face her pity. "They've hunted us since that first night."

"Then we shall have to get you away from here." She rose, gathering her traveling coat around her. "I shall explain to the captain."

"Please, ma'am," Alek said, trying to keep his voice from shaking. "Don't tell anyone else who I am. It might complicate things."

Dr. Barlow looked thoughtful for a moment, then said, "I suppose this can be our secret, for now. The captain will be happy enough with your offer of engines."

She opened the door, then turned back. Alek wished she would just leave. The emptiness was welling up now unstoppably, and he didn't want to cry in front of a woman.

But all she said was, "Take care of him, Mr. Sharp. I shall return."

THIRTY-FIVE

Alek's sadness had been obvious from the beginning, Deryn reckoned.

She'd seen it when he'd woken her up the night of the wreck, his dark green eyes full of sorrow and fear. And yesterday when he'd told her about being an orphan—she should have known from his silences how raw the heartache was.

But now it was all in the open, tears running down his face, his sobs heavy. Somehow, revealing himself had loosened Alek's mastery of his sadness.

"Poor boy," Deryn said softly, kneeling beside him. Alek was huddled against the cargo box, his face buried in his hands.

"I'm sorry," he snuffled, looking ashamed.

"Don't be daft." She sat beside him, the box warm at her back. "I went half mad when my da died. Didn't talk for a month."

Alek tried to say something, but failed. A hard swallow wracked his frame, as if his throat were glued shut.

"Shhh," Deryn said, and pushed a lock of hair from his face. His cheeks were wet with tears. "And don't worry, I won't tell anyone."

Not about his crying, nor who he really was. That was obvious now. She'd been a ninny not to see it before. Alek had to be the son of that duke fellow who'd started all this. Deryn remembered the day she'd come aboard the *Leviathan*, hearing how some aristocrat had got himself killed, riling up the Clankers.

All this bother over one barking duke, she'd thought so many times. Of course, it probably didn't seem that way to Alek. Having your parents die was exactly like the world exploding, like a war being declared.

Deryn remembered after Da's accident, her mother and the aunties trying to turn her back into a proper girl— skirts, tea parties, all the rest. As if they wanted to erase the old Deryn and everything she'd been. She'd had to fight like mad to stay who she was.

That was the trick—to keep punching, no matter what.

"The boffin will get the captain on our side," Deryn said softly. "And then we'll be out of here in no time. You'll see."

Not that she was entirely sure that Alek's engine plan would work. But anything was better than sitting here hoping for a lucky breeze.

Alek swallowed again, trying to get his voice back.

"They poisoned them," he finally managed. "They tried bombs and pistols first, to make it look like Serb anarchists. But it was poison in the end."

"And it was just a way to start this war?"

He nodded. "The Germans thought the war *had* to come. It was just a question of when—and the sooner the better for them."

Deryn started to say that sounded barking crazy, then remembered all the crewmen who'd been so eager for battle. She supposed there was always some sod spoiling for a fight.

But it still didn't make sense. "Your family are in charge of Austria, aren't they?"

"For the last five hundred years or so, yes."

"So if the Germans killed your da, why is Austria helping them instead of giving the kaiser a good kicking? Doesn't your family know what really happened?"

"They know—or at least suspect. But my father wasn't very popular with the rest of the family."

"What in blisters did he do wrong?"

"He married my mother."

Deryn raised an eyebrow. She'd seen family squabbles over who the children married, but they usually stopped short of bomb-throwing.

"Are your relations completely barking mad?"

"No, we're rulers of an empire."

Deryn reckoned that amounted to pretty much the same thing, but didn't say so. Talking about it seemed to be helping Alek get control, though, so she asked, "What was so wrong with her?"

"My mother wasn't from a ruling house. She wasn't exactly *common*, mind you—she had a princess among her ancestors. But to marry into the Hapsburgs you have to be proper royalty."

"Well, of course," Deryn said. Alek's superior manner suddenly made a lot more sense. She supposed that with his father dead the boy was a duke on his own—or an *arch*-duke, which sounded even loftier.

"So when they fell in love," he said softly, "they had to keep it secret."

"Well, that's dead romantic," Deryn exclaimed. When Alek gave her a funny look, she lowered her voice a bit and added, "You know, sneaking about."

Something like a smile appeared on his face. "Yes, I suppose it was, especially the way my mother told it. She was a lady-in-waiting for Princess Isabella of Croÿ. When my father began to visit, Isabella thought he must be courting one of her daughters. But she could never figure out which one he liked. Then one day he left his watch behind on the tennis courts."

Deryn snorted. "Aye. Back home I'm always leaving my watch on the tennis courts."

Alek rolled his eyes at her, but kept talking. "So Isabella opened the watch, hoping to find a picture of one of her daughters inside."

Deryn's eyes widened. "And there was a picture of your mother instead!"

Alek nodded. "Isabella was very cross. She dismissed my mother from service."

"That's a bit rough," Deryn said. "Losing your job just because some duke fellow likes you!"

"Losing her 'job' was the least of it. My granduncle, the emperor, refused to permit the marriage. He wouldn't even talk to my father for a year. It rattled the whole empire. The kaiser, the czar, even the Holy Father tried to patch things up."

Deryn raised an eyebrow, wondering again if Alek was mad, or simply full of blether. Had he just said that the *pope* had meddled in his family business?

"But finally they came to a compromise—a left-handed marriage."

"What in blazes does that mean?" she said.

Alek wiped the tears from his face. "They could marry, but the children could inherit nothing. As far as my granduncle is concerned, I don't exist."

"So you're not an archduke or anything?"

He shook his head. "Just a prince."

"Only a prince? Blisters, that's *rough*!"

Alek turned to her and narrowed his eyes. "I don't expect you to understand, Dylan."

"Sorry," she muttered. She hadn't really meant to make fun of him. The family split had cost Alek his parents, after all. "It just all sounds a bit odd."

"I suppose it is," he sighed. "You won't tell anyone, will you?"

"Of course not." She stuck out her hand. "Like I said, your family's no business of ours."

Alek smiled sadly as they shook. "I wish that were true. But I'm afraid we've become the whole world's business."

Deryn swallowed, wondering what *that* must be like— to have your family squabble turn into a barking massive war. No wonder the poor boy looked so stricken all the time. Even if none of it was Alek's doing, tragedies always scattered seeds of guilt in bucketfuls.

Deryn still replayed Da's accident in her mind a dozen times a night, imagining what more she could have done to save him, wondering if somehow the fire had been her fault.

"You know you're not to blame, right?" she said softly. "I mean, to hear Dr. Barlow tell it, it took a hundred politicians to stuff things up this bad."

"But *I'm* what split my family," Alek said. "I unsettled everything, and that gave the Germans their opening."

"You're more than just that, though." Deryn took his hand. "You're the one who came across the ice to save my bum from frostbite."

Alek looked at her, wiped his eyes, and smiled. "Maybe that too."

"Alek?" came Dr. Barlow's voice from nowhere, and the boy jumped half into the air.

Deryn smiled as she stood, pointing at the message lizard up on the ceiling.

"The captain has agreed with your proposal," the beastie continued. "Please meet me at your walking machine. We need at least two translators to coordinate our engineers with your men."

Alek just sat there staring up at the lizard in horror. Deryn smiled and pulled him up. "It's waiting for an answer, you dafty."

He swallowed, then said in a nervous voice, "I'll be there as soon as I can, Dr. Barlow. You should also ask Count Volger for help. He can speak perfectly good English when he wants to. Thank you."

"End message," Deryn added, and the beastie scampered off.

A shudder went through Alek. "I'm still not used to talking animals, I'm afraid. It seems a bit ungodly, making them so much like human beings."

Deryn laughed. "Have you never heard of parrots?"

"That's quite different," he said. "They're *meant* to speak that way. But I . . . want to thank you, Dylan."

"For what?"

Alek raised his empty hands, and for a moment Deryn thought he would cry again. But he only said, "For knowing who I am."

He put his arms around her then, a rough embrace that lasted only a moment. Then he turned and hurried from the machine room, headed for the fallen Stormwalker.

As the door swung shut, Deryn shivered, the strangest feeling creeping through her. Where Alek's arms had wrapped around her shoulders an odd kind of tingling was left behind—like the crackle along the airship's skin when distant lightning kindled the sky.

Deryn put her own arms around herself, but it didn't feel the same.

"Barking spiders," she muttered softly, and turned to check the eggs again.

◦ THIRTY-SIX ◦

The next afternoon's watch Deryn and Newkirk were posted on the spine.

Overnight the ship had swelled, the *Leviathan*'s gut in full roar from the beasties' day of gorging. Down on the snow the last of the ship's stores were splayed out, swarmed with feasting birds. Deryn felt her own stomach rumbling with her breakfast of greasy biscuits and coffee. The crew were allowed to eat only what food the animals wouldn't touch.

But a few hunger pangs were worth the bounce of the membrane under Deryn's feet—taut and healthy again. The lumps along the airbeast's flanks were smoothing out. At around noon the wind had started to drag the lightened ship across the glacier, forcing the riggers to fill the ballast tanks with melted snow.

But Dr. Busk had said it would be a close thing,

lifting the weight of the Clanker engines along with five extra men.

"He's moving," Newkirk said. "He must still be alive."

Deryn glanced up at the Huxley. Mr. Rigby had insisted on taking a watch aloft, saying he couldn't bear his last two middies getting frostbite from long hours in the icy sky, even if it meant sneaking out of the sick bay.

"We best pull him down soon," Deryn said. "Dr. Busk will skin us if he freezes up there."

"Aye," Newkirk said, blowing on his hands. "But if he comes down, one of *us* will have to go back up."

Deryn shrugged. "Beats egg duty."

"At least egg duty's *warm*."

"Well, you might still be on it, Mr. Newkirk, if you hadn't killed one of the boffin's barking eggs."

"It's not my fault we're stuck on this iceberg!"

"It's a glacier, you ninny!"

Newkirk grumbled something unpleasant and stormed away, stomping his feet on the hard scales of the spine. He'd claimed the egg disaster had been Dr. Barlow's fault for not explaining Clanker temperatures, but a number was a number, Deryn reckoned.

She almost called him back to apologize, but only swore. Might as well see how work was going on the new engine pods.

Deryn lifted her binoculars. . . .

The forward engines were partway down the airship's flanks, thrusting out like a pair of ears. The tops of both pods had been removed, and a muddle of oversize Clanker machinery stuck out in all directions. Alek was working on the port side, along with Hoffman and Mr. Hirst, the airship's chief engineer. They were all in animated conversation, arms waving in the cold wind.

The whole business seemed to be going slowly. At about noon the starboard engine—where Klopp and Bauer were working—had sputtered to life for a few noisy seconds, the membrane rumbling under Deryn's feet. But something must have cracked. The engine had shut down with a shriek, and the Clankers had spent the next hour tossing bits of burnt metal down onto the snow.

Deryn turned to scan the horizon. It had been more than a day since the Kondor attack. The Germans wouldn't give them much longer. A few recon aeroplanes had already peeked over the mountains, just making sure the wounded airship hadn't gone anywhere. Everyone said the Germans were taking their time, assembling an overwhelming force. The assault could come at any minute.

And yet Deryn's eyes drifted back to Alek. He was translating for Hoffman now, pointing at the front end of the engine pods. He spun his hands about like props, and Deryn smiled, imagining his voice for a moment.

Then she lowered the field glasses and swore, empty-ing her mind of blether. She was a *soldier*, not some girl twisting her skirts at a village dance.

"Mr. Sharp!" came Newkirk's shout. "Rigby's in trouble!"

She looked up. Newkirk was at the winch already, cranking madly. A yellow distress ribbon fluttered from the Huxley, and Mr. Rigby's semaphore flags were moving. Deryn raised her field glasses.

The letters whipped past at double speed, and she'd missed the beginning, mooning dafty that she was. But the sense of the message soon became clear.

. . . D-U-E—E-A-S-T—E-I-G-H-T—L-E-G-S—A-N-D—S-C-O-U-T-S

Deryn frowned, wondering if she'd misread the signals. "Legs" meant a walking machine, of course, but there weren't any eight-legged walkers listed in the *Manual*. Even the big-gest Clanker dreadnoughts needed only six to move about.

And this was Switzerland, still neutral territory. Would the Germans dare attack by land?

But as Rigby repeated the signals, the words flashed past again, clear as day. Along with another bit of news:

E-S-T-I-M-A-T-E—T-E-N—M-I-L-E-S—C-L-O-S-I-N-G—F-A-S-T

Suddenly Deryn's brain was fully back into soldiering.

"Can you get him down without me, Newkirk?" she called.

"Aye, but what if he's hurt?"

"He's not. It's barking Clankers . . . and they're coming by *land*! I've got to raise an alert."

Deryn pulled out her command whistle and piped the signal for an approaching enemy. A nearby hydrogen sniffer perked up its ears, then began an alert howl.

The wailing spread down the ship, sniffer to sniffer, like a living air-raid siren. In moments men were scrambling everywhere. Deryn looked about for the officer of the watch—there he was, Mr. Roland, running toward her across the spine.

"Report, Mr. Sharp."

She pointed up at the Huxley. "It's the bosun, sir. He's spotted another walker coming!"

"Mr. Rigby? What in blazes is *he* doing aloft?"

"He insisted, sir," Deryn said. "The walker's got eight legs, he says—I checked that part twice."

"*Eight?*" Mr. Roland said. "Must be a cruiser at least."

"Aye, it's big, sir. He's spotted it from ten miles away."

"Well, that's lucky. The big ones aren't so quick. We'll have an hour at least before it's here." He turned, snapping at a message lizard scuttling past.

"Begging your pardon, sir," Deryn said, "but Mr. Rigby said 'closing fast.' Maybe this is a nippy one."

The master rigger frowned. "Sounds unlikely, lad. But check with the Clankers. See if they know anything about this eight-legged business. Then bring word to the bridge."

Deryn saluted, spun about, and headed down.

Drop lines were hanging all along the spine, so she clipped a carabiner onto one and rappelled, bouncing down the flank. The rope hissed through her gloves, the metal carabiner turning hot as she slid.

Deryn's blood began to race, the rush of coming battle erasing everything else. The ship was still defenseless, unless the Clankers could get their engines going.

When her boots clanged against the metal support struts of the pod, Mr. Hirst looked up from the jumble of gears. He was hanging off the edge of the engine, no safety line in sight.

"Mr. Sharp! What's all this howling about?"

"Another walker's been spotted, sir," she said, then turned to Alek. His face was streaked with grease, like stripes of black war paint. "We're not sure what kind. But it's got eight legs, so we reckon it's big."

"Sounds like the *Herkules*," he said. "We passed her at the Swiss border. She's a thousand-ton frigate, new and experimental."

"But is she fast?"

Alek nodded. "Almost as quick as our walker. You say she's here in Switzerland? Have the Germans gone *mad*?"

"WARNING THE NEW ENGINE TEAM."

"Mad enough—she's ten miles east, and has scouts with her. How long do you think we've got?"

Alek spoke to Hoffman a moment, translating into German and metric. Deryn felt her foot tapping as she waited, her stinging palms wrapped tightly around the rope. One jump and she'd be sliding toward the bridge.

"Maybe twenty minutes?" Alek finally said.

"Blisters!" she swore. "I'm heading down to tell the officers. Is there anything else they should know?"

Hoffman reached out and took Alek's arm, muttering in hurried Clanker. Alek's eyes widened as he listened.

"That's right," he said. "Those scout craft you mentioned—we saw them too. They're armed with spotting flares, full of some sort of sticky phosphorous!"

Everyone was silent for a moment. Phosphorous . . . the perfect stuff to roast a hydrogen breather.

Maybe the Germans didn't plan on capturing them after all.

"Well, get going, lad!" Mr. Hirst shouted at Deryn. "I'll send a lizard to the other engine. And you two, let's get this contraption started up!"

Deryn took one last glance at Alek, then stepped from the strut. She dropped toward the bridge, the rope sizzling hot between her gloved hands.

○ THIRTY-SEVEN ○

"But the engine's not warmed up yet!" Alek cried. "We could crack a piston in this cold!"

"It'll work or it won't," Hirst shouted back at him. "The ship's going up either way!"

The *Leviathan*'s master engineer had a point. Below them ballast sparkled in the sunlight as it spilled from the forward tanks. The metal deck rose beneath Alek's feet, like an ocean vessel lifted by a wave. Men were streaming back toward the airship across the snow, the howls and whistles of godless animals echoing like a jungle around them.

The airship shifted again, ice snapping from the ground ropes as they stretched and tightened. Mr. Hirst was darting about outside the pod, cutting the pulley lines they'd used to haul the engine parts up. In a few moments all connections with the earth would be severed.

But the engine wasn't fully oiled yet. Half the glow plugs were still untested, and Klopp had forbidden starting up before he'd personally inspected the pistons.

"Will it run?" Alek asked Hoffman.

"Worth a try, sir. Just start it slow."

Alek turned to the controls. It was still strange, seeing the Stormwalker's needles and gauges out of their usual place in the pilot's cabin, and the gears and pistons that belonged in the walker's belly splayed in the open air.

When he primed the glow plugs, sparks flew around his head.

"Slowly now," Hoffman said, putting his goggles on.

Alek took hold of the single saunter—the other was over on the starboard engine with Klopp—and pushed it gently forward. Gears caught and turned, faster and faster, until the rumble of the engine set the whole pod shivering. He glanced over his shoulder to see the plundered guts of the Stormwalker spinning before his eyes, black smoke rising from the exhaust tubes.

"Wait for the order!" Mr. Hirst called above the roar. He pointed at the signal patch on the airship's membrane. It was made of cuttlefish skin, the master engineer had explained, connected by fabricated nervous tissue to receptors down on the bridge. When the ship's officers placed colored paper on the sensors, the signal patch would mimic the hue exactly, like a camouflaged creature in the wild. Brilliant red meant full speed ahead, purple meant half power, and blue meant quarter speed, with other shades in between.

But with these untried engines, Alek doubted that his notion of "half speed" would be the same as Klopp's. It might take days to get the balance right, and the Germans would be here in minutes.

The ground ropes were flailing as riggers cut them loose, and Alek felt another lurch beneath his feet. The cold wind was tugging at the ship now, the great beast skidding sideways along the glacier.

"Quarter speed!" Hirst yelled. The signal patch had turned dark blue.

Alek slowly pushed the foot pedal down. The propeller engaged. It spun lazily for a moment, and then gears meshed and caught, the blades disappearing into a blur.

Soon the propeller was drawing an icy wind across the uncovered pod. He ducked lower, pulling his coat tight. What would *full* speed feel like?

"Down a notch," Hirst cried.

Alek looked at the signal patch, which had turned paler. He eased the saunter back a bit, careful not to stall the engine.

"Hear that?" Hoffman said in the relative quiet. "Klopp's engine."

Alek listened hard—and made out a distant roar. While

his own engine idled, Klopp's was going strong, pushing them into a gradual left turn.

"It's working!" he cried, amazed that the Stormwalker's engines could move something so vast through the sky.

"But why are we turning east?" Hoffman asked. "Isn't the frigate coming from that way?"

Alek translated the question for Mr. Hirst.

"It might be that the captain wants to build up speed down the valley. We're a bit heavy, thanks to your engines, and forward motion gives the ship lift." Hirst hooked a thumb over his shoulder. "Or it might be that he's spotted those blighters back there. . . ."

Alek turned, peering through the blur of propeller blades. Behind them a fleet of airships was rising over the mountains—Kondors, Predator interceptors, and a giant Albatross assault ship dangling gliders from its gondola. A vast aerial attack, timed to descend just as the *Herkules* and its scouts arrived from Austria.

The master engineer leaned back on the struts, lazily resting a foot on the main joint. He slipped his goggles on and said, "I hope these noisy contraptions of yours are ready."

"I hope so too." Alek adjusted his own goggles and turned back to the controls. The *Leviathan's* nose swung slowly eastward, till finally the airship was aimed down the length of the valley.

"FULL THROTTLE."

The signal patch turned bright red.

Alek didn't wait for Hirst's command. He pushed the saunter forward hard. A sputter erupted for a moment in the tangle of gears and pistons. But then the engine roared back to life, the propeller spinning into a shimmer of sunlight.

"Check your bearings!" Hirst yelled over the noise.

Alek saw what the man meant—the airship was veering to starboard, his engine pushing harder than Klopp's. The black teeth of the mountains loomed ahead.

He pulled the saunter back a bit, but a moment later the ship was swinging too far the other way. Klopp must have also seen the turn and pushed his own engine to compensate.

Alek growled with frustration. It was like two men trying to pilot a walker, each with control of one leg.

Mr. Hirst laughed and shouted, "Don't worry, lad. The airbeast has the idea now."

Alek squinted against the icy headwind. Stretched out beside him the creature's flank had come alive. Waves traveled down its length, like a field of grass rippling in a strong wind.

"What's happening?"

"They're called cilia. Like tiny oars stirring the air. The beast will steady us, even if your Clanker engines can't."

Alek swallowed, unable to take his gaze from the undulating surface of the airbeast. Working on the engines, he'd tried to think of the airship as a vast machine. Now it had become a living creature again.

Somehow the tiny cilia were guiding them down the valley. It was like riding a horse, Alek supposed. You could tell it where to go, but it chose where its own footsteps fell.

Hoffman nudged his shoulder. "Say farewell to our happy home, young master."

Alek looked to his left. The castle was shooting past beside them. Provisions for ten years, and he'd spent all of two nights there. . . .

But it was much too close—the castle walls were almost level with the engine. Below Alek the dangling drop lines were still dragging along the snow. And they were headed straight toward the frigate and its scouts.

"We're not climbing!"

"Looks like we're carrying an extra half ton or so," Hirst shouted. "The boffins can't have been this wrong! Are you certain these engines aren't heavier than you told us?"

"Impossible! Master Klopp knows the exact weight of every piece of the Stormwalker."

"Well, *something's* holding us down!" Hirst yelled.

Alek saw flickers of light before them—more ballast spilling from the forward tanks. Then something solid spun past below.

"God's wounds!" Hoffman swore. "That was a chair!"

"What's going on?" Alek yelled at Hirst.

The master engineer watched another chair flutter toward the ground. "They've sounded a ballast alert. Everything we can spare, over the side." He pointed ahead. "And there's why!"

Alek squinted against the icy wind. A white haze was rising in the distance. Metal limbs flashed in the sunlight, churning up a cloud of snow.

The *Herkules* was hurtling up the valley toward them. At this altitude the *Leviathan*'s bridge would crash straight into its gun deck.

Alek's instinct was to pull back on the saunter. But the signal patch was still red. Losing speed meant losing lift, which would only make things worse. And turning about would take them into the guns of the pursuing zeppelins.

Hoffman grasped his arm, leaning in close and muttering in fast German, "This may be the wildcount's fault."

"What do you mean?" Alek asked. He'd hardly seen Volger since their argument the day before. The count had sourly agreed to the plan, but hadn't helped at all with the engines. He'd spent the day hiking to and fro from the wrecked Stormwalker, transferring the wireless set and spare parts to their new cabins in the *Leviathan*.

"We were moving things to your cabin, sir. Twice he

had me wrap up a gold bar in your clothes. And heavy they were too."

Alek closed his eyes. What had Volger been *thinking*? Every bar of gold weighed twenty kilograms. A dozen hidden bars would be like having three stowaways aboard!

"Take the controls!" he cried.

THIRTY-EIGHT

The struts leading to the airship were vibrating like piano strings, pulsing in time with the engine. The metal shivered in his hands, and Alek held tight against the icy winds, climbing quickly past the startled master engineer.

"Where are you going?" the man shouted.

Alek didn't answer, his gaze fixed on the ground slipping past below. He couldn't see how Dylan scrambled about on those ropes so casually. The leather safety harnesses the Darwinists wore hardly seemed thick enough to hold a man's weight. Of course, they were probably made of *fabricated* leather, but that was only more unnerving.

The cilia rippled wildly on the creature's flank, an ocean of shimmering grass, the ratlines fluttering in the wind. At least he wouldn't have to dare the ropes. The struts led straight to an access hatch, which sat between the two ribs supporting the engine's weight. Alek crawled through and headed down.

After the freezing wind outside, the warmth of the creature's innards was welcoming, even with its odd and bitter smells. The ribs had a set of cross-ties between them, so Alek could imagine he was simply climbing down a ladder instead of crawling beneath the skin of a huge beast.

He'd been a fool not to realize that Volger would smuggle everything he could aboard the airship. The man never stopped scheming, never left the next step unplanned. Volger's preparations for this war had taken fifteen years, after all. He wasn't going to leave a quarter ton of gold behind without a fight.

Alek reached the bottom of the ladder, then dropped through another hatch into the main gondola. But then he paused, looking up and down the swaying corridors of the ship. . . .

Where was Volger's cabin? Working all night on the engines, Alek hadn't even slept in his. It didn't help his sense of direction that crewmen were running everywhere, carrying furniture and spare uniforms to be tossed overboard.

Then he noticed that the gondola floor was tipping slightly to the left. Of course. The cabins they'd been given were all on the port side. And toward the bow—so the gold was dragging down the airship's nose!

He ran forward until he spotted the familiar corridor. He threw open the door of Volger's cabin. It was empty, except for a bed, a storage locker, and the Stormwalker's wireless receiver on the desk.

Volger hadn't left the gold in plain view, of course. Alek pulled out the desk drawers, but found nothing. The locker held only clothes and weapons from the castle stores.

Dropping to the floor, he spotted a map case under the bed. Alek reached underneath and tried to drag it out, but it wouldn't budge—as heavy as a solid block of iron. He braced his feet on the bed and pulled at the case with both hands, but it still wouldn't move.

Then Alek realized that the bed had to be far lighter than the gold, and flung it aside. But the latches of the map case were locked. He'd have to throw the whole thing out. Alek stood and pushed open the window, then tried to pick up the case.

It wouldn't lift a centimeter off the ground. It was far too heavy.

"God's wounds!" he swore, kicking at the lock.

"Looking for this?"

Alek looked up. Count Volger stood in the doorway, holding a key.

"Give me that, or we're all dead!"

"Well, obviously. Why do you think I'm here?" Volger

shut the door and crossed the room. "Beastly business, getting down from those engine pods."

"But why?"

Volger knelt by the map case. "Klopp needed some translating."

"No!" Alek groaned. "Why did you *do this?*"

"Bring along a vast fortune in gold? I should think that would be self-evident." Volger unlocked the case with a flick of the key, then opened it.

The gold bars shone dully, a dozen of them—more than two hundred kilograms. Volger lifted a bar with both hands, grunting as he hurled it through the window. They both leaned forward, watching it flash in the sunlight as it fell.

"Well, that's seventy thousand kroner gone," Volger said.

Alek bent and lifted one, the muscles in his hands screaming as he heaved it up and out. "You almost got us all killed! Are you mad?"

"Mad?" Volger grunted, lifting another bar. "For trying to save what little of your inheritance you haven't already thrown away?"

"This is an *airship*, Volger. Every gram makes a difference!" Alek pulled another bar from the case. "And you bring gold bullion aboard?"

"I didn't think the Darwinists would cut it so close." Volger grunted again, another gold bar spinning away.

"And just imagine how pleased you'd have been if I'd been *right*."

Alek groaned. Working alongside the *Leviathan*'s crew, he had absorbed the airmen's mania about weight. But Volger thought in terms of heavy cannon and armored walkers.

Alek pushed another bar through the window—only six left.

"But we may as well finish the job," Volger said. "Throw it all out, like the walker and the castle and ten years' worth of supplies!"

"So *that's* what this is about?" Alek said, lifting another bar. "That I've thrown away all your hard work? Don't you realize we've gained something more important?"

"What could be more important than your birthright?"

"Allies." Alek pushed the gold bar out the window. As it fell, he thought he felt the deck leveling beneath him. Maybe this was working.

"Allies?" Volger snorted, then lifted another bar and flung it out. "So your new friends are worth throwing away everything your father left you?"

"Not everything," Alek said. "All my life you and my father prepared me for this war. Thanks to that, I don't have to hide from it. Come on, there are only four left. The two of us can lift them all at once."

"Still too heavy." Volger shook his head. "Your father

was an idealist and a romantic, and it cost him dearly. I always hoped you'd inherited a bit of your mother's pragmatism."

Alek looked down at the case.

Only four gold bars. . . . He wondered what a boy like Dylan would say to such a fortune. Maybe it wasn't entirely mad, what Volger had done.

"Well," he said, "perhaps we could save one."

Volger smiled as he knelt, pulling one of the bars out and sliding it back under the bed. "There may be hope for you after all, Alek. Shall we?"

Alek knelt across from him, and together they heaved the case up, Volger's face turning red with the effort. Alek felt his own muscles throbbing in his arms.

Finally the case was resting on the windowsill. Alek took a step back, then threw himself against the case as hard as he could.

The last three bars spilled out as they fell toward the snow, spinning wildly and glittering with sunlight. Alek felt Volger's grip on his shoulder, as if the man thought he would go tumbling after them. The airship pitched up beneath Alek's feet, rolling to starboard as the weight of his father's gold fell away.

"But I truly didn't think it would matter, not on a ship this huge," Volger said quietly. "I never meant to endanger you."

"JETTISONING THE LAST INGOTS."

"I know that," Alek sighed. "Everything you've done has been to protect me. But I've chosen a different path now—one less safe. Either you recognize that or we part ways when this ship lands."

Count Volger took a deep, slow breath, then bowed. "I remain at your service, Your Serene Highness."

Alek rolled his eyes, and started to say more. But a light flickered outside, and they both leaned out the window again.

Flares were arcing up from the ground. The *Leviathan* had reached the first German scouts. Their mortars were firing, sending bright cinders aloft. Alek breathed in the sharp, familiar scent of phosphorous, and the rumble of nearby cannon reached his ears.

"I just hope we weren't too late."

◦ THIRTY-NINE ◦

"Off your bums, beasties!" Deryn shouted, sending another cluster of bats fluttering into the air.

Mr. Rigby had sent the middies forward to lighten the bow. Something heavy was holding the airship's nose down. Either that or the forward hydrogen cells were leaking like mad. But the sniffers hadn't found the slightest rip.

From up here Deryn could see the whole valley, and the view was barking dire. The Clanker walking machine had come to a halt a few miles away. Its scouts stretched in a line across the glacier, waiting for the airship to fly into their guns.

Suddenly the membrane reared beneath Deryn's feet. The nose had tipped up a bit.

"Did you feel that?" Newkirk yelled from across the bow.

"Aye, *something's* working," she called back. "Keep rousting the beasties!"

Deryn unclipped her safety line and ran toward another cluster of bats, shouting and waving her arms. They turned to stare at her skeptically before scampering—they hadn't been fed their fléchettes yet.

And they wouldn't be anytime soon. When the ballast alert had sounded, Mr. Rigby had tossed two whole bags of spikes over the side. If the zeppelins caught up, the *Leviathan* would be defenseless, her flocks stuffed with plenty of food—but no metal—and now scattered to the winds.

At least the borrowed Clanker engines were working, so far. They were noisy and smelly, and threw out enough sparks to give Deryn the mortal shivers, but blisters could they push the ship along!

The old motivator engines had only nudged the airbeast in the right direction, like a plowman flicking a donkey's ears. But now that was upside down: The cilia were acting like a rudder, setting the course while the Clanker engines propelled the ship.

Deryn hadn't realized the whale could be such a clever-boots, adapting to the new engines so quickly. And she'd never seen an airship move this fast. The pursuing zeppelins—some of them small, nippy interceptors—were already falling behind.

But the German land machines still waited dead ahead.

The ship bucked again, and Deryn lost her footing,

skidding down the slope. Her foot caught in a ratline, jerking her to a nasty halt.

"Safety first, Mr. Sharp!" Newkirk called, snapping the shoulder straps of his harness like suspenders.

"Pretty smug, for a bum-rag," Deryn muttered, snapping her clip back onto a ratline. She gave the bats another halfhearted shout, but the ship didn't seem to need it anymore. The airbeast's nose was pulling up in starts, another jolt skyward coming every ten seconds or so.

It felt as if they were chucking officers out the bridge front window! But at least the ship was climbing.

Deryn eased forward a bit, until she had a good view of the Germans.

The little scout craft, skittering machines like metal daddy longlegs, were shooting off their mortars. But the barrage was only flares, which weren't designed to climb very high. They arced a few hundred feet up and burned there uselessly, singeing the air beneath the gondola's belly.

But now the big eight-legged walker's guns were elevating, tracking the airship but holding their fire. At the speed the *Leviathan* was making, they'd only get one shot before she flew past them.

A command whistle began to scream, one long note, pitched almost too high to hear. The all-hands-aft signal!

Deryn turned and ran. On either side of her, sniffers scuttled along the membrane, headed toward the tail. The spine was crowded with men and beasts all running in the same direction, the air gun crews pulling up their weapons to carry them along.

It was a last, desperate attempt to move every squick of weight to the rear of the ship. Done all at once, it would tip the ship's nose up, driving her still higher into the air.

Halfway back, Deryn saw flickers on the snow below, and glanced over her shoulder. The muzzles of the walker's guns were blazing, smoke billowing out in clouds.

Before the rumble even reached her ears, the airship bucked again—harder this time, as if someone had tossed a grand piano overboard. The nose flew up, hiding Deryn's view of the German walker, and the deck rolled hard to starboard. Whatever they'd tossed away, it had been on the port side.

She heard the tardy thunder of the guns then, and shells started arcing past. They were huge incendiaries, igniting the sky like gouts of frozen lightning.

One flew past so near that Deryn felt its heat on her cheeks and forehead. The air was instantly burned dry, her eyes forced half shut by the shell's fury. The light from the flaming missiles threw the shadows of men and beasts across the membrane, stretched and misshapen by the airship's curves.

But the entire barrage was flying too far to port.

The sudden loss of weight, whatever it had been, had rolled the airship out of the way just in time. And the riggers' work over the last few days had held—not a squick of hydrogen was flaring from the skin.

But Deryn kept running for the ship's tail, as did the rest of the topside crew. Not just to pull the ship up harder, but to see behind them.

There it was again, the eight-legged walker, now sliding into the distance astern. Its guns were swiveling, trying to spin around and fire once more. But the *Leviathan*'s new Clanker engines were carrying her away too fast.

By the time the guns blazed again, the burning shells fell hundreds of feet short. They dropped into the snow and expended their anger there, the walking machines vanishing behind a veil of steam.

Deryn joined the cheer that rose up along the spine. The hydrogen sniffers howled along, half mad from all the ruckus.

Newkirk appeared, panting and covered with sweat, and clapped her on the shoulder. "Blistering good fight! Eh, Mr. Sharp?"

"Aye, it was. I just hope it's over."

She raised her field glasses to gander at the zeppelins, now silhouetted by the setting sun. They'd fallen still farther behind, hopelessly outmatched by the Stormwalker engines.

"They'll never catch up now," she said. "Not with night falling."

"THE *HERKULES'* SHELLS GO WIDE."

"But I thought those Predators were fast!"

"Aye, they are. But we're faster, now that we've got those engines on us."

"But haven't they got Clanker engines too?" Newkirk asked.

Deryn frowned, looking down at the *Leviathan*'s flanks. The cilia were stirring madly, weaving the airflow around the ship, somehow adding the currents of the sky to the raw power of the engines.

"We're something different now," she said. "A little of us and a little of them."

Newkirk thought a moment, then *hmph*ed and clapped her on the back again. "Well, frankly, Mr. Sharp, I don't care if the kaiser himself gives us a push, as long as it gets us clear of this iceberg."

"Glacier," Deryn said. "But you're right—it's good to be flying again."

She closed her eyes and took a deep breath of freezing air, feeling the strange new thrum of the membrane beneath her boots.

Already, her air sense told her, the beast was veering south, setting course for the Mediterranean. The zeppelins behind were an afterthought; the Ottoman Empire lay ahead.

Whatever sort of tangled crossbreed the Clankers had made her into, the *Leviathan* had survived.

◦ FORTY ◦

The pistons were the trickiest bits to draw. There was something about the way they fit together—the Clanker logic of them—that blistered Deryn's brain.

She'd been sketching the new engines all afternoon, imagining the drawings in some future edition of the *Manual of Aeronautics*. But even if no one ever saw them, the warm day was excuse enough for lounging here. The airship was only a hundred yards above the water, the afternoon sun bouncing from the waves and setting everything aglitter. After three nights shipwrecked on a glacier, it seemed the perfect afternoon to lie in the ratlines, soak up the heat, and draw.

But even with the Mediterranean Sea stretching out in all directions, the Clankers never seemed to relax. Alek and Klopp had been busy down on the pods since noon, fashioning windshields to protect the engine pilots. That's what they were calling themselves—*pilots*, not engine men or any proper Air Service term. They'd already forgotten that the real pilots were on the bridge.

Then again, she'd heard it rumored that the ship didn't *need* pilots these days, Darwinist or Clanker. The whale had developed an independent streak, a tendency to choose its own way among the thermals and updrafts. Some of the crew wondered if the wreck had rattled the beastie's attic. But Deryn reckoned it was the new engines. Who wouldn't feel feisty with all that power?

A bee was crawling across her sketch pad, and she waved it away. The hives had come out of their three-day hibernation hungry, gorging themselves on the wildflowers of Italy as the *Leviathan* headed south. The strafing hawks

looked fat and happy this afternoon, full of wild hares and stolen piglets.

"Mr. Sharp?" came the master coxswain's voice.

Deryn almost snapped to attention. But then she saw the message lizard staring at her, its beady eyes blinking.

"Please report to the captain's quarters," the lizard continued. "Without delay."

"Aye, sir. Right away!" Deryn winced as she heard her voice squeak like a girl's. She lowered it and said, "End message."

Gathering her pad and pencils as the beastie scampered away, Deryn wondered what she'd done wrong. Nothing bad enough to earn an audience with the captain—not that she could remember. Mr. Rigby had even commended her on taking Alek hostage during the Stormwalker attack.

But her nerves were twitching nonetheless.

The captain's quarters were up near the bow, next to the navigation room. The door was half open and Captain Hobbes sat behind his desk, the wall charts rustling in the warm breeze from an open window.

Deryn saluted smartly. "Midshipman Sharp reporting, sir."

"At ease, Mr. Sharp," the man said, which only made her more nervous. "Please come in. And shut the door."

"Aye, sir," she said. The captain's door was a solid piece

of natural wood, not fabricated balsa, and it thumped shut with a heavy finality.

"May I ask you, Mr. Sharp, your opinion of our guests?"

"The Clankers, sir?" Deryn frowned. "They're . . . very clever. And quite determined about keeping those engines running. Good allies to have, I'd say."

"Would you? Then it's lucky they aren't officially our enemies." The captain tapped his pencil against the cage that sat on his desk. The carrier tern inside it fluttered, its tongue slipping out to taste the air. "I've just learned that England is not at war with Austria-Hungary, not yet. At the moment we need only concern ourselves with the Germans."

"Well, that's handy, sir."

"Indeed." The captain leaned back and smiled. "You're rather friendly with young Alek, aren't you?"

"Aye, sir. He's a good lad."

"So he seems. A young boy like that needs friends, especially having run away from home and country." The captain lifted an eyebrow. "Sad, isn't it?"

Deryn nodded, saying carefully, "I suppose so, sir."

"And all quite mysterious. Here we are at their mercy, mechanically speaking, and yet we don't know much about Alek and his friends. Who are they, really?"

"They are a bit cagey, sir," Deryn said, which wasn't a lie.

"THE CAPTAIN'S QUARTERS."

"Quite so." Captain Hobbes picked up the piece of paper before him. "The First Lord of the Admiralty himself has become curious about them, and requests that we keep him informed. So it might be useful, Dylan, if you kept your ears open."

Deryn let out a slow breath.

This was the moment, of course, when duty required her to tell the captain all she knew—that Alek was the son of Archduke Ferdinand, and that the Germans were behind his father's murder. Alek had said it himself: This wasn't just family business. The assassinations had started the whole barking war, after all.

And now Lord Churchill himself was asking about it!

But she'd promised Alek not to tell. Deryn owed him that much, after setting the sniffers on him the first time they'd met.

For that matter, the whole barking ship owed him a debt. Alek had revealed his hiding place to help them fight the zeppelins, giving up his Stormwalker and a castle full of stores. And all he'd asked in return was to stay anonymous. It seemed impolite for the captain even to be asking.

She couldn't break her promise—not like this, without even talking to Alek first.

Deryn saluted smartly. "I'm happy to do whatever I can, sir."

And she left without telling the captain any of it.

◉   ◉   ◉

That evening when she went to find Alek on egg duty, the machine room was locked.

Deryn gave the door a couple of loud raps. Alek opened it and smiled, but he didn't stand aside.

"Dylan! Good to see you." He lowered his voice. "But I can't let you in."

"Why not?"

"One of the eggs is looking pale, so we've had to rearrange the heaters. It's all very complicated. Dr. Barlow said that another person in the room could affect the temperature."

Deryn rolled her eyes. As Constantinople drew closer, the lady boffin grew more and more protective of her eggs. They'd survived an airship crash, three nights on a glacier, and a zeppelin attack, and yet she seemed to think they'd shatter if anyone looked at them sideways.

"That's a load of yackum, Alek. Let me in."

"Are you sure?"

"Yes! We're keeping them close enough to body temperature. Another person in there won't hurt."

Alek hesitated. "Well, she also said that Tazza hasn't had a walk all day. He'll be tearing down the walls of her cabin if you don't see to him."

Deryn sighed. It was amazing how the lady boffin could be so tiresome without even being *in the room*.

"I've got something important to tell you, Alek. Shove aside and let me in!"

He frowned but relented, letting her squeeze past into the sweltering machine room.

"Blisters, are you sure it's not *too* hot in here?"

Alek shrugged. "Dr. Barlow's orders. She said the sick one needed to be kept warm."

Deryn looked at the cargo box. Two of the surviving eggs were nestled together at one end; the other was alone in the middle, surrounded by a pile of glowing heaters— far too many. She took a step forward to check the thermometer, then frowned. They were Dr. Barlow's barking eggs. If she wanted to cook them, fine.

Deryn had more important things to worry about.

She turned to Alek. "The captain called for me today. He asked about you."

Alek's face darkened. "Oh."

"Don't worry. I didn't tell him anything," she said. "I mean, I wouldn't break my promise."

"Thank you, Dylan."

"Even though he . . ." She cleared her throat, trying to sound casual. "He told me to keep an eye on you, and said I should tell him anything I find out."

Alek nodded slowly. "He gave you a direct order, didn't he?"

Deryn opened her mouth, but no words came out—

something was shifting inside her. On her way here she'd hoped Alek would give her permission to tell the captain, solving the whole dilemma. But now an entirely different desire was creeping into her mind.

What she really wanted, Deryn realized, was for Alek to know that she'd lied for him, that she would go on lying for him.

She suddenly had that feeling again, the same as when Alek had told her his parents' story—a crackling in the overheated air. Her skin tingled where he'd hugged her.

This wasn't going right *at all*.

"Aye. I suppose he did."

Alek sighed. "A direct order. So if they find out you've hidden my identity, they'll hang you as a traitor."

"Hang me?"

"Yes, for consorting with the enemy."

Deryn frowned. In all her weighing of promises and loyalties, she hadn't thought that far ahead. "Well . . . not *quite* the enemy. We're not at war with Austria, the captain says."

"Not yet. But from what Volger's heard on the wireless, it'll only be a week or so." He smiled sadly. "Funny, all those politicians trying to decide if we're enemies or not."

"Aye, barking hilarious," Deryn murmured. *She* was the

one standing here, not some politician. This was her decision. "I promised, Alek."

"But you also took an oath to the Air Service, and to King George," he reminded her. "I'm not going to make you break that oath. You're too good a soldier for that, Dylan."

She swallowed, shifting on her feet. "But what will they do to you?"

"I'll be locked up tight," Alek said. "I'm too valuable to let escape into the wilds of the Ottoman Empire. And when we get back to England, they'll put me somewhere safe until the war's over."

"Blisters," she said. "But you *saved* us!"

The boy shrugged. The sadness was still in his eyes. Not brimming over into tears again, but deeper than she'd ever seen it.

She was taking his one squick of hope away.

"I won't tell," she promised again.

"Then I'll have to give myself up," Alek said sadly. "The truth has to come out sooner or later. No point in you getting yourself hanged."

Deryn wanted to argue, but Alek wasn't making it easy. He was right about disobeying orders in wartime. It was treason, and traitors were executed.

"This is all Dr. Barlow's fault," she grumbled. "I wouldn't have found out who you were if she weren't so nosy. She's not telling either, but of course they'd never hang a clever-boots like her."

"No, I suppose not." Alek shrugged again. "She's not a soldier, after all. On top of which, she's a woman."

Deryn's mouth dropped open. She'd almost forgotten— the Air Service *wouldn't* hang a woman, would they? Not even a common soldier. They'd boot her out, certainly, take away everything she'd ever wanted—her home on this airship, the sky itself. But they'd never execute a fifteen-year-old girl. It would be too barking *embarrassing.*

She felt a smile on her face. "Don't worry about me, Alek. I've got a trick up my sleeve."

"Don't be stupid, Dylan. This isn't one of your madcap adventures. This is serious!"

"My adventures are *all* barking serious!"

"But I can't let you take the risk," he pleaded. "Enough people have died because of me already. I'll go with you to the captain now and explain everything."

"You don't have to," Deryn argued, but she knew Alek wouldn't listen. He wouldn't believe she was safe from hanging unless he knew the truth. Strangest of all, she almost *wanted* to tell him, to trade her secret for his.

She took a step closer.

"They won't hang me, Alek. I'm not the soldier you think I am."

He frowned. "What do you mean?"

Deryn took a deep breath. "I'm not really a—"

A sound came from the door—the jangling of keys. It opened and Dr. Barlow strode in, her eyes darkening as they fell on Deryn.

"Mr. Sharp. What are *you* doing here?"

⚙·FORTY-ONE·⚙

Alek had never seen such a cold look on Dr. Barlow's face. Her eyes flicked from Dylan to the eggs, as if she thought the boy had come to steal one.

"Sorry, ma'am," Dylan muttered, swallowing whatever he'd been about to say. "I was just heading up to see Tazza."

Alek grabbed his arm. "Wait. Don't go." He turned to Dr. Barlow. "We have to tell the captain who I am."

"And why would we do that?"

"He's ordered Dylan to keep an eye on me, and to tell him everything he learns. Everything." Alek stood up straighter, trying to summon his father's voice of command. "We can't ask Dylan to disobey a direct order."

"Don't worry about the captain." Dr. Barlow waved her hand. "This is *my* mission, not his."

"Aye, ma'am, but it's not just him," Dylan said. "The

Admiralty knows we've got Clankers aboard, and the First Lord himself was asking about them!"

Dr. Barlow's face darkened again, and her voice dropped to a growl. "*That* man. I should have known. This crisis is all his fault, and yet he still dares to interfere with my mission!"

Dylan tried to sputter some response to this, but failed.

Alek frowned. "Who is this fellow?"

"She's speaking of Lord Churchill," Dylan managed. "He's the First Lord of the Admiralty. He runs the whole barking navy!"

"Yes, and you'd think that would be enough for Winston. But now he's gone beyond his station," Dr. Barlow said. She took a seat beside the eggs, pulling a few of the heaters away from the sick one. "Sit down, both of you. You may as well know the whole story, as the Ottomans will find out soon enough."

Alek shared a look with Dylan, and they both settled onto the floor.

"Last year," she began, "the Ottoman Empire offered to buy a warship being built in Britain. It is among the most advanced in the world, with a companion creature strong enough to change the balance of power on the seas. And it is ready to sail."

She paused, peered at a thermometer, then moved a few more heaters around in the straw.

"But the day before you and I met in Regent's Park, Mr. Sharp, Lord Churchill decided to seize that ship for Britain. Even though it was already paid for in full." She shook her head. "He suspected that the Ottomans might wind up on the other side in this war, and he didn't want the *Osman* in enemy hands."

Alek frowned. "Well, that's just plain thievery!"

"I suppose so." Dr. Barlow flicked a piece of straw. "More important, it was a shocking bit of diplomacy. That annoying man has made it nearly certain that the Ottomans will join the Clankers. It is our mission to prevent that from happening."

She patted the sick egg.

"But what's that got to do with my secret?" Alek asked.

Dr. Barlow sighed. "Winston and I have been at odds about the Ottomans for some time. He doesn't appreciate that I'm trying to fix his mistakes, and he'd love to get in my way." She looked at Alek. "Finding out that we have the son of the Archduke Ferdinand as our captive would provide him with an excuse to turn this ship around."

Alek set his teeth. "A captive? Our countries aren't even at war! And may I remind you who runs the engines for this ship?"

"That is precisely my point," Dr. Barlow said. "*Now* do you see why I don't want you and Dylan blabbing to the captain? It would cause a great deal of trouble, setting us all against one another. And we've been getting along so splendidly!"

"Aye, she's right," Dylan said. The boy looked relieved.

Dr. Barlow turned and adjusted the egg again. "You can leave Lord Churchill to me."

"But it's not just your problem, ma'am," Alek said. "It's Dylan's as well. You say you'll protect him, but how can you promise to . . ." He frowned. "Who exactly *are* you, madam, to take on this Lord Churchill?"

The woman rose to her full height, adjusting her bowler hat.

"I am exactly as you see me—Nora Darwin Barlow, head keeper of the London Zoo."

Alek blinked. Had she said Nora *Darwin* Barlow? A new trickle of nerves began to grow in his stomach.

"You m-mean," Dylan stammered, "your grandfather . . . the barking *beekeeper?*"

"I never said he was a beekeeper," she laughed. "Only that he found bees inspiring. His theories wouldn't have achieved nearly such elegance without their instructive example. So stop your worrying about Lord Winston, Mr. Sharp. He's nothing I can't handle."

Dylan nodded, looking pale. "I'll just go see to Tazza, then, ma'am."

"An excellent idea." She opened the door for him.

"And don't let me catch you here again without permission."

The boy started to slip out the door, then cast Alek one last look. For a moment their eyes locked. Then Dylan shook his head and disappeared.

He was probably as astonished as Alek. Dr. Barlow wasn't just a Darwinist; she was *a Darwin*—the granddaughter of the man who'd fathomed the very threads of life.

Alek felt the floor shifting beneath him, but he doubted it was the airship turning. He was standing beside the incarnation of everything he'd been taught to fear.

And he had entrusted himself to her completely.

Dr. Barlow turned back to the eggs. She was rearranging the heaters, stacking them near the sick egg again.

Alek clenched his fists to keep the quaver from his voice.

"But what about when we get to Constantinople?" he said. "Once you and your cargo are safely there, what's to stop you from locking me up?"

"Please, Alek. I have no intention of locking anyone up." She reached out to ruffle his hair, which sent a shiver down his spine. "I have other plans for you."

She smiled as she walked to the door.

"Trust me, Alek. And do keep a close eye on those eggs tonight."

As the door closed behind her, Alek turned to look at the softly glowing cargo box, wondering what was in the eggs that was so important. What sort of fabricated creature could replace a mighty warship? How could a beast no bigger than a top hat keep an empire out of this war?

"What's inside you?" Alek said softly.

But the eggs just sat there, not answering at all.

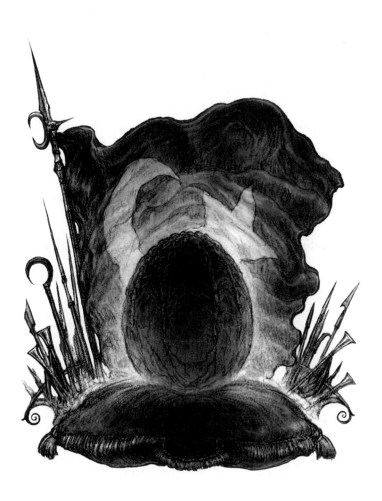

AFTERWORD

Leviathan is a novel of alternate history, so most of its characters, creatures, and mechanisms are my own inventions. But the book's time line is based on the actual summer of 1914, when Europe found itself lurching toward a disastrous war. So here's a quick review of what's true and what's fictional in the story so far.

On June 28, Archduke Franz Ferdinand, heir to the throne of Austria-Hungary, and his wife, Sophie Chotek, were assassinated by young Serbian revolutionaries. In my world they survived a first pair of attacks, but were poisoned later that evening. In the real world, however, they were killed in the afternoon. (I wanted my book to start at night.) Just as in *Leviathan*, the assassinations led to war between Austria and Serbia, which spread to Germany and Russia, and so on. By the first week of August the globe was embroiled in the Great War—now called World War I. These two tragic deaths, and some appalling diplomacy among the great powers of Europe, resulted in millions more.

There were rumors at the time that the Austrian

government, or perhaps that of Germany, had secretly
arranged the murders—either as an excuse to start a war
or because Franz Ferdinand was too peace-minded. Few
historians believe this conspiracy theory now, but it took
decades to be disproved. Certainly the German military
was determined to get a war started, and used the assassinations to do exactly that.

Franz and Sophie had no son called Aleksandar,
though. Their children were named Sophie, Maximilian,
and Ernst. But just like Alek in my story, these three
were forbidden to inherit Franz's land or titles, all thanks
to their mother's less-than-royal blood. And, just as in
Leviathan, their parents had implored both the Austro-
Hungarian emperor and the pope to change this situation. In the real world, though, Franz and Sophie did not
prevail.

The romantic story that Alek tells about the tennis
game and the pocket watch is entirely true.

Charles Darwin really did exist, of course, and in the
mid-1800s made the discoveries that are at the core of
modern biology. In the world of *Leviathan* he also managed to discover DNA, and learned to reach into these
"life threads" to create new species. In our own world the
role of DNA in evolution wasn't fully understood until
the 1950s, however. We are only now fabricating new life

forms, and none so grand as Deryn Sharp's airship home.

Nora Darwin Barlow was also a real person, a scientist in her own right. The columbine Nora Barlow flower is named after her, and she also edited many definitive editions of her grandfather's work. But she was neither a zookeeper nor a diplomat.

The Tasmanian tiger is an entirely real beast. You could have seen a thylacine much like Tazza at the London Zoo in 1914, but no longer. Despite having been the top predator of the Australian continent only a few thousand years ago, the species was hunted to extinction by humans in the early twentieth century.

The last known Tasmanian tiger died in captivity in 1936.

As for the Clankers' inventions, they are somewhat ahead of their time. The first real armored fighting machines didn't enter battle until 1916. They couldn't walk, but used tractor treads, just as tanks do today. The world's militaries are only now beginning to develop useful vehicles with legs instead of treads or wheels. Animals are still much better at walking over rough terrain than any machine.

So *Leviathan* is as much about possible futures as alternate pasts. It looks ahead to when machines will look like living creatures, and living creatures can be fabricated like machines. And yet the setting also recalls an earlier time in which the world was divided into aristocrats and commoners, and women in most countries couldn't join the armed forces—or even vote.

That's the nature of steampunk, blending future and past.

The conflict between Winston Churchill and the Ottomans over seized warships is also based in fact. But that is best left to the second book, which follows the *Leviathan* to the ancient city of Constantinople, capital of the Ottoman Empire.